"A CRIME-NOVEL TRIUMPH."
-KIRKUS REVIEWS

Blending her marvelous skill as a story-teller with her fourteen years of experience as a New York City police officer, Dorothy Uhnak has written a searing, powerful novel about a terrifying crime and the way it changes the lives of the victim, the investigators, and the criminal himself. From its first page, when a beautiful, sexy female TV news star is the victim of a savage rape and mutilation, to the final spine-tingling bombshell of a climax, FALSE WITNESS is a spellbinding revelation of human passions that brilliantly confirms Dorothy Uhnak's reputation as one of America's best writers about crime and the law.

ABOUT THE AUTHOR

Dorothy Uhnak, a native New Yorker, spent fourteen years as a police officer — years during which she was promoted three times and twice awarded medals for "services above and beyond."

Ms. Uhnak, an Edgar winner in 1968, had her first book, *Policewoman*, published while she was still a detective. She is also the author of *Law and Order* and *The Investigation*.

False Witness

by

Dorothy Uhnak

FAWCETT CREST • NEW YORK

*This book is dedicated with deep affection and grati-
tude...*

to Tom O'Rourke, for a lifetime of friendship

to Jack O'Brian and Barry Farber for consistent kind-
ness and generosity from the very beginning through
the long years

Special thanks to my daughter, Tracy, not only for the
hours of typing and deciphering, but more importantly
for offering encouragement and strength when I faltered

and to Dr. Marvin J. "Chick" Schissel, as fine a racon-
teur as he is a dentist

Prologue
Crime Scene

As she lay near death, Sanderalee Dawson was spared the pain of her terrible injuries by shock.

She swallowed the salty thin blood that filled her mouth. It was an instinctive attempt to keep the life force inside her, as was her attempt to breathe in small, short, careful gasps rather than in huge lung-filling expansions, which she might then be unable to exhale. There was a slow dull consciousness working, devoid of panic: if her attempts to breathe made a lot of noise, he might hear her, might still be nearby, would realize she was not yet dead, might return to hurt her again.

Having made the decision to survive, she experienced one quick electric shock of pain so total, so devastating that the cry caught in her throat, seemed about to strangle her. She was suffocating and it was not gentle or easy. It was terrifying and she fought against it.

She opened her eyes and gazed without understanding at the pendulum motion of the telephone receiver as it skimmed the floor, dangling from the end of the uncurled white rubberized cord.

There was a hand holding the receiver, the fingers locked in a rigid grasp. It was a severed hand and a thick trail of blood followed the back and forth swaying motion, in a bright red pattern on her white ceramic tile kitchen floor. It was hers.

Part One

The Victim

1

She had been left for dead. Had Sanderalee Dawson been, in fact, dead, a great many lives and reputations and careers and ambitions and relationships would now be quite different. Including mine. Especially mine.

When my phone rings in the middle of the night, I have a facility for becoming not only awake but instantly, totally, sharply alert. For some stupid, dark-based reason, I try to convince not only the caller but myself that I wasn't asleep, I was just lying there in the darkness waiting for an emergency call.

As Bobby Jones attempted to control his obvious excitement, his voice expanded with the Nebraska flatness that four years in New York City had not totally obliterated. Where anyone else quickens, he slows down.

"Lynne, I've sent a patrol car to pick you up. It should be at your apartment within the next five minutes or so. I'm calling from Roosevelt Hospital. They might have to move her for special surgery and it looks very bad. She's lost a lot of blood. I'm heading for her apartment and I'll meet you there. Your driver knows where it is—that old Holcroft Hall building near Carnegie Hall."

I don't see the graveyard-shift doorman, Giorgio, very often. It is unusual for me to dash out of my building and into a New York City Police Department squad car at four in the morning. But Giorgio handled it with great aplomb: he arrived at the curb before I did and held the car door open, sweeping aside with a semi-bow as though it were your standard black limo. There wasn't any traffic at all. We made the trip from lower Fifth, where I live, to 58th and Seventh Avenue in record time.

Bobby Jones appeared from the shadows and escorted me into the entrance area of the building, holding open the heavy iron-scrolled glass door, which led into a small cubicle that provided the doorman a good view out. The uniformed doorman was seated behind his battered wooden desk, his job taken over by a large, thuggish-looking detective who squinted with professional suspicion.

"This is Bureau Chief Lynne Jacobi, D.A.'s office," Bobby informed the detective. The introductions seemed to stop on that one-sided note.

"And your name and command, officer?"

He sucked on a tooth while making up his mind. I've met his kind before. Many times.

"Detective Arthur Godley, Homicide. Godley. Not Godfrey."

"Uh-huh. And this gentleman?"

The doorman was instantly on his feet. "I'm Timothy Doyle, ma'am," he told me in a soft, aged, melodious brogue.

"Tim here was on duty the whole night, Miss Jacobi. He's given me a statement, which is being typed up right now for him to sign."

"*Mr. Doyle*, I'd like to talk to you after I come back from upstairs. I could use a cup of strong wake-up tea and I have a feeling you could brew just the thing."

Timothy Doyle's face lit up and he nodded enthusiastically. He was an Irishman from another era: one of the proud-humble, tough-gentle, devoted-independent, reliable-to-the-death immigrants who considered being "in service" an honorable and respectable profession.

Bobby Jones handled the old-fashioned elevator as

though he'd been doing it all his life. He brought the rumbling old car flat even with the eighth-floor hallway and held it steady with one hand on the control as he pulled at the folding gate.

I walked directly into Detective Arthur Godley's twin brother, or his clone.

"Sorry, lady," he growled. "Unless you live on this floor you can't come up here. This is a sealed-off crime-search area."

Neither Bobby nor I had to go through the identifications again. Chief of Detectives Jim Barrow swept from the open door of Sanderalee Dawson's apartment. I was enclosed momentarily in his embrace: a hard, smothering hug followed by a quick cheek kiss of friendship and I thought, fleetingly, of what the reaction of my young female staff members would have been. Oh God, that kind of chauvinistic crap. And you *allow* it! They have yet to discern what you allow and go with and what you put a sharp stop to. Barrow and I are equals. We work together on occasion and we have worked together very successfully through the years as each of us has risen through the ranks of our respective organizations. His division of the New York City Police Department prepares cases for consideration for my division of the New York County District Attorney's Office. My people, in effect, evaluate and pass judgment on the work done by his people. We are the ones who have to go before the jury and present, in an orderly and convincing fashion, what they have come up with. There have been times when we've disagreed. There have been bitter and unpleasant moments. There have been times when Jim Barrow and I would gladly have paced off against each other, turned and fired. Except, of course, as an advocate of strict gun control, I do not carry.

I accept the friendly embrace from my professional equals. At times, a good hug can be very reassuring. I am nearly forty years old and I have been doing battle for many, many years without too many compromises along the way. My young female associates haven't

13

been in the war long enough to learn that there are necessary times of truce.

The small square entrance foyer to Sanderalee's apartment was dark and cavelike with shiny dark brown ceramic tile flooring, darker brown walls, small dull wall lights. By comparison, the huge living room was a blaze of light caused not merely by the lamps and raw bulbs set up by the investigators but by the decor: soft pale monochromatic beige sweep of couch leading to a subtly blending series of velvet chairs in just slightly darker shades, all set on wall-to-wall very thick, pale, mushroomy carpet in the identical hue of the walls and ceiling. Beautiful wooden accent pieces: a desk, a small antique armoire lit from within to display a precise arrangement of exquisite collector's items—porcelains, paperweights, small silvery treasures.

The room was out of a magazine. Every item decorator perfect. Everything calculated to set off the main occupant. Sanderalee Dawson would serve as the centerpiece. The recessed spotlights would glance off and enhance her warm beige honey-gold complexion. Even in the confusion caused by the police technicians and photographers, one could see that the professional set designer had selected with great calculation every painting on the walls, every art book and flower arrangement. There was nothing impulsive or spontaneous. The only color selected for the room came from a wonderful collection of pillows; all sizes, all shapes, all designs.

The discordant, unanticipated color, dominating all the overturned furniture and tossed-about lamps, was the darkening brownish-red thickly shimmering blood. Sanderalee's life force was sprayed and splattered and pooled all over the room in a way that would have reduced her decorator to suicide. There could be no cleaning up. There would have to be a complete cleaning out.

Jim Barrow's heavy arm wrapped around me as he guided a path carefully around the forensic people who

14

gathered, collected, photographed, measured, traced, paced, calculated, guessed, estimated, noted and gossiped. It was all routine to them, although rarely are they called upon to perform their rites in such a lush setting. From time to time, one or another hummed or whistled or stopped work to glance admiringly at the floor-to-ceiling collection of photographs of Sanderalee Dawson along one wall. The blank and beautiful face of the professional high-fashion model watched them without expression: a haughty dark beauty, mysterious, remote, slightly threatening in the distance created by the turn of her chin. And then, the surge of life and spirit caught by an excellent photographer who had created a playful mood: a let's have some fun with this damn thing babe, show us what ya got Sanderalee, yeah Sanderalee yeah yeah yeah. A series of quick click-click-click living shots. And then, a new Sanderalee Dawson: important lady. First black woman hostess of her own important 11:15 to midnight, five nights a week, live talk show. Important lady: beauty now merging with a keen intelligence, an in-charge, don't try to kid me, sucker, expression. The photographer had captured the essence of this phase of Sanderalee's personality. I'd been on her show a few times; I'd watched her on and off. Some of these photographs revealed some deep essence of the woman beyond what a snap-click-gotcha could find. I noted his name: Alan Greco.

They had entered the apartment, Sanderalee Dawson and unidentified male, stopping while she hung her angora hat and scarf and navy blue jogging jacket on the old-fashioned railroad-car hat rack in the hallway: brass antique, barely turn of the century. They had moved into the perfection of the living room. She had taken some things from the small refrigerator behind the bar and set them on a large tray: a bottle of white wine; a bottle of Perrier water; a bowl of limes, uncut; some cheeses ready on a small china plate. There were two tall crystal glasses set on the bar, the ice cubes melting, the mineral water not poured, the elegant green bottle opened by a sterling silver opener and a sterling silver bottle cap for recapping.

"She seems to have been preparing for a social evening, at least for a friendly snack. They never got to it. It's a little hard to trace the sequence," Jim Barrow admitted. He turned and pointed to a small heap of silky undergarments. "Those, the bra and bikini underpants, were found right there. But the victim was found in the kitchen dressed in her lightweight ski sweater and jogging pants. Peculiar."

It was peculiar. Jim pointed to a small object on the rug beside the bar. We both knelt, careful not to touch anything. It was a beautiful silver unicorn with about two inches left of what probably had been a four-inch silver horn. There was blood on the remnant of the horn and on the beautiful body of the fallen good luck symbol.

"My guess is that he attacked her suddenly, without warning, since she was getting ready for a quiet drink of soda water." Jim Barrow shook his head. "That's the trouble nowadays, Lynne, everyone drinking damn bubble water instead of something sensible like Scotch. I'd say the unicorn was on the counter and she grabbed it. My guess is that she connected. Unless we find that broken-off piece of silver horn, the 'male-unknown' might have it imbedded in him somewhere. The blood on the unicorn could be his or hers."

We stood up. Barrow's voice was soft and intense. It ignored the presence of all the technicians, the police personnel in the room, and created a lonely intimacy. I faced into the room with him as he described, from the condition of the victim, the assault: beating, tearing, ripping; rape, sodomy, the near-murder which yet may have been accomplished.

It lingered; something of the dark passions remained and intensified the thought of Sanderalee alone with some madman. She, the center of this carefully created place of beauty and serenity, the reason for this place, this setting, had been the sole and isolated and vulnerable target of a terrible and unanticipated force.

16

Barrow led me to Sanderalee's bedroom. It was a quiet oasis, which she had obviously created for herself and to hell with the decorator. There was a feeling of controlled chaos: yes, it's cluttered, but damn it, it's my clutter and I know where everything is. There was a stack of papers and notebooks and magazines on the glass-topped desk; there was a small dish of penny-candy on the table next to the bed; a fancy French telephone; a doodle pad; stuffed teddy bears and pink elephants and rag-dolls on the bed. A shelf of Madame Alexander dolls, black and white, elegant, expensive, untouched, their lovely little eyes seeing everything with disdain and disinterest.

"You got dolls in your bedroom, Lynne?" Barrow asked.

"I had my last doll when I was about eight or nine. And then I realized the trap that was being set for me."

"And so you turned to law books and university applications. What's your bedroom look like, Lynne?"

"Steel furniture. Japanese mat on the floor. You know."

"Oh, Lynne, Lynne, were I a few years younger. And not married and the father of ten fine children and grandfather of six. You and I could have had a fine time of it. Here, take a look at this bathroom. Must have imported the whole damn thing from Hollywood."

There was, indeed, the look of Hollywood. A large redwood tub with all kinds of interesting devices: brushes, hoses, controls, little seating platforms or whatever. The room itself was huge—a swinger's family room. There was a conventional stall shower; the toilet was carefully concealed in its own little compartment. Mirrored walls on two sides of the room. Actually they were sliding doors, which hid closets containing more clothes than your local friendly department store.

And a lovely round sink, a flowered bowl set on a marble pedestal. The flowers in the bowl were covered with a bright, watery red. Sanderalee's date had washed some of the blood off his hands in this room.

"My guess is he left her unconscious in the kitchen. She never made it in here. He seems to have gone exploring for God knows what reason." Jim pointed to blood smears on the mirrored doors and on the doorframe. They were smudges, as though made by the brushing of a bloody sleeve. "Then, he washed his hands in here. Doesn't seem to have touched anything. See that bloody washcloth? He used it to turn on the water faucet. Very careful about his fingerprints. I don't think we'll find any from the 'alleged perpetrator.'"

"All the blood, Jim? My God, what the hell did he do to her?"

Barrow looked at me in surprise and, apologetically, he said, "I thought you knew about all the injuries, Lynne. I assumed your man, Jones, told you." His firm arm around my shoulders led me into the hallway, through the living room, past the small expensive little custom bar into an antiseptic kitchen: a glaringly white room. Floors, walls, ceiling, cabinets white. Butcherblock countertops; stainless steel sinks; restaurant large freezer and refrigerator and stove. Brightly lit. More blood than I had ever seen in one place before. And I have been on the scene of some very gory homicides.

There was a heavy meat cleaver on the floor, professional type. Bloody.

White telephone receiver swinging slightly along the floor, covered with blood.

"It's still hard to trace the action, but I'd say the sexual assault took place in the living room. Now, her getting those clothes on—that's a puzzle, but she was dressed when she came into the kitchen. At least, that's an assumption; makes more sense than that he came in and put the clothes on her afterward. Well, at any rate, she made it into the kitchen and apparently there was a further struggle. Can't say who grabbed the cleaver first; maybe she did, but he sure had it last.

"He hacked off her left hand." Jim Barrow's right hand chopped through the air smartly toward his left wrist. "Whack-o. Severed clean at the wrist. Her hand was clutching the service telephone receiver when the uniformed men arrived."

Jim Barrow was a large bear-type man, the kind who probably never in his life had to get involved in personal violence. Just his size, his presence, would discourage any challenger. He was a gentle man: strong, warm, reassuring. I leaned into him for a minute, grateful that I could do this. It was one of those woman-perks and I was grateful for it.

His arm turned me from the spectacular red and white horror.

"Gee, I thought you knew, kid. I would have prepared you a little. Her *other* injuries are pretty bad. This guy came on like Attila the Hun, at least. From what I got so far, he slugged her hard enough to break the jawbones both sides of her face, her cheekbones, several of her teeth." His strong pushing led us back into the living room where we both stared at the mess and Jim released me and pointed into the kitchen. "I'd say that somehow, probably in a state of shock, she managed to get back into the living room. Hence, this particular pool of blood. Then, I guess she wandered back inside the kitchen, where Mr. Doyle, the doorman, and the two uniformed men found her. She would have strangled if that young cop hadn't reacted fast."

"Strangled? She would have strangled?"

"Oh," Jim Barrow said softly. "I didn't tell you about her other...injury."

"My God, besides rape and sodomy and dismemberment and broken face bones and teeth, Jim. Besides all that, what the hell else could he have done to her?"

"Well, this she might have done to herself. No, not really, I mean during the course of the struggle. She put up a hell of a fight." Jim rolled his lower lip between his teeth, then pantomimed a blow to his chin. "Bit her lower lip off," he said.

2

Timothy Doyle was a lovely man with a Mickey Rooney face and thick white theatrically long hair. He watched me carefully as I examined the titles of the paperbacks that filled three shelves on the wall of the little cubby just off the entrance vestibule. His shrewd bright blue eyes sparkled at my surprise.

He had impressed me properly and we sat across the tiny table from each other, hands wrapped around mugs of tea.

"I hope it's not too sweet, my dear. I lace it with honey and lemon that I prepare special for the energy it gives. Not with your standard Irishman booze. I'm your oddball, sober, non-drinking non-stereotype, though that dummy Arthur Watsizname out there keeps asking wasn't I maybe off dozin' or boozin' and missed seein' this . . . attacker leave the building."

"I've just glanced at your statement. Now you tell me. Don't worry about exact times or anything. Not right now. Right now, I just want to hear you tell me."

He nodded and took one noisy sip of tea, held it in his mouth for a moment, then swallowed.

"Ms. Dawson came home from the studio at her usual time, maybe one-twenty, one-thirty or so. The studio limo brought her."

He hesitated.

"Okay, she was brought home by the studio limo. You took her up to the eighth floor. Alone at this time?"

"Yes, ma'am. Alone. About fifteen minutes later," he waved a hand, "as you said, you can check the times with my statement—well, she buzzed the elevator and I went up and brought her down."

"Do you always escort passengers? No one rides up or down alone?"

"That's exactly right. It's an old-fashioned building; nothing automatic or modern. We just do things as we've done things all along. Now, then: she was dressed in her jogging clothes. Navy blue outfit with the green and white stripes; light blue fluffy knit hat and scarf—angora, is it? the kind of fluffy that gets all over you."

Noted.

"How did she seem to you? Her mood."

"Tense. Tight. Wound up."

"Say anything to you?"

"Not a word; nothing. Nor I to her. So off she goes. I held the door open and she started off to the right, toward the Circle."

"How far did you watch her go?"

He shook his head. "That was it. Just the direction: toward the Circle. Okay. It's about two-thirty now and she's back. And she's got a runner with her."

I took a deep breath. Timothy Doyle described him to me.

"I'm five-nine, so I measure everyone up or down from me, as I'm a middle-sized man, you might say. He was close to six feet, give or take an inch." He held up his hand, interrupting himself. "Most important fact: he was a *white man*."

"All right. What did he look like? Light hair, dark hair, color of his eyes? Just in your own words, Mr. Doyle."

"I never examined his face, Ms. Jacobi. I never even took more than a quick glance. I noticed his white hands. I could say only that he was white and that is exactly all I can say about what he looked like." Sadly,

21

he added, "I could not identify him at all, Ms. Jacobi, as I did not look at his face."

Terrific. A wonderful dream witness; but he had not looked at the perpetrator's face. Mr. Doyle had been, as always, discreet.

"Did they talk about anything in particular in the elevator, Mr. Doyle?"

He closed his eyes for a moment; his wide forehead crumpled with thought. He shook his head.

"They never said a word, Ms. Jacobi. Not a single word. Neither him nor her; nor did I. Beyond maybe a nodding acknowledgment, you know, when I let them in, 'Ms. Dawson, ma'am.' It wouldn't have been the thing, do you understand, for me to have given the man the once-over."

"All right, then. You took them up to the eighth floor. Neither of them spoke to you or to each other. They got off and headed for her apartment and you went back down to your desk. And then?"

And then about an hour or so later, the light on his switchboard flashed and flashed, on and off sporadically. He plugged in to answer Sanderalee's summons and heard the terrible sounds. Sounds that he'd never heard before, but so terrible that he had not a moment's doubt of disaster.

"It's a strange and funny thing, but I had a kind of *déjà vu* experience," he told me with solid simplicity. "I felt a premonition. I heard the sounds coming from that poor girl's telephone and without even thinking about it, I went right to the front door and as if it was all arranged, there was a patrol car parked not twenty feet away. It's not a usual thing; I doubt it's ever been just at that spot. Anyway, I just called out to them to come quickly. I guess something in my voice told them this was serious. They came. Two young patrolmen. Oh, so very young; the older of the two not more than twenty-five, or -six, but the youngster maybe twenty-two or -three, poor lad. Not prepared for what we walked into. As if you could prepare for such a sight. But anyway..."

22

I held up my hand and he waited politely. "You went with them, into the elevator, right? You, in effect, left the door unguarded, right?"

He drew himself up stiffly, vaguely insulted. "Yes, in effect."

"Mr. Doyle, you and the patrolmen went up to the eighth floor and got off the elevator. From that point on, tell me everything you saw. Everything you heard. Slowly."

He crossed himself swiftly; I wondered when was the last time he'd done that. It seemed an act of superstition rather than of faith.

"Ah, Jesus God, it was that terrible." His brogue went thick and soft; almost a different voice—a different man. His bright blue eyes clouded over; his tongue licked dry lips and his large, strong hand squeezed the tea mug tightly, then trembled as he set it on the small table. He looked directly at me, but he was seeing the eighth floor: the apartment that reeked of Sanderalee's agony.

"At first, we couldn't find her, you know. We heard the noise, the soft groaning, like a wee animal; softer even, like a hurt little bird. And of course, I realized and told the policemen: the kitchen. That's where the intercom phone is and she'd been calling down and that's where she'd be. We walked right through that room, the living room, right through, right past all that upset, the chairs knocked over, the things pushed aside. The blood."

He stopped speaking.

"There was a great deal of blood, Mr. Doyle. Yes. I saw that myself. It must have been very shocking for you to walk in on that. And Sanderalee, Mr. Doyle. Tell me. *Tell me.*"

His eyes glazed. "There she was, you see, that poor child, all broken, all...broken, all torn and bleeding, everything covered with blood and her hand, her poor hand was clutching the telephone like a vise." He blinked and said to me, "It was hard to realize then, what we were seeing, how terrible it was. How hurt she'd been. Only her eyes seemed alive: her eyes, so wide-open, dear God, what her eyes had seen. And the poor younger cop, the twenty-two or twenty-three-year-old, Christ, he went whiter than the walls and the older policeman, he took over and he said, 'Petey, get on the phone in the other room and get an ambulance' and then...I guess he realized what neither of us, the younger one or I, had realized. He said to me...funny, this policeman's voice was so strong and so calm. He took charge, very snappy like—like a soldier—he said to me, 'Pop, you find a plastic bag in one of the cupboards here and you fill it with ice from the freezer. Just do it,' he said, although I didn't realize why. Like 'boil water, the baby's coming.'" Timothy Doyle laughed. It was a nervous, inappropriate laugh and we both knew it but he couldn't help it. He laughed a little more; then he coughed and put his head down. When he raised his face, there were long running tears trickling down his cheeks. I reached out and pressed his arm. He was trembling.

"Mr. Doyle. You did that, what the policeman told you to do? The ice, the plastic bag?"

"Oh, yes. I did that. And then the younger cop came back in and said the ambulance was on its way and then there was a terrible gagging sound. Yes. That's what it was: a dying sound. Ms. Dawson was strangling right there on the floor and the three of us looking down at her. And the younger of the policemen, white-faced and shaken, he knelt down and just, it seemed to me anyway, he covered her face with his, he was face down to her. I couldn't tell, of course, but I knew anyway, he was helping her to breathe and...he looked up all of a sudden and—" Mr. Doyle stopped speaking.

He put his face in his hands and his shoulders heaved convulsively. I dug into my pocketbook and came up with a wad of tissues, which I separated: half for him, half for me. I felt a wave of sympathetic sobbing deep inside my chest, which is where it would have to stay for now. That's all I needed: to sit and get hysterical with my witness.

"Okay, Mr. Doyle. Take a deep slug of that tea of yours. Okay. *Tell me, Mr. Doyle.*"

He regained control. It was even worse than when he'd been emotional. He spoke in a dead steel voice; by rote, he described the indescribable.

"When the young policeman tried to help her to breathe, he realized there was something blocking her windpipe, or whatever. He...put his mouth over hers and sucked hard and then he raised his face and spit something into his hand. At just about that moment, the medics arrived. They burst into the apartment. They took one look and thought the young policeman was wounded. His face was covered with blood. His mouth...and then he looked at what was in his hand. It...it was what had blocked the girl's breathing. He screamed. The young policeman. He leaped up as though an electric prod had touched him." Mr. Doyle studied his clasping and twining fingers for a moment and then said softly, "It was her lip, you see, the flesh that she had bitten off. It had come loose and slipped into her throat and he sucked it out and cleared her breathing passage. And saved her life, if the poor girl will live after all that's happened. And the policeman, he suddenly keeled over with his hands clutching his stomach, frantic as to where he could...he was convulsed, you see, and my God, he didn't want to add to...I grabbed his arm and turned him to the kitchen sink. Now maybe I destroyed some evidence, I hope to God not, but I turned on the cold water and sloshed the boy's face and washed away the vomit from the sink. And from his face. And the blood from his mouth."

"And then what, Mr. Doyle?"

"And then, they took over is all. The medics. She was breathing with short gasping sounds and they bundled her up and took her out on a stretcher. And then. Yes. Then the older one, the older patrolman, he helped the medic pry the telephone receiver from—from her—her hand and..."

"And put it into the plastic bag you'd filled with ice?"

He nodded.

"From the moment you saw her until they took her away on the stretcher, did she say a word? Anything that sounded like a word?"

"Not a word, ma'am. Just a small baby sound, a sighing when she breathed. Not a word."

Okay. We'd gotten the shock stuff over with; he'd survived it. It was out in the open. Now. Backtrack.

"Mr. Doyle. When you took Sanderalee Dawson and this man up in the elevator, and they didn't speak at all, and you didn't look directly at either of them, where did you look?"

He closed his eyes tightly, then snapped them open. "At his feet. At his running shoes. He was wearing a navy blue runner's suit. I said that in my report. But I'd forgotten about the shoes."

"What about the shoes?"

"They were...different. Not your usual Adidas or Nikes. They were different. I've never seen shoes exactly like that before."

"Mr. Doyle, are you familiar with running shoes?"

"I am. In this building alone, I can't tell you how many of them run. It's the thing now, you know, and they get all decked out just so. Dear God, I wish I could tell you more, but just that one thing: his shoes were...different. Special."

"Okay. We'll get some catalogues to you. Maybe they were imported or something. It might be very important, Mr. Doyle." I stood up.

"Mr. Doyle, did you see this man come back downstairs? Did you see him again, after bringing him up to the eighth floor?"

"No, miss. He never came through the lobby."

There was a back door—a service exit that opened outward; it had a safety lock so that it could not be opened from the outside. It backed onto an alley. Bloodstains had been found at the door, which had been shoved open and left ajar.

"Mr. Doyle, thank you for the tea, and for all your time. I will probably come back and talk with you again." We walked into the small entrance hall and I

26

looked up at the high ceiling for the first time. There was a lovely, shining crystal chandelier hanging from a gleaming brass chain. Dimly, I could make out angels on the ceiling, frolicking in a large circle.

"I'd like to really take a good look at Holcroft Hall. I've passed it many times through the years, but never really looked at it."

"I can give you its long and interesting past, Ms. Jacobi," Timothy Doyle told me. "This place here, it's the real genuine article, Ms. Jacobi. You come back another day and I'll tell you," he said, love and pride in his voice.

Bobby had his car ready at the curb and we headed toward Roosevelt Hospital. The morning light was grayish blue, dampish, raw with a March wind that had played around with Bobby's yellow hair. A farm-boy's cowlick stood up dead center, defying the big-city hairstylist's efforts. His handsome face was drawn and thoughtful. The scattering of freckles over the bridge of his nose was ridiculous: a man of thirty-two with freckles. Huck Finn. Bobby Jones. He sucked on the corner of his mouth, which activated two deep cheek dimples. We stopped for a red light, and he turned to me, his honest, open, midwestern face astonished at the evil one human being had visited on another.

"My God, Lynne. My Lord, what he did to her."

"They don't do things like that in Lincoln, Nebraska, do they, Bobby Jones?"

"Except in wartime, I don't think they do things like that anywhere in the world, Lynne."

I smiled sweetly and then asked him, "Bobby, dear, have you ever heard of a mass murderer named Charlie Starkweather? I do believe he was a near neighbor of your'n."

3

Within three minutes of our arrival at the Roosevelt Hospital Emergency Unit we learned that Sanderalee Dawson had been transferred by ambulance to New York Hospital for special surgery. Within the next three minutes, it became crystal clear to me that a prosecutor's nightmare was unfolding in the large public waiting room.

In the center of the room, Deputy Police Commissioner in Charge of Public Relations Fred Mandell stood beaming and nodding and grinning and becoming serious and dramatic by turns, in response to his former colleagues from two of the major national television networks.

"Want to try that again, Freddie?"

"Turn the kid in to the camera, Fred. Damn. I'm not picking up on the blood enough."

Deputy Police Commissioner Fred Mandell was not a police officer. He had never been a police officer and he could never begin to qualify as a police officer. Yet he took his high appointed role as Public Relations Commissioner very much to heart. Rumor was he carried a pearl-handled .32 and even knew how to use it. He was handsome, personable and went out of his way to accommodate the cameramen assigned both from the networks and from the newspapers. He was posing and positioning one of my primary witnesses, the young patrolman who had apparently saved Sanderalee Dawson from strangling on her own lip.

I had spotted a small empty office on our way in and I told Bobby Jones, "Get that jerk over here right away. And get that young police officer off to a corner and don't let him open his mouth—not to show his bloody fangs or to make one more remark."

Deputy Police Commissioner Fred Mandell approached me with a pleasant expression, his arms opening wide for one of those European side-to-side embraces with kisses flung into the air. I slid away from him and slammed the door closed. The puzzled, slightly worried expression wiped the stupid grin from his face.

"Been holding a little free-for-all press conference out there, have you, Fred?"

"Lynne, Lynne. They are our best friends in the long run. We've got to keep them on our side."

"How much did you let that poor dopey-looking kid with the blood on his mouth say?"

"Hey, Lynne, wasn't that kid something?" Fred shuddered. "Yuk, imagine sucking out a thing like that. And he's able to laugh and clown around about it now, just like it's an everyday thing. He couldn't have more than a year on the job, and he handled himself beautifully."

Wonderful.

"You keeping notes for your book, Fred: my three most wonderful cases as a police commissioner? You signed up with anyone yet? This will be one hell of a case. It's got all the elements: beautiful victim, a racial angle, sex-sex-blood-and-gore. Just one thing, Fred. You put a lid on. Right now. A very tight, not-another-single-word lid. Not one single leak. Nothing, without my approval. Got that, Fred?"

"You're a very uptight lady, Lynne, you know that?"

"Fred. Commissioner Mandell. Your fun is over for the night. Don't make me get an injunction. Smile a lot and wink at your pals out there, but open your mouth once more, say one more word about my case without my permission, and I'll take away your pearl-handled revolver."

His handsome face tightened and then relaxed. He reverted to the anxious-to-please former television executive he had been before the Mayor, for God knows what reason, made him a police commissioner.

"How could I refuse such a charming request from such a charming lady?"

"You can't. Now tell that little patrolman to get his butt in here."

That cop would have broken Mr. Timothy Doyle's kind heart, the little jerk. He had had his moment. He had behaved properly and selflessly. But now he had reverted to his more basic self. I could see him twenty years from now; the smug lines had begun in the corners of his young mouth. His eyes narrowed and measured me with a cool and distant wariness: who the hell was I?

"Sit down, officer. I'm Assistant District Attorney Lynne Jacobi, Bureau Chief of the Violent Sex Crimes Division."

"Oh? I'm Police Officer Peter Delaney. Me and my partner were the first on the scene with that woman..."

"Tell you how we're going to do this, officer. *I'm* going to ask you a question and *you're* going to give me an answer. Clear?"

His brows climbed slowly up his forehead and a grin played around his lips and he shrugged. He still didn't have the vaguest idea who I was; *he* was the hero of the moment.

"Where did that blood come from, officer? That blood that's smeared on your mouth?"

His hand reached up and his fingertips delicately traced the evidence of his glory. "From that Sanderalee-whatever's mouth, lady. Didn't no one tell you about what happened?"

I leaned against a desk and folded my arms and regarded this kid from the distance of nearly twenty years; measured him; let him enjoy a few more seconds of his glory.

30

"Officer Delaney, don't mess around with me, because if you do I'll wreck you so totally, so completely that you'll spend the next eighteen or nineteen years plucking drunks from public toilets from one end of this city to the other. And no one, sonny, no one at all, will want to see your face smeared with vomit on their front pages. You got that? You ready to sit up straight and start behaving like a professional police officer?"

He had gone a little pale; a little tighter; a lot more resentful. His fingers touched the corners of his mouth again.

"Look, lady, I..."

"*Chief.* You call me *Chief*, because that's my title. Got it?"

"Yes, sir. Uh-uh-Chief. I'm...well, you see, me and my partner were the first on the scene and..."

"No, we'll get to all that when I ask you. You tell me where that blood came from that's on your mouth right now. Or you want me to tell you how it happened? Did someone out there say 'Hey, officer, show us how it was'? Did someone suggest you dip your eager little fingers into the blood on your tunic and smear it on your mouth so it would look more dramatic for the cameras?"—

Right on target. The kid started to fall apart. I let him because he had it coming, even though it wasn't totally his fault.

"All right. Now we're being honest with each other, Police Officer Delaney. You will speak to *no one* without the permission of someone from my office, whether it be me or one of my subordinates. Got it? Good. Now, I spotted a washbasin over there behind the screen. Go over and wash your face, then come back here and show me your memo book."

"My memo book?"

"You haven't filled in your memo book? You were too busy giving press conferences? Where's your partner?"

"He stayed with the chick. He went in the ambulance up to New York Hospital."

31

"He went with the '*victim*.' He went with *Ms. San-deralee Dawson*. She is not a '*chick*.' You got a way to go, officer. For God's sake, close your mouth and wash your face."

It took another five minutes to discover that at no time, from the moment he and his partner had entered that blood-awful kitchen until she had been taken on a stretcher out of his sight, had Sanderalee said one single word. She had only made groaning, cackling sounds.

"Why do you suppose your partner stayed with her in the ambulance on the way here? And in the ambulance when she was being transferred? Why do you think he did that, officer?"

He blinked, then nodded. "In case she says something? In case she comes to and says something of value?"

"You got it. Officer, you stay in here all by yourself and you write up your memo book. I want you to put down the exact times involved; the exact moves you made; what you saw. Everything. Put it in your memo book, not on the front page of the *New York Post* or the *Daily News*. You took very commendable action to-night. You very likely saved Ms. Dawson's life, if she survives all this. You don't mean zilch to those people out there. You're good for a picture, that's it. They really don't give a damn if you put your career in jeopardy by giving out information you should not give out. You are tomorrow's front page to them. Period."

His face lit up. "Jeez. You think I might have my picture on the front page of the *News* tomorrow? Jeez."

4

The chaos and excitement at New York Hospital was far more controlled and institutionalized. They were accustomed, at this huge uptown East Side installation, which was associated with Cornell University Medical School, to the unusual: to caring for the rich, the famous, the infamous, the exotic.

There was a Briefing Room and all the control of a Presidential Press Conference as a spokesman for the hospital fielded questions from media people and "interested parties."

The medical bulletin was brief and nonexplicit. Surgery was in progress at this very moment. Microsurgery of the most delicate kind. Involving the attempted reattachment of Ms. Dawson's severed left hand.

"It looks good as of right now," the bland hospital spokesman said. "The severed hand was kept under optimal conditions. Surgery commenced approximately ten minutes ago; the three-man surgical team of Doctors David Cohen, Adam Waverly and Frank Esposito is in service." How long would the surgery take? "That depends. However long is necessary." What about Ms. Dawson's other injuries? "I cannot comment in any detail at this time."

Chief of Detectives Jim Barrow stood head and shoulders over the milling crowd. He extricated himself from several worried-looking television types and signaled me to a corner in the back of the room.

"I got your note about Timothy Doyle's handling of the cold water faucet, Lynne. Thanks. We've printed him and checked it out. That'll save us something, anyway." He turned and faced into the room. "Behold the glamorous people. That little clique around the doctor are network executives. One of them actually asked if it would be advisable to cancel Sanderalee's live show tonight."

"God, she's really wiped out," we overheard. "I mean, there goes the whole bloody sweeps week right down the old toilet."

Jim Barrow winked at me. "Nice, huh? That bitch up there has really let them all down."

"And in a rating sweeps week," I added. "Terrible. Listen, Jim, I'm going to assign a full staff to this assault. And either Bobby Jones or Lucy Capella—you know my investigator, Lucy Capella?"

"Little dark-haired girl, used to be a nun?"

"That's Lucy. Either or both of them will be my liaisons. Where are we at right now?"

Detectives were tracking down and interviewing all of the guests on Sanderalee Dawson's talk show of last night; members of her crew; her chauffeur; her neighbors; street people who might have seen her assailant.

"And we're starting at scratch with a big fat Rolodex of names of her contacts: friend and foe. The lady has collected a lot of both over the last few years. Especially over the last six months, when she's gone slightly wacko politically. Listen, kiddo, I have my guys doing floor plans and sketches and the usual up at her apartment. We're gonna seal it for the present, but if you want access just let me know and I'll leave word."

Barrow knew me; I always found it valuable to return to the scene of the crime—if it was an indoor setting—long after everyone had gone. I found it valuable to wander around, to get the feel of the place: to absorb it totally, so that months later, maybe even years later, I could reconstruct it accurately in a courtroom, presenting the jury with more than technically correct perfect-to-scale floor plans.

"Good, Jim. Thanks, yes, I'll want to do that. What the hell is all that commotion?"

There was a soft, heavy purring sound emanating from groups of white-uniformed hospital personnel: nurses and doctors, suddenly transformed into movie fans. All were focused on the smaller-than-life-sized but terribly intense figure of Eric Roe, seethingly inarticulate movie star of the moment. He swept majestically into the crowded room with his entourage of flacks who chanted, "C'mon now, girls, don't crowd Eric. Give him a break, kids. Eric's a friend of Sanderalee, so no autographs, have a heart, can't you see Mr. Roe is very distressed."

Mr. Roe stayed around long enough to be photographed being very distressed and then he and his drumbeaters were gone. There was an excitement in the room: who's going to be next? Paul Newman? Naw, he don't know Sanderalee. Does he? Hey, look, there's what's-his-name, the singer.

The cameramen flashed on anybody who might be somebody. After all, this was salable stuff all over the world.

"C'mon Lynne," Barrow said, "I'll buy you a cup of coffee. Let's get the hell out of here before we both get arrested."

5

Jim Barrow gave me a lift back to my apartment. He couldn't resist commenting on the beauty of the rising sun, the unique cloud formations over the East River, and the anticipated number of winter-murdered bodies that would start bobbing up once the thaw was definitely over.

"I like the sunrise in the cloud-swept skies part, Jim. Thanks for the lift. I'll be at my office in an hour or so or I'll leave a number where I can be reached."

"Sure you don't want me to come upstairs with you and warm you up a little, babe?" he asked good-naturedly.

"Jim, here's exactly what I'd like you to do." I leaned over and whispered terrible and dirty things in his ear. He pulled back startled, then laughed.

"You young women of today. My God!"

Hot shower—cold shower, towel wrapped around my head as I rushed to answer the expected, excited tapping at my door. Sometimes I cannot quite believe what has happened to my living room: years ago, I literally "bought a room" right off the floor of Bloomingdale's and had it installed in this nice large main room of my four-room apartment overlooking Washington Square Park. Somehow, through the years, Bloomie's had disappeared, been swallowed up and lost beneath the clutter of my books and periodicals and clippings and case files.

My next-door neighbor, Jhavi, was standing there, as expected. He reached up and took the towel off my head.

"Blow dry, Lynne. It's cut for blow-dry." He looked around in his usual lost way at my chaos. "Want me to fetch you a dryer?"

"No, no. Mine's in the bedroom. I'll get it. Turn off the coffee. The cups are set out."

I heard him fiddling at the television set, then the controlled-excited voice of the newsman telling about Sanderalee. Jhavi turned to me.

"Were you out early this morning? On this? My God, you were out on this?"

As we watched the *Today* show, Jhavi fussed and fingered my hair into place, turning the blow dryer on and off during commercials.

My next-door neighbors and closest friends in the building are what my old Aunt Belle would call "very strange people" and what are now called "gay people." Harley Alton is a powerhouse of a black man who was once a famous linebacker in New York. He now owns and operates a very successful midtown restaurant and has various other flourishing businesses, which he discusses with me periodically. While I am not his attorney—I do not moonlight—I do help him out a little. I check up on his attorney, whom he does not trust completely and at times with good reason.

His lover is an exotic named Jhavi. I have been tempted at times to check him out and feel somewhat certain he could be located in some little corner of Brooklyn, but I prefer his own history: a Far Eastern childhood in a tiny, hardly known but strategic border kingdom, threatened by all the major powers, which forced his father—an important member of the royal family—to send Jhavi and his sister to America for education and asylum.

Jhavi is one of the top set designers on Broadway and my apartment is one of his major despairs. He has done many sketches, but so far, everything he suggests seems to me like a Persian whorehouse, complete with tented fabrics coming from the ceiling, or else an exact duplicate of the set he is currently working on, most recently a revival of *A Streetcar Named Desire*.

He is a rare and physically lovely man, small and perfectly proportioned, graceful as a dancer, with flashing black eyes in his mysteriously dusky face.

He often studies me with the despair of an artist facing a not very promising subject. But he has taught me the high art of makeup: I can literally put on my entire face, start to finish, blank eyes and thin lips brought to life and prominence, high cheekbones accented, switcheroo, presto, change-o—dull, dopey-looking Lynne to bright, intelligent and attractive woman-attorney on her way. All in ten minutes flat.

As we watched and listened, he flipped and fluffed and smoothed my straight black hair into a sort of Japanese schoolgirl's casualness; snapped his fingers for a clip. Then, implacably, he rolled out my exercise mat.

"On the floor, love, on the floor. No indolence. Once that starts it ends here; look. There you are, my dear Lynne. That's you." He held the photograph of my roly-poly parents, who in their plump middle age, in the faded picture, looked like stuffed merry twins.

I exercised, which I hate. I also diet, which I doubly hate. There are times—many times—when I think, What the hell. It might be fun to become rounded and fat along the edges. And then I would look like my parents, and maybe even begin to talk like them—the way I remember them sounding—a soft, excited mixture of Hungarian-English-Yiddish. I would enjoy life and eat rich foods and deprive myself of nothing delicious. It was how they lived and they didn't die of heart trouble or high cholesterol or fat-based diseases. They died together in an exploding TWA jet en route to Florida: their first flight ever, in celebration of their twenty-fifth anniversary. Some lunatic of a boy had packed explosives into his parents' luggage so that he

38

could collect enough money to live in California for the rest of his life because he could see no other way out of Brooklyn. He was nineteen: just my age. He didn't get to go to California, but the flight insurance enabled my brother to go to dental college and me to go to law school.

I arrived at my office at 10:15. At 10:30, as expected, I was summoned to the office of the District Attorney. He had been at his desk for nearly an hour—my intelligence system was excellent. He had had his first briefings of the day: been regaled with the crime horrors of the last twelve hours. What damage had been inflicted on innocent people, on guilty people, on family members by other family members; what police officer had been accused of what illegal deed; what accused crime lord had attempted to fly out of the country; what case was court-ready; what citizens' group was meeting and hoping for his presence; what out-of-town jurisdiction was requesting the assistance of his people; what law-school symposium was asking his cooperation.

Who in the world was this Sanderalee Dawson and, aside from the dreadful injuries inflicted on the young woman, why was there such a public outcry and why was his office being swamped with phone calls from as far away as the State Department in Washington, D.C.? In fact, why was this being treated as an international incident? Who, indeed, was this Sanderalee Dawson?

"Lynne?"

If you were to stop one hundred fifty people at random on the streets of New York, one hundred forty of them would know at least some passing gossip about Sanderalee Dawson; some would know—or think they knew—a great deal about her personal/sex life as revealed in publications from *TV Guide* to *People* to the *National Enquirer*. Among the other ten would be one congenital idiot; a deaf-blind man; two people who spoke no English; four people who claimed they never watched television; one who swore allegiance only to NET; and then there would be Jameson Whitney Hale,

District Attorney of New York County, who would look a little vague and shake his head.

He had appeared as a guest on both the Cavett and Susskind shows, yet could distinguish between them only by the clues he'd picked up: Cavett is the little fellow who tap-dances for a hobby and Susskind is the little fellow with white hair who pretends he knows everything. Right? Ah, yes, and Sanderalee Dawson is that pretty young black woman who used to turn up on the Carson show every now and then. And she has her own talk show now? Amazing. The world of television personalities is a vague reality to him; he deals with so much raw flesh and blood, so many real lives and deaths, he must be excused his ignorance of the make-believe world.

Jameson Whitney Hale settled comfortably into the depths of his leather wing chair and motioned me to his comfortable leather couch, which meant he was prepared to give me enough time to bring him up to date.

Mr. Hale is the third of his name, although he doesn't use the number. He is the result of the proper breeding, the proper educational background—Groton, Harvard and Harvard Law School. He had the proper stint in the Navy during the Korean conflict and had spent enough time in his family's enterprises up in Boston to realize he had no great interest in any of the Jameson or Whitney or Hale interrelated corporations. Years ago, at a proper dinner party, he was introduced to the dynamically energetic, newly elected governor of the State of New York, Nelson A. Rockefeller, who just happened to be in the process of putting together the very best goddamn staff in the country. To be located in New York City. Why not give it a try, Jameson? Why not indeed, Nelson?

The third Jameson took to public life and public service and his young wife and young family settled into their Central Park West duplex where they balanced all the expenses of living in New York City against all the cultural and social advantages. Finally, after years of appointive positions, Jameson Whitney Hale elected to be elected: he ran, virtually unopposed, for the office of District Attorney. He followed in the hallowed steps of Mr. Frank Hogan, and carried on the spirit of honor, trust, cleanliness, decency and objectivity in the running of his office that had made Mr. Hogan's career the paradigm for elected officials everywhere.

I have worked in every one of the eight bureaus under his jurisdiction, after a one-year stint in Legal Aid, defending the very cretins I now prosecute. I decided early on to make this office my career; to catch the attention of the boss not by the fact of being one of the very few women around at the time, but by being one of the very best assistant district attorneys working for the office.

Even after fourteen years on his staff, there is still occasionally the small slight catch in the throat, the abrupt flood of adrenaline, the thump in the pit of the stomach when you are sent for to discuss what you have done, or failed to do, in the course of an investigation or court case. There is the ever-present need to gain the rarely bestowed nod of approval. Every staff member knows when the "Old Man" has given you the dazzling quick grin or the murderous shaft.

For me, Jameson Whitney Hale's approbation is essential. I am ambitious; totally and with great determination, a step at a time, I have been working and moving toward a definite goal.

I want Jameson Whitney Hale's job.

While my present ambition, given its historical setting in the age of upward-and-onward-let's-make-up-for-lost-time women, is not remarkable, Jameson Whitney Hale's commitment to my ambition is very remarkable. He backs me completely and totally. He was never consciously a male chauvinist; it was just that his entire upbringing—education, social environment, generational outlook—precluded any serious consideration of female abilities in a male world. My success in his domain had been singular—not so much because I am a singular woman (although I do have

41

claims in that area) as because I was the *only* woman to break through the various barriers that had been placed before me. At a time when such intrusion was not only unfashionable but downright outrageous, my success in handling assignments within the diverse bureaus of the District Attorney's office became known. My experience ranged from prosecution of fraudulent accident cases all the way to indictments/convictions of organized crime lords.

Had I been a man, my successes would have been noted favorably and placed in my résumé folder against the time when I would, as my predecessors had done, venture into the world of private practice or higher governmental office. The judicial system is so staffed with judges whose initial training was the D.A.'s office, it has been almost a mandatory prep school for ever-higher appointive offices. Except there were no women visible in the scheme of things, unless you were to consider the occasional motherly, elderly woman justice serving in Family Court until her sixty-fifth retirement birthday party and gold wristwatch.

I did not want Family Court. I do not like gold wristwatches. I had decided, early on in my career with the District Attorney's office, to get my credentials, my validation, in every area possible. My expertise, in hope that my day would come.

Had I been a man, my request for transfer from one bureau to the next on the heels of some marked achievement would have seemed highly questionable. Since I was a woman—and who can figure them out in the first place?—it seemed like a harmless enough idiosyncrasy. My mobility was my preparation for my ultimate goal; the time for its attainment had finally arrived. Women were leaders now on the international scene, the national scene, the state and local scenes. I was ready to crack that sacrosanct male-defined domain: the District Attorney's office.

Jameson Whitney Hale had been approached several times with offers for other public office. In the past, he had considered carefully and declined. This year, the proposals put to him were very serious and had strong bipartisan backing. They were offering him the United States Senate. He had until late spring to declare himself, to be tested in the primary. He would be damned certain of his victory before committing himself.

His office would then become available. He would resign as soon as he declared and would appoint an interim District Attorney: either a sitting incumbent with his strong endorsement, who would be a sure thing in the fall elections, or a sitting incumbent from an outside agency who would just be keeping the chair warm until a wide-open election.

Mr. Hale's chief assistant, Max Phelan, was in his early sixties and had long been preparing his retirement home on Hilton Head Island, South Carolina. That left all the bureau chiefs; most of us had eyes for the office. There was that one other possibility—unlikely, but hovering around in the background. He could appoint an outsider: a former State Attorney General or Congressional Investigator or eminent professor of criminology, for reasons of political expediency.

There were many forces working on behalf of Jameson Whitney Hale, including a strong, politically active contingent of women's organizations who would commit to him all-out in the senatorial race, should he appoint a woman incumbent.

I was the only woman fully qualified.

In our preliminary discussions, we had a verbal agreement: all things being equal, nothing rocking the boat, no major catastrophic scandal erupting around me, should he get the definite nod to run for the U.S. Senate, he would back and endorse me fully not only as the incumbent but as the candidate most qualified, most suited.

So much for the silly girl, hopping from bureau to bureau to bureau—let her, what harm can it do, after all, what difference does it make, as long as she does her work properly.

Our relationship, over the long years and through

many different encounters, has always been strictly asexual.

Practically always.

There was a moment, years ago, when the air between us as we considered endless charts of data and evidence, alone late at night in his office, was suddenly charged with electricity. When we each became uncomfortably aware of the other, when a casual brushing of hand against sleeve, the accidental eye contact, had a strange, tense and unanticipated significance.

There had been an isolated fragile moment, caused by great exhaustion from hours of uninterrupted overwork, when we were surprised by the power of the awareness we both experienced at exactly the same time.

We kissed. Just once. Just our lips touching. No hands, no embrace, no fumbling. Just a rather cool meeting of our mouths that formed both the question and the answer at the same time. Then we both experienced a great sense of relief.

Without either of us saying a word about it—ever—we knew the moment had come and gone and we were in no danger whatever each from the other. Our relationship would continue along its professional, asexual course.

"Lynne?"

Who is this Sanderalee Dawson? I am exactly the right person to answer his question in depth and for a particularly shallow, silly, embarrassing reason.

Sanderalee Dawson and I were born on the same day of the same year, within fifteen minutes of each other. This information came to me when we found ourselves sharing a dais, guest speakers about to inform our intense audience of women-achievers how it was for us: how each of us had taken her place in the man's world and succeeded and widened the spaces around us for others to follow. During a break in a totally nauseating luncheon—something greenish and shimmering beneath an ugly, glutinous yellow sauce, which neither of us tried to penetrate—she turned to me and absently

44

asked, "What's your sign?" Taurus, I told her, and her face lit up.

I am nearly forty years old. I am actually thirty-eight years old, but for the last two years I have been describing myself as nearly forty, so that when I am in fact forty, I will be used to the whole idea of it. Sometimes I wake up in the middle of the night and, for a frightening moment, I hear my own voice say "I'm ten years old. Little undersized Lynnie, ten years old. How come I can get away with it, fooling all these people who think I'm someone else? Can't they see I'm ten years old and scared of the dark?" I get up in the morning and look in the mirror and say to my tired face, "Hey. You're nearly forty years old." And I believe it. The kid got lost somewhere in the dark.

Of course, I never told Sanderalee Dawson any of this. I just looked at her and wondered how she could so easily pass for twenty-five, twenty-six at the most, when we were to the hour what she called astrological twins.

And so I have had a rather proprietary if passing interest in her career and life. After all, sharing an exact birth moment with someone is something of an intrusion.

Sanderalee Dawson's publicized background was Hollywood-romantic, though how much of it was true I wouldn't know. A girl from the Deep South, sent to live with an aunt in New York City, she had been "discovered" at the age of eighteen by the well-known French director Jacques Gerard, who had been filming in Harlem as a background for his classic three-continent study of youth in the early sixties. She had been a typist in a storefront insurance office on 125th Street when Jacques and crew spotted her and from then on: fairy tale.

Under the guidance of Gerard, to whom she was later married, Sanderalee Dawson became the most popular, highest-paid fashion photographer's model in Europe.

Her features were as delicate and mysterious as those of an Egyptian princess. Her cheekbones caught

45

light and shadow in extraordinary ways. Her eyes were an astonishing shade of pale green, the slight upward tilt emphasized by outrageous makeup. Her hair, thick and heavy, took easily to the avant garde styles required. The fact that she seemed more a deeply tanned white woman with hints of the exotic in her background was all to the good: it was not yet known that "black is beautiful."

Her body might have been created specifically for modeling: it was long and thin, perfectly proportioned, flawless with photographically essential bone structure. After a few years of great success in the European fashion world, after she split up with Gerard, Sanderalee was discovered by *Vogue* and brought home to be the first major black model in the United States.

The early, most famous photographs showed an ice-cool woman with smoldering interior or, perhaps, just the opposite: smoldering woman with ice-cool interior. She could flash in any direction. The camera never detracted from nor enhanced her. It *captured* whatever role she chose to play.

Inevitably, she tired of being someone's mannequin. She went to Los Angeles where an adventurous young ad agency took a chance: to use a beautiful black woman in an out-and-out sexual come-on TV commercial for perfume.

The scene was an all-white bedroom, satins, silks, furry rugs, a great musical background; wordlessly, the camera panned the length, the *endless* length of this golden tan fantastic creature in an unbelievable white evening dress, clinging as she lay stretched and poised, back to camera, facing an obligatory fireplace. The camera explored her body, reached her back, shoulders, neck, then her head turned slowly and sensuously as she propped her cheek against her hand. Sanderalee made love to the camera, her eyes offered the invitation, her mouth, lips parted lustfully, as in a maddening whisper, she named the perfume: *Woman*. Quick blackout.

It became the most popular, sensational, criticized,

46

copied and satirized commercial of its day and led to Sanderalee's appearance on the talk show circuit: Carson and Griffin; a chance to swap wisecracks on Mike Douglas, where an ogling group of fellow guests let it be known they couldn't care less for her wit, just let us look at her, right, fellas?

Within a year of the commercial and the guest shots, Sanderalee Dawson had her own half-hour talk show on the Coast.

Depending on her mood, her guests, her whim of the moment, Sanderalee slipped back and forth from Carolina niggergal to New York Bloomie's dream woman. Anger, which had sparked through many of her early photographs as something strong and mysterious, was no longer the I'll-show-*them* sort of thing. In recent appearances, both on her show, which was now New York–based and network-syndicated, and in the political arena, into which she was dipping now and then, Sanderalee's anger was real and a little frightening.

She and Gerard had been separated for years, although the marriage hadn't been dissolved until Sanderalee became deeply involved in a search for racial identity. Her fellow-seeker was a well-known black entertainer who abandoned Hollywood and Las Vegas, gave up his open shirts, gold chains and tight pants in favor of matching dashikis. Although physically they were very different, Sanderalee and friend seemed to have gone to the same hairdresser for a tumbleweed natural; the same speech teacher, from whom they emerged with a slow, cadenced, measured way of talking, as though mentally translating from a much older language into a careful, unfamiliar English.

They had picked up on the same type of condemnation of all things white. Under her new lover's careful guidance—he became co-producer of her show—there was a self-consciously "black" atmosphere on her set; her selection of guests and topics ranged from angry black welfare mothers to disheveled white civil libertarians who heaped abuse on the white establishment from which they had recently removed themselves. And she surrounded herself with surly, head-shaven black ex-cons. Members of her crew, both black and white, were rumored to be getting edgy.

When this affair ended, the entertainer returned to the Coast, ordered a new wardrobe of expensive but subdued clothing, to be worn minus the gold chains, and resumed his temporarily abandoned career. Sanderalee took off her dashiki, had her hair straightened back to normal and moved in another direction: that of outspoken political observer.

In point of fact, Sanderalee's political savvy was very shallow and could not stand the test of intelligent interrogation. That makes more astonishing the fact of her tremendous popularity not only with the public, who loved her fresh, daring, what-the-hell-do-I-care attitude, but the lineup of eager potential guests who ranged from Secretary of State to hopeful candidates for the state assembly. An appearance on Sanderalee's *Let's Take a Stand*, 11:15 to midnight, five nights a week, guaranteed more public exposure and more followup press and weekly magazine coverage than any publicist could possibly arrange.

During the last six to eight months, Sanderalee's interests had veered sharply toward a fascination with terrorism as a viable weapon against intolerable conditions of life affecting vast numbers of people.

Her guide, instructor, mentor, was a fully qualified Ph.D. in Education: Dr. Regg Morris, a highly visible, clearly vocal, outspokenly determined advocate of the aims, policies and methods of the PLO. Although he kept carefully in the background, and was glimpsed only rarely on the subsequent TV special, it was public knowledge that the force behind Sanderalee Dawson's highly publicized, filmed, photographed, magazined and editorialized trip into Arafat-land had been set up, guided, managed and arranged by Dr. Regg Morris.

On her ninety-minute TV special, *Search for Peace in the Mid-East*, we were treated to the sight of Sanderalee Dawson, radiant in the hot dusty sunlight, carelessly dressed in her chic Ralph Lauren western

48

outfits, dancing and gun-waving joyously with Arafat and his band of forty machine-gun-armed thieves; slinging an unwelcome, unholy arm around semi-veiled women, probably damning them forever into unimaginable hells for being photographed over and over again with this strangely vibrant, highly excited American woman with pale green eyes. Willing male teachers, grinning boyishly—they were mostly teenagers—instructed her in marksmanship and helped her to sight her automatic rifle. Painted on the targets were the familiar, graspingly evil, large-nosed, Zionist-Jew thugs, and as she fired her weapon, jumping with the kick to her shoulder, as she slaughtered the enemy of the peoples, there was great joy among the Palestinians.

On the basis of her ten-day visit, spent hopping, dancing, shooting, embracing, cheering, being photographed touching and singing with groups of dirty little children with runny noses, and seething at the refusal of the Israeli government to grant her status other than that of a visiting tourist or working journalist (she felt herself to be an ambassador-at-large, at least), Sanderalee Dawson was metamorphosed into a full-bodied, strong-voiced advocate of Palestinian rights.

She sat and listened, indifferently, to representatives of our government explaining the delicate situation, the balance of rights, emotions, the quiet, unpublicized talks that were continuously going on; the Camp David accords; the tremendous difficulties and subtleties involved. Finally her eyes hardened into glass that sparkled with passion and fury at her startled guest as she reverted to Sanderalee-perfect, bell-ringing oratory that by its force and delivery, if not by its content, devastated her victim. She managed it all with a superb sense of timing. After all, the television studio was her home ground and she knew how to get the final word in, the unanswerable accusation, the cutting remark that destroyed all that had gone before. As soon as the cameras were off, a good-natured, smiling, gracefully light-handed Sanderalee would help her furiously impotent, insulted, besmirched guest to disengage himself from wire and microphone.

She had one or two bad days, even with the control she was able to exert. One of her most controversial shows, which had brought forth the most mail, the highest ratings, the most anger, the most vicious amusement, had been her straight forty-five-minute interview with a former newsman who had written a book documenting Arab-Israeli relationships over a period of twenty years.

The newsman tried to draw parallels and to explain differences between the two peoples. He was earnest and seemingly nonpartisan except for his abhorrence of terrorism.

Sanderalee Dawson seemed hardly to listen to him; failed to respond to any of his gentle questions. She played with the rings on her fingers and the bracelets on her arm, with the scarf around her neck, with the long silk of her shoulder-length hair. She waited. At the last possible moment, when even her crew thought Sanderalee had been bested and silenced at last by a kindly, well-informed, eminently qualified and universally respected journalist, Sanderalee smiled at her guest, and everyone who knew her tensed and waited. Her producer, in the control room, bit down on his thumb, hard.

"Tell me something, Philip," Sanderalee spoke softly, turned directly to her guest, leaned forward as he regarded her politely, "*you're a Jew*, aren't you?"

There was a split second left. Sanderalee turned fullface into the camera, shrugged expressively and in a hard, cold, deadly tone she said, "*I rest my case.*"

Cut to black.

A followup to this incident was carried in the *New York Post* and was also acknowledged by the journalist himself. As soon as the screen went dead, there was a stunned silence in the studio, a total lack of sound or movement. Sanderalee looked up, startled, to see the stricken face of her guest, the deathly white complexion of her director, the frozen positions of the crew.

"Oh, my God," Sanderalee had said, rushing to her

guest's side, "oh my God, Philip, I'm so sorry how that came out. It was just the...the absolutely theatrically *perfect* thing to say. You know I love and respect you, my dear."

The funny part was, the journalist believed her and later stated that she was a woman totally innocent of the possible effects of what she said or did.

6

Jameson Whitney Hale laced his long white fingers over his long flat stomach. His custom-made three-piece suit hiked up slightly at the ankle as he stretched his basketball player's legs, then repositioned himself thoughtfully. He was an aristocratic-looking man; genes did, indeed, tell. Fifty-eight years of good clean living and earnest dedication to the task at hand had carved themselves on his classic features: in another time and place he'd have made a nifty king.

"Do you think," he asked me carefully, "there is a possibility that this attack was politically motivated? Or do you think that it's just a case of out-and-out sexual assault?"

Automatically the response rushed from my lips. "Sexual assault, in and of itself, has been a politically motivated act throughout all of history."

He frowned at my lapse into the semantics of the women's movement. Surely, we were far beyond that;

his arched eyebrows, his intelligent light brown eyes, showed disappointment.

"Well, you asked me."

"Really, Ms. Jacobi. I am merely asking you for *an informed guess* in this *specific* case. Are we dealing with a political matter or with a lunatic nut?"

"We are dealing *either* with a politically motivated act or with the act of a depraved lunatic nut."

"Thank you. We'll see if events justify your initial guess." He gestured to the neat, systematically stacked case folders on his desk with a shake of his head. He went over to his memo pad and made a check mark, probably next to my name; consulted his wristwatch and then his appointment calendar. "Keep me closely informed. I assume you of course have someone at the woman's bedside." I nodded. He walked around his beautiful antique desk, avoiding his genuine leather chairs, stepped lightly on his Oriental rug and led me to the door. "Lynne, good morning." He peered down at me, frowned. He was a very attentive, critical man. "You should get more sleep, Lynne. You've circles under your eyes. Shame about this Dawson woman. Very beautiful, judging from her pictures. Lives it up pretty good, according to the *News*. If one is to believe the *News*. I'll await your word on her condition."

I heard the door close softly behind me and found myself in the long marble-floored corridor that led to his assistant's and his secretary's offices. It was a softly lit, portrait-lined walk past the former District Attorneys of New York County. Their faces all looked very stern, very masculine and very self-righteous. Some of them had been low-down crooks. Most of them had been honest and decent. I could feel their cold eyes slide over me, then glance at one another in indignation: how dare she aspire to join us? Is there no end to their ambitions?

I thought about Mr. Hale's remark, "Lives it up pretty good, according to the *News*." That reminded me of my bone-marrow belief that somewhere engraved in the deepest, darkest recesses of Jameson Whitney

Hale's psyche exists the unalterable conviction impressed on male children the day they are told about female children: *She asked for it*.

It is what is in the minds of most male jurors and too often in the conditioned response of female jurors when we deal with rape or sexual assault.

It is not just a street-common, uneducated belief. My gynecologist once gave me, gratis, a physiologically oriented lecture on the impossibility of such a thing as rape (barring a dead or unconscious woman). At some crucial moment, *he told me*, the woman makes a conscious decision to the effect that What the hell, it isn't worth losing your life over. At that crucial moment, *he told me*, she becomes an active participant in a sexual act, so how the hell could this be rape? *he asked me*.

As a Legal Aid attorney for one less than shining and glorious year, I defended against the charge of rape in the ludicrous days when corroboration by a third person was required. So tell me, Johnny, was there anyone else in the dark alley where you took the girl, or were there any windows facing into the clump of bushes, did anybody see what the hell you were doing to her, was there a possible witness? Thank God, then you've got nothing to worry about.

Every now and then—not often, but every now and then—to the consternation of my colleagues (after all, a guilty plea is a conviction, is a loss-column item), I would advise the perpetrator, the alleged perpetrator, the defendant, my client, to cop a plea. Say, Yeah, I did *something* to her; we'll work out what it was later; we'll bargain it out so you won't have to spend too much time at Riker's or upstate; so you won't be out of action in your alley/park/subway/stairwell for too long. Do you think I really ought to do this, counselor, I mean, after all, if you really look at this in a certain way, it was almost like, ya know, like what the hell was she doing on the street at that time of day/night/morning or on that particular street at any time, day or night, or going into that elevator or that park or that building or that subway station and dressed like she was in a long/short/

loose/tight/dress-skirt-slacks, what *right* did she have? It was almost like, you know, *she asked for it.*

I was well schooled in the traditional male response to any and all sex crimes against and perpetrated on the female body. Except, of course, where tiny little girls were concerned: they hadn't yet learned to *ask for it.*

I had used the Legal Aid experience the way most young attorneys did: to gain experience, insight, savvy— rather than to serve justice. I applied for a position in the District Attorney's office when I had learned all there was for me to know on the loser's side of the fence. My one year among the rapists and the smug, nearly universally defensive reaction of all the men with whom they came in contact, from the arresting officer to attorney to court clerk to judge, taught me that there was an underlying leer and brotherhood summed up in those immortal words: *She asked for it.*

7

The name on Bobby Jones' birth certificate was Michael Bobby Jones; the father's name: William Arthur Jones; mother's name: Mary Anne Bobby. Since there were two other boys named Michael Jones at the grammar school he attended, one already called Mike and the other Michael, and since he did not want to end up a Mickey, he opted for the use of his mother's maiden name. Hence: Bobby Jones.

Bobby Jones grew up in Lincoln, Nebraska, doing all those things only Gentile kids in the Midwest did. He played on his high-school baseball team. He marched with his high-school marching band, playing a trumpet as he high-stepped in his school's uniform. He went skiing in the winter with a bunch of his blond, blue-eyed, well-adjusted pals; went off shooting up deer and rabbits with his dad and big brother, and they actually *ate* what they killed. They had a real fireplace in their small two-story house; a real live Sis who played the piano for them so they could sing Christmas carols and "Onward Christian Soldiers." He also had a kid brother. Bobby's father was a small-town "doc"; his uncle was an Assistant State Attorney General. Both men had been decorated heroes in World War II and one of Bobby's oldest cousins had been killed in Korea.

Bobby's older brother, Billy Jones, enlisted in the Marines and was sent off to Vietnam even though no one in the family could quite figure out what Vietnam was all about. Two weeks after his family was notified of Billy's death, Bobby received his last letter ever from his brother. In a cramped and hard to read P.S., his brother told him "Don't let them get you into this fucking war; it sucks."

Bobby Jones served in Vietnam for two years and then he came home with his long hair, his captain's bars, his changed eyes, his foul mouth, his hardened heart, his air of puzzled displacement and hardly contained anguish.

Why did you come to New York, Bobby Jones?

"My hair; my language; my general appearance; my attitudes; my recreational habits. I...was no longer able to cope with the innocence of Lincoln, Nebraska."

"And so you went to Columbia Law School?"

"And so I went to Columbia."

"And so you made the *Law Review*. And then spent a year and a half at a church-funded counseling service for Vietnam vets."

"Until I couldn't take it anymore. The frustration, the indignation, the sense of separation."

"And so you looked around."

"And so I looked around."

"And so you applied to the District Attorney's office."

"And so you interviewed me. My first lady boss."

His face in repose is so perfect that it hurts me to look at him at times. I feel overwhelmed by the pain of not having known him when I was fifteen years old and in desperate need of him. When I would hide, red-eyed, in the ladies' room and leave the school dance early, claiming to any girlfriend who would ask that I had sudden cramps. That ubiquitous, irrefutable excuse for all things. Because there was no one to lead me onto the dance floor. No one to take me out of the dark, shameful corner. No Bobby Jones.

He is, at thirty-two, in full masculine splendor. Were he stupid, empty-headed and a fool, it would still be fun to be around him for the sheer esthetic pleasure of his physical beauty. But there is a wonderful, exciting intelligence behind those seemingly guileless, childishly blue eyes: there is an alertness, a sharpness, a weighing and measuring that shows in the depths of those sky-eyes. There is a calculation and a scheming quality also. I am aware of that; I am wary of it; I am suspicious of and alerted to it. Yet I discount it for the pleasure he gives to me.

He has worked for me for nearly three years. We have been lovers for just over a year. His promotion to the position of Chief Investigator was entirely coincidental to the escalation of our interest in each other. Yet he is in a somewhat off, possibly uncomfortable position: was it for his professional competence or for his personal prowess that he earned his current status? That is his question, not mine.

I wonder how he handles office speculation. I wonder if it makes him uncomfortable. I wonder if it makes him question his abilities. We do not discuss any of this; I am amused and yet sympathetic to his situation. After all, for nearly fourteen years, with every advancement I attained, I encountered and dealt with the same speculation from those around me.

We neither flaunt nor deny our relationship. The matter is never alluded to in any way within my Bureau.

I am proud of the composition of my Bureau. It is a generally acknowledged fact that I have only the best people working for me. It is interesting to note the position of women in my squad of assistant district attorneys and investigators. I am the only Bureau Chief who has the option of turning down a female candidate who I feel is not qualified, not the best. No one can point a finger at me and claim discrimination or violation of equal opportunity. I am the only one with a real option when it comes to this selection; therefore, I have the very best, the cream of the crop, the hands-down, flat-out best women not among the women but among all the applicants. They know; I know; my other people know. It makes for a smoother running, more efficient group effort.

Most of the time, within the boundaries of a working day, I am able to regard Bobby Jones from a cool and professional distance.

In private, it is an entirely different matter. In bed, we are equals. I am delighted by his seeming lack of vanity. He does not make a temple of his body; he does not run, jog, do push-ups or sit-ups or lift weights. He tells me that leanness and good health are family traits like thick hair, excellent eyesight, and good teeth.

He tells me very little about his short marriage to a high-school sweetheart just before he shipped out. It consisted of a filmy-white bride, a flight to L.A., a few days in a hotel. Letters: hers chatty, newsy, gossipy; his stilted, careful, vague. Homecoming: differences; disappointments; disillusions; changes. Quiet divorce.

He does not pry into my dead marriage; we merely exchange the information: file and forget.

Only about sex is he obsessive: that is the one physical activity to which he claims a strong commitment and expertise. He is skilled and playful and clever and considerate; he is adventurous and experimental and mysterious and exciting. He has introduced me to certain games; new techniques. He can surprise me and reassure me.

We are well-matched in bed.

There is a certain precision in our spoken language. We are, after all, both attorneys and therefore careful and wary of forming unwanted commitments. We never say "I love you"; we do say "I love *that*": that which you have done, are doing to me; that which you make me feel; this moment; this time with you. As though our moments, our time together, were separate and sealed off and remote from our own persons. Games. We play games.

At the sound of the pounding on the door to my apartment, Bobby shook his head and held a pillow over his face: make him go away. It was Jhavi, shouting, excited. He rushed past me as I opened the door. He dashed across the living room directly to the television set, annoyed that it wasn't turned on.

"My God, Lynne, you're on TV. Why aren't you taping it on your Betamax? Where is the damn thing?" He whirled around, checked it out, disgusted to learn that we had a tape of *Casablanca* on the recorder. "Oh, for God's sake, Lynne, how corny can you get? Hey, Nebraska, look at Lynne. She's on the tube."

8

Jameson Whitney Hale interrupted my morning update on the Sanderalee Dawson case with a vague, puzzled, distracted question.

"Lynne? Lynne, did I see you on the television news
last night?"

"You saw a brief clip of me from a show I did about
two or three years ago. Sanderalee was having at law
enforcement in general and the D.A.'s office in particular. The old song: you only prosecute black men. In
the clip they showed, she was accusing me of being part
of a genocidal plot."

Mr. Hale looked over the tops of his reading glasses,
his dark eyebrows raised in surprise. "Good God, *are*
you part of a genocidal plot?"

"As an advocate of the death penalty, I guess I'm
subject to a lot of name calling. 'Genocidal lunatic'—
'legal murderer of black men.' That was how Sanderalee Dawson characterized me."

"Yes. I caught all that. What was it all about? I guess
I tuned in about halfway through. I missed the beginning."

"Well, since Sanderalee Dawson is entering day four
of her coma, and since we're not giving them any tidbits
about our investigation, and since her time slot has to
be filled, some bright-heads over there put together a
rather rushed half-hour of cuts and clips. I'm afraid the

purpose was to show the wide range of enemies Ms. Dawson has publicly collected."

"Ah. So that puts you in the public position of being a known antagonist of Ms. Dawson's? As I remember it, your closing lines were rather strong."

What had happened was, the more I tried to present my case calmly, unemotionally, professionally, the more black, down-home, co'npone little nigger gal Sanderalee Dawson became. Finally, she interrupted my assurances that a convicted murderer's life span of several years would guarantee him the fullest protection of the law and that the death penalty would only be resorted to in the most outrageous, specific circumstances.

"And once he's dead, baby, he dead, that black man you gonna murder, right? And whut the hell, another black man gone down the road, ri'?" It was her "jes-a-lil-ole-nigrah-gal-fuhm-down-home" best; it's very effective in walking all over your words to her. I had kept going, then finally had held up my hand and interrupted her bluntly. "You want to do your shuffle-on-home number now or you want an opinion? Is this to be a discussion or a vaudeville routine, because I didn't bring my dancing shoes."

They had left that part in. Without the lead-in or any preliminary discussion. I came over as a cold-blooded bitch to Sanderalee's wounded girl routine.

They were in there working for her, Sanderalee's crew. Guest after guest, in the clipped and put-together show, was shown "having at Sanderalee." Although in actuality she always emerged at the top of the heap, in this special thirty-minute tribute to "Our Sanderalee; our brave, outspoken lady whose integrity against all odds has never been questioned," we slammed at her, mashed her down, in one way or another attacked Sanderalee Dawson.

"Yes, it was a pretty cheap shot, but all of a piece with the way this matter is being handled in the media. Wait, before I forget..." He stood motionless for a split second, nodded, lifted up a stack of papers and found the small note to himself, which he extended to me. "Glori Nichols, name ring a bell? About a month ago, she approached us through the public relations office. She's a television producer. Does documentary things. She said along the lines of the Maysles brothers, does that mean anything to you?"

"They're very good. Maybe too good. They get in very close to their subjects. Live-in close. I remember something about a city hospital."

"Well, she spoke to me briefly a month ago, but at the time, it just seemed an intrusion. She called this morning, directly as a result of that clip of you last night, in fact."

"Oh? And...?"

"Seems she's been putting together a documentary featuring three women who are succeeding in occupations generally dominated by men. So far, she's been filming a woman commercial pilot and a woman who is one of three top financial advisors in a Wall Street brokerage house. And... she seems to feel you'd be a good third subject."

He took off his glasses and thoughtfully tapped them in the palm of his hand. There was something more on his mind; I knew Mr. Jameson Whitney Hale. I waited. He sighed. He motioned me into a leather wing chair, then leaned against the edge of his desk, his face close to mine.

"Lynne. This is strictly confidential: file it and forget it. For now."

"Right."

"I've been given a definite offer by the Republicans; they can almost guarantee conservative party backing. And strange as it may seem, they feel fairly certain they can count on a large portion of the liberal vote. That would pretty well tie it up in a neat package."

"U.S. Senate."

He sighed and smiled tightly. "U.S. Senate. And that leaves us with you. I think we should begin preliminary work to get you known. Your public work for the ERA and non-partisan backing by various statewide women's groups is all to the good, but what we've got to do is concentrate on this one small tight overpopulated island of Manhattan. This Nichols woman informs, me that her documentary has the backing of a major network; it is tentatively scheduled for early fall airing. The timing could be extremely fortunate for you. You would by then be in place"—he leaned back and nodded to the chair behind his desk—"and your name could become at least familiar to the less sophisticated voter before he encounters it on the ballot in November. This could be the kind of publicity it would be impossible to purchase.

"And if by some fortunate set of circumstances you can resolve this Sanderalee Dawson matter favorably with an arrest and an indictment during the filming of this documentary, why I think it would be a foregone conclusion that you'd be the first of your sex to sit on this chair: the first woman District Attorney of New York County." He stepped back and with a sweep of his hand indicated the ornate, expensive antique chair.

"I thought all this furniture was yours, Mr. Hale. You will take it with you when you resettle in Washington, won't you?"

He walked behind the desk chair and rested his large and competent-looking hands on the intricate carving. "This will be my gift to you, my dear."

We held that for a moment, he reaching for his dream and I for mine. Simultaneously, since we are both hardheaded realists, we exhaled and got on with the business of the day.

I brought him up to date as far as our investigation was concerned. Just before I left his office, he reminded me to get in touch with this Ms. Glori Nichols.

9

Sanderalee Dawson lay deeply comatose and the doctors would not commit themselves as to her condition should she regain consciousness. Her injuries were deep and severe. There was as yet no way of measuring or evaluating possible brain damage; her emotional wounds were speculative.

The three-man microsurgery team was headed by Dr. David Cohen, a tall, slender, low-key personality of surprising good humor. He was comfortable in front of the cameras and easily fielded the questions tossed at him by the medical reporters assigned by the news media. Dr. Cohen had come to international fame a few years ago while he was attending a medical conference in London. As a leading practitioner of the new microsurgery techniques, it was a lucky coincidence that he was nearby when one of the "royals" (one of the endless persons in line for the throne should an unimaginable catastrophe overtake and eliminate most of the immediate royal family of Great Britain) had an extremely unfortunate accident while attempting to saddle a rather jumpy polo pony. There were pictures of a grim-faced Dr. David Cohen being escorted into the ancient private wing of a large public hospital, which frequently housed an injured royal or two—they were such energetic people. There were rumors and wild stories of detached major limbs. There was even speculation in one of the more lurid journals of a nearly severed head. Within an hour after his arrival, a smiling, relaxed Dr. David Cohen emerged to face the mobs of journalists. He gracefully fended off specific questions with the well-received statement: "Surely you gentlemen know I am honor-bound not to discuss any injury incurred by a member of the royal family." When told that the news had been leaked that it was a royal thumb that had been cleanly detached and successfully reattached, Dr. Cohen shrugged roguishly and gave a winning thumbs-up signal, which was flashed around the world. Without any violation of British ethics, he had confirmed what the journalists already knew and he had done it with style, dash and good taste.

Dr. Cohen had trained most of the world's specialists in the techniques he had perfected. He was consulted via long distance middle-of-the-night telephone hookups and occasionally was whisked away via private jet to supervise the reattachment of a disconnected limb in places ranging from Mexico to Saudi Arabia.

"This surgery was not unique," Dr. Cohen told the newspeople. "Fortunately for the patient, her hand was quickly and intelligently preserved, and the fact that there was a minimum time lapse between the severing and the restorative surgery is all to the good."

He introduced his colleagues: Dr. Adam Waverly, an overweight, verbose, oddly ugly man who was anxious to discuss his surgical experience in Vietnam, which was, in his words, "a marvelous field experience for any surgeon."

The third member of the team was Dr. Frank Esposito. He was young, good-looking, snappish, brisk and tense. He literally elbowed Dr. Waverly out of camera range as he shoved his way out of the news conference with a quick "No comment. Dr. Cohen and Dr. Waverly have covered all pertinent information."

Dr. Cohen ended the conference with his statement that he had no comment at this time relative to the work that would have to be done to repair the cosmetic damage inflicted on Sanderalee Dawson.

"That is a separate matter for future consideration. Gentlemen, thank you."

Thumbs up and grin. He was as skilled and controlling as a movie star handling a media event.

The New York Times ran a three-section "Man-in-the-News" feature article on the backgrounds of the doctors who worked on Sanderalee Dawson. They were instant media heroes and the correct answer to one of the questions in *The New York Times* weekly quiz was Esposito-Cohen-Waverly.

For us, however, as in any homicide, the most immediate person we had to work on was the victim, Sanderalee Dawson. I decided on a "day-of-birth—day-of-death" background investigation. I spent about thirty minutes with A.D.A. Wesley Copeland, who was flying down to Greensboro, North Carolina, en route to Cullen, where Sanderalee had been born.

Wesley Copeland had been born and raised in Atlanta; he spent three years in Korea, mustering out as one of a very few black Army captains. He moved to New York, passed the Civil Service exam for patrolman, put in his twenty years, retired with a first-grade detective's pension, which—along with his Assistant District Attorney's salary—comfortably took care of the remaining mortgage on his brownstone in Brooklyn.

When Wesley Copeland applied for a spot in my Squad, my first reaction was that he was overqualified. He had a bachelor's and a master's in Criminology from the John Jay College of Criminal Justice and a law degree from NYU. Most of his academic work had been done at night. He told me, quite frankly, that he wanted no more than two years' experience and then planned to go into private practice. I considered that we were lucky to have him in the Squad: another best of the best.

One of Wes's finest qualities is his easy, Southern-soft manner of gathering information. He is a good listener and people tell him more than they intend. His

65

background reports read like short stories: people take on flesh and style. He assured me he would feel at home in North Carolina.

"I have the good sense," he told me with a slow, wise smile, "not to arrive in Cullen in a long purple Cadillac. None of the folks, white nor black, would approve. I'm just passing through town and thought I'd look for a particular tombstone of an old granny I'd heard about all my life but never met. The old folks love to talk about long ago. They'll know all about Sander lee Dawson and her family."

We spot-checked the people who immediately came to mind as potential murderers/assailants: her ex-husband was now in Australia with some film company, shooting a documentary about aborigines. One or two of the men from her show, with whom she'd been seen occasionally, seemed set with verifiable alibis.

Among the people who established themselves as a "waiting entourage" at the hospital, some difficulty developed when three self-proclaimed PLO honor guards became involved in a pushing-shoving argument with some of the network people. One of the honor guards pulled a gravity knife and behaved in a "menacing way." Another displayed a .357 Magnum revolver casually stuck into his waistband. The police waded in. Everyone was disarmed. The weapon carriers were carted off to the precinct. Cries of favoritism and Zionist plot rent the air. Dr. Regg Morris—he of the Ph.D. in Education—showed up with a small army of civil libertarians, white and black, and they caused a small commotion of their own. Some heroes of the Jewish Defense League showed up unbidden and began to chant and wave placards outside the precinct. When asked to leave, they refused. Once taken into custody, face to face with the PLO warriors, the precinct turned into the Golan Heights. Reinforcements of both persuasions—aroused Arabs and indignant Jews—showed up in masses of angry bodies. From the TV news tapes, it was hard to tell who was doing what to whom, but everyone denounced the fascist police.

My staff was systematically working its way through a seemingly endless list of Sanderalee Dawson's acquaintances and was trying to reconstruct, on a minute-by-minute time table, her movements on the night of the attack from the moment she was brought home by the studio chauffeur until she was found by Timothy Doyle and the two uniformed police officers.

While she had been seen publicly with any number of men, both black and white, most of the dinners, disco appearances, theater dates and parties were all, in one way or another, job related. Since the dissolution of her marriage with the Frenchman, Sanderalee was not known to have been involved in any personal way with a white man. Being seen publicly with a white man was one thing; privately, it seemed, it was a thing of the past.

The only man she had been linked with for nearly a year was Dr. Regg Morris, and he was hardly white.

We showed a few catalogues of running shoes to our only eyewitness (from the knees down), but Timothy Doyle absolutely, stolidly rejected every picture shown to him: No, no, no, none of them resembled the special, dark blue, oddly "different" running shoes of the man with Sanderalee Dawson that night. Bobby Jones was to meet with both a heart specialist who had a book out about running and an orthopedist who dealt with the whole new category of "runner's problems" to see what sort of shoe he might come up with.

Meanwhile we dealt with the confessors: those perpetual full-moon characters who have some deep-seated need to describe in lurid detail the gory things they'd done to whatever victim hit the headlines. Three of them were shipped off to Bellevue very quickly. The fourth was more than a little scary. He brought in a carefully wrapped left foot in a serious state of decay—claimed he'd chopped it off some woman's leg. Was it possibly Sanderalee Dawson's? We turned him over to Chief Barrow's people.

* * *

Sanderalee Dawson's nighttime slot was filled with endless discussions about what had happened to her, what was being done about it, who was behind it all. A roundtable discussion, being led by a pacifist intellectual black minister of somewhat tender years, was taken over by that instant media hero Dr. Regg Morris, he of the marvelous voice and flashing eye; he who had accompanied Sanderalee Dawson on her trip among the gallants of the PLO; he who loved her best and would have his revenge.

"And it was nothing less than a *Zionist attempt* to silence Ms. Dawson," he told us, speaking quickly, not pausing for breath, "and to so silence the freedom-loving peoples of the Third World and to wreak Israeli havoc and viciousness on the newly acclaimed spokeswoman of a people who have come to love her, to count on her, to recognize hers as a voice to the conscience of the world, and the perpetrators of this carefully calculated deed"—quickly, quickly, the man never seems to breathe—"have to know, *have to know* that force begets force, violence begets violence, destruction begets destruction, attack begets attack. The PLO is the military arm of that temporarily silenced voice of that purely beautiful black woman. Hold on there a minute, Reverend" (this to the hapless "leader" of the discussion group who was trying desperately to put in a word of his own), "you just hold on, you'll get your chance to preach that old Zionist-implanted Christian propaganda: Turn the other cheek. Sanderalee Dawson don't have no more cheek to turn, brother, and I surely ain' turnin' mine, no more, no way, baby."

New York—born, raised by an English-teacher mother and an attorney father, Columbia Teachers College—educated, he can "get down home" with the best of them when it serves his purpose.

The horrified producers—mostly Jewish by birth or by association—were aghast at what passions they had loosed. The next night they tried for a learned discussion among psychologists and psychiatrists, to probe the sort of mentality that could perform so gross and dreadful an attack on a woman like Sanderalee Dawson. The wrong guests were placed together in a semicircle. The women ended up calling their male colleagues chauvinist pigs. The males maintained their smugly superior attitude and deferred to the biggest mouth among them, who declared: "All you *women* could go back for a little therapy to examine the reasons for your blatant hatred of men. Remember: 'Lesbians are *made*, not born.'"

The next night, the producers decided to run an old movie. But their ratings had never been higher and they were getting unbelievable press coverage. There was a gold mine under their feet if they could only decide how to get the stuff out.

Two letter bombs were received at the office of the Federation of Jewish Philanthropies. One elderly black woman clerk lost the tips of the fingers on her right hand and her eyes were injured when her glasses shattered. The second bomb was a dud.

A large box of honey candy was delivered to the New York home of the United States representative from the United Arab Republic. A telephoned warning from the "Never Again Committee of Ten" sent the bomb-squad detectives, wearing lead vests, into the mansion, and mobs of veiled women and dark-eyed children into the streets. But the bomb went off with a whimper rather than a bang.

The evening television news shows at both six and eleven picked up and featured every incident that could possibly be connected, in any way, to the attack on Sanderalee Dawson. There were endless, earnest speculations, theories, opinions, outrages, pleas for calmness from religious leaders of all persuasions; sometimes veiled hints of more trouble to come. There were satellite pickups by the major networks throughout the world: our overseas friends and allies had a marvelous time questioning the fate of those citizens of the United States who had had the courage to voice and publicly champion unpopular political causes. The word "conspiracy" raced through the air.

I called the hospital and checked with Lucy Capella.

Status quo: Sanderalee Dawson was in a deep, meticulously monitored coma. Neither better nor worse; life signs were steady. She was in the Intensive Care Unit with a police officer on duty at her bedside twenty-four hours a day. Listening for the slightest word. We'd even settle for a sound at this point.

There were private-duty nurses in attendance in relays, around the clock, in addition to all the regular hospital staff.

There was a uniformed police officer assigned around the clock in the small medical office immediately adjoining the ICU. There was a uniformed police officer assigned to patrol the hallway of the fifth floor, where the ICU was located. His job was to stop, question and identify any person or persons who were in the area without a legitimate reason. He was responsible for stairwells and elevators, corridors and rooms in the vicinity.

Hospital personnel maintained a scrupulous checklist of who went in or out of the ICU. Only those medical personnel previously checked and cleared by hospital authorities and the police were permitted in. There were no other patients in the ICU at this time, although it was understood that should an emergency occur and all other facilities be filled, after a careful screening, the room could be shared. Under rigid guidelines.

Both Jim Barrow and I—as well as the Police Commissioner and the Mayor of the City of New York—were totally committed to the premise that no one, absolutely no one who was not authorized was going to have an opportunity to "get at" Sanderalee Dawson. One of my people arrested a well-known hotshot columnist who had paid fifty dollars for a mop and bucket and had bulled his way into the room backward, humming sweetly and mopping broadly. He was just a little clumsy and got his feet tangled up in his dirty pail of water and he went down in a heavy heap, right on top of his camera which flashed, just once, in his own startled face. But he had gotten enough of a glimpse to wing a column on "The Inside of the ICU: Sanderalee Dawson, Kept Alive by Tubes."

His information was inaccurate. Sanderalee's own vital signs were strong; she was holding her own with nothing more than dextrose, vitamins and some anticoagulants. Deep deep down inside the coma, she was beginning to stir.

I had nearly a dozen of my people assigned exclusively to the investigation, working with Police Department detectives. I glanced over the growing stack of reports: nothing new, nothing I didn't already know.

I left a message with the office secretary where I could be reached. The telephone number was Sanderalee Dawson's. I figured it was time for me to revisit the apartment at Holcroft Hall under quieter, more orderly circumstances.

10

I've never had any really great quarrel with the New York City subway system. It is a relatively convenient, relatively inexpensive method of transportation. I've never been mugged, pushed to the tracks nor witnessed anything more violent than a lot of shoving and pushing.

However, I did feel the slow building sense of anger and frustration as I surveyed the filthy violence implied by the formless spray-paint graffiti. It had been called "people's art" a few years ago, by a well-known writer who should have known better. To me it is space filled with the uncontrolled anger and contempt of a generation of destroyers.

The burst of whirling wind at Columbus Circle felt good. A little dusty, a little grimy, a little bit of biting cold air, a little sting to the eyes, but the sky was clear blue at four-thirty of an early March afternoon and any day with an unpolluted sky can't be all bad.

It looked to me as if some dealers were settled onto the benches at the entrance to Central Park, but that was an educated guess. They might just have been jumpy guys bursting with energy and that was why they kept turning around, looking behind them, "shaking hands" a lot with casual passersby in quick encounters. If you got close enough, you'd probably hear the chant: Waddaya want? grass? coke? Colombian-Jamaican-Hawaiian, name it you got it. Only the best, man, after all, I gotta be back here tomorrow. I wouldn't screw ya, right?

A few old ladies in layers of clothing set their bulging shopping bags on the ground and scattered dried corn for the dirty pigeons.

Across from the wide sweep of Columbus Circle, Central Park South offers another world entirely: expensive hotels with wide-windowed restaurants on the second floor to offer a marvelous park view; towering apartment houses whose tenants use chauffeured limousines the way most people use buses.

I pulled my coat collar up against the blast of wind and began regretting having taken such a less than direct route to Holcroft Hall. I knew I was trying to stall; that I was not terribly anxious to close myself up in Sanderalee Dawson's apartment. Instead I walked over to Fifth Avenue; the wind was down, the sky was streaked with long orange clouds and directly ahead of me were the gleaming windows of F.A.O. Schwarz, practically a landmark on 58th Street. There were more adults than children looking into the window at the fantastic display of stuffed animals. I looked through the jungle of lions and leopards and monkeys and camels and seals and there he was: a six-foot giraffe with long black lashes and bright green glass eyes and a coy but knowing smile. There was something about him that was so appealing; so ridiculous; so expensive. Maybe for my fortieth birthday. Maybe upon my election as District Attorney. Bought secretly of course, in the dead of night. I stood there, wondering how I would get him home.

Then I turned down Fifth Avenue and right at 57th Street. I was walking in a huge circle. Across Sixth Avenue, to Seventh Avenue, another right turn, quick glance at the art gallery posters, past Carnegie Hall, continuing uptown to Holcroft Hall at Seventh Avenue and 58th Street. A direct route from the subway station would have taken about three minutes. But I was in no particular hurry.

Holcroft Hall is one of those dark gray historic buildings that most New Yorkers have never even heard about, even those who work in office buildings directly across the street. It has become so gray, so darkly set into its location as to be almost invisible. It is a fifteen-story Gothic monstrosity built in the early 1920s. Beneath the black filth and years of city grime is a marvelous storybook facade consisting of gargoyles with protruding eyes and evil pointed tongues, cherubs with slightly wicked expressions, warped angels and knights, and swords crossed over shields with an occasional Latin motto thrown in. The building swarms with devils and dragons and suns and moons and scaly, slimy, crawly things with sleepy faces and innocent expressions. When your eyes grow keen enough to trace out the various forms, the building seems to pulse with strangely suggestive, mildly sexual activity. Or maybe not. There is nothing clearly defined.

Mr. Timothy Doyle, when he stopped by the office to sign his finalized statement, had told me what to look for, as if confiding a secret that he wouldn't tell to many others. It is a special building, he said, and we keep quiet about it.

It is luxurious by the standards of the twenties, with

73

high ceilings, large rooms; constructed by a group of multimillionaires who wanted the convenience of a place in the city instead of returning to their mansions in Darien or Kings Point. It was not for corporate use, but for the pleasure of a chosen group. Originally, each of the fourteen owners—the first-floor lobby area was jointly owned—purchased an entire floor of the building.

With changes in the economy, with the rise and fall of private, corporate and individual fortunes, with wars and conflicts, with different lifestyles, with changes in the social structure, there were many changes within the interior of Holcroft Hall, though the outer facade remained untouched. The huge apartments were redesigned, subdivided; kitchens added, bathrooms, entrance doors. The smaller apartments were then sold quietly, carefully and for a great deal of money.

There was still one apartment—one entire floor, the seventh—that was mysteriously maintained intact. All fourteen rooms, plus servants' quarters, kept clean and polished and modernized with new facilities through the years, television and stereo systems, occasional additions or replacement of furniture, but untouched otherwise. Even Timothy Doyle was vague about—or at least unwilling to discuss—the owners. Periodically the apartment was occupied, but nothing more could be learned about the owners. Except that the apartment was definitely vacant on the night of Tuesday, March 6, 1979, when the terrible attack on Sanderalee Dawson was taking place directly overhead.

The arrangement of apartments was different on each floor. There were some floors with just two large apartments: eight rooms and six; a more subdivided floor of smaller apartments: a studio with kitchen and bathroom; a two-bedroom and living room; each different, each designed by different owners. Sanderalee Dawson had bought her large five-room apartment about two years ago. She had the smaller of the two bedrooms turned into the luxurious bathroom Jim Barrow had shown me when I was first in the apartment.

Across the hall from her was a six-room apartment whose walls did not touch hers at any location. To the back of her apartment was a three-room apartment, bedroom wall to Sanderalee's bedroom wall. The owners, a movie star and his film-producer wife, were in Europe. Occasionally they gave their key to their manager, but he had been on the West Coast since January.

The occupants of the six-room apartment were staying at their condominium in Florida.

Sanderalee Dawson had come home to her luxury apartment, set dead in the center of nearly total isolation. Directly overhead were portions of two smaller apartments. The extremely gifted pianist daughter of a well-known industrialist had sublet one of them from a well-known conductor, who was on tour and who occasionally made arrangements for the convenience of students or teachers at nearby Carnegie Hall. The young woman had been at home, asleep in her bedroom, which nowhere made contact with Sanderalee's apartment. The occupant of the other apartment was a writer, off on tour with his latest bestseller. The pianist next door had a key to his apartment and twice weekly checked on his plants.

The doorman on duty now, not as warm and intelligent as Timothy Doyle, was in a hurry to get back downstairs to continue his conversation with the detective still assigned to safeguard the apartment.

"He's been tellin' me things like you wouldn't believe about some a them sex crimes. Beggin' your pardon, miss. But I guess you wouldn't be shocked, seein' as how you're a policewoman yourself sort of, aren't you?"

I thanked him, but no thanks, to his offer to "stand guard" outside. I assured him I wasn't frightened and that I would be fine.

Not true. I was frightened. The minute I stepped into the dark brown entrance hall, leaned my back on the door, heard the doorman's heavy footsteps and the clanky old elevator leave the floor, I felt a stomach-deep fear. I took two deep breaths and surveyed the small room. Actually, the foyer wasn't as small as I had

75

remembered it. It had been very cluttered that early morning, filled with policemen and technicians and fresh evidence of horrors. It was a well-used space: handsome book shelves reached from the waist-high narrow cabinets up to the ceiling. Filled mostly with books: a serious book-place, not for odds and ends with an occasional book or two placed just so.

Sanderalee Dawson was a reader. Some of the classics were well handled. There was a collection of poetry: hardcover college textbook-type; some modern paperbacks. There was a system to the arrangement and I began to trace it around the three sides of the room: history—ancient, European, American; wars—ancient and modern; English novels—eighteenth and nineteenth century. A section of photography books. Decorating guides; piles of expensive decorator magazines. Large collection of bestsellers, fiction and nonfiction. Shelf of screenplays, softbound shooting scripts. An album of Polaroid snapshots. I would look at that later.

I had flicked on the master light switch in the foyer and flooded the entire apartment with light: from table lamps, from recessed spots, overheads, track lights.

Sanderalee's housekeeper had been given the go-ahead yesterday to hire a staff of heavy-duty cleaning men. They had come and rubbed and scrubbed and shampooed and bleached and sanitized everything in the place. Walls had been scrubbed clean; furniture looked pretty good, unless you looked very carefully, unless you were aware of where the blood had accumulated. They had done a good job, but my guess was that Sanderalee, should she one day come back to this place, would throw everything out and get herself a decorator.

I think, if I were Sanderalee, and survived, I would walk away from this place and start all over again. Far away.

Because it lingered in the room: in the very air of the room, in the spaces of the room. I felt the movement of what had happened, visualized it as it had raged

76

from one room to the other, across the lush mushroom-colored carpeting, against the walls, crashing into the furniture, overturning tables, lamps. Had she grabbed at a pillow, anything, to try to fend him off? Yes, the small statue of the unicorn. The six-inch silver unicorn with the blood-stained horn. Apparently, she made a stabbing, puncturing wound somewhere on her assailant. We weren't sure: the blood type—B positive—was the same as Sanderalee's blood type. Which was a dirty trick on us. Ten percent of the people in the world have B positive; Sanderalee and her attacker fell into that category. As did I, her astrological twin.

Had that maddened him further, that poor defensive jab, that small needle of a unicorn horn? Unicorns are magical, mythical creatures, supposed to bring wonderful good things. Had that stab, jab, pushed the lunatic into further madness: into grabbing the cleaver in the kitchen?

The kitchen looked like something in a science fiction movie: stark, severe, sterile. Hospital-clean; functional; cold white ceramic brick floor, white walls, stainless steel equipment. No touch of color or warmth. That was why the blood had seemed so shocking: the richness of color splashed all over this icy white room. Had this been some kind of childhood dream, this spartan hard-edged room?

I went to Sanderalee's bedroom, the only room besides the foyer that contained any warmth, any trace of personality. He hadn't taken her into the bedroom. He had come alone, through this room, into that crazy Hollywood bathroom, to wash his hands, to rinse off her blood.

There was the collection of dolls, blank gleaming little eyes, rigid little arms and stiff little fingers, expensive little outfits. The stuffed toys weren't expensive; they looked old and loved, something from the past. I fingered the collection of perfume bottles on the glass-topped dresser, then leaned closer and saw the collection of photographs that had been slid under the glass. I turned on the dresser lamp; these were old photographs. Elderly people, small children, blurry faces; there was one picture of a tall lanky girl, rigid and tense, thin arms folded, elbows sharp, eyes staring straight ahead. Sanderalee at age ten? twelve? There she was again, this time half-hidden by other children, her hands resting on the shoulders of an old woman seated on a chair. Nothing you could really see, all so out of focus, vague. Snapshots of the past. I wondered what kind of child she had been. There was a certain, discernible sadness.

I went back into the living room and stood quietly, not moving, trying to absorb the silence, to penetrate the silence, to get through the silence to the agonized cry that must have filled this room. I wanted to remember this room... and the kitchen. I wanted to memorize the feeling of that kitchen: the absolute coldness and isolation in which he had left her.

So that I could force a jury into this place: to experience what she had felt in this apartment. To experience, through my presence, the action of this crime.

When the phone rang, I nearly jumped out of my shoes. It was a loud, startling sound: unexpected. A screaming sound.

"Jacobi here."

"Jones here. Listen, can you borrow some running clothes from your little elf of a neighbor? There's an interesting nightspot I want you to case with me tonight."

"Running clothes for a nightspot? What is this, Bobby Jones, one of your more exotic nights on the town?"

"Could be. Stick with me, Chief, and see the world."

"What time?"

"Pick you up your place at nine. Then later, we'll double back to your place. It's Friday, boss. Tomorrow is a lazy day... yes?"

"We'll see what tomorrow is after tonight."

I turned off all the lights with the master control switch in the foyer.

I don't know why, but I stood in the absolute silence

of that soundproof pitch-dark room and, very softly, called her name.

"Sanderalee."

Later, I learned that at approximately that moment, she said her first audible words. They were "*Help me.*"

Part Two

The Accusation

II

We were dressed in identical dark blue jogging suits: a matched set of health nuts. Bobby Jones had even managed to borrow a pair of authentic running shoes. He shook his head at my beat-up old sneakers. As soon as we got out of the cab, he began running in place, stretching and moving his muscular body with shrugs and feel-good stretches. He looked sensational and I wanted to get back in the cab and take him home.

But I went along with him without protesting because of the gift he had brought me: an oversized, soft-cover book of photographs of Luciano Pavarotti in rehearsal. The one hundred fifty pages explored the singer's charm, pain, delight, exhaustion, playfulness, sensitivity, robustness, boyishness, sex appeal. Everything was captured and recorded but the glorious voice: mood after mood probed, revealed. The total concentration, the exhilaration, the encompassing exuberance of that wide-open, arm-flung, handkerchief-clutching smile after the achievement of a difficult aria: it was all there. The photographer was Alan Greco—he of the Sanderalee series. Bobby Jones promised I would return home with an autograph from the photographer, who had also done the sensitive and revealing narration for this book.

The place was called the Jog-gon-Inn. Very cute. Among the things in this world I hate is cute. I admit, it was a fairly original setup, which is difficult to come up with in New York City. It was divided into two separate and distinct places. The front room was a health bar, featuring a long help-yourself counter of salads and nut dishes and yogurts and cheeses. There were little hand-printed notes to recommend and describe some of the stranger offerings. All drinks were mineral water or fruit or vegetable juices. Everything was calorie-counted, healthy, good for you. The atmosphere was clean, fresh; the two chefs looked like Ivory soap commercials as they took orders for wonderful, natural, quick-cooked surprises. Table service was provided by young, rosy-cheeked kids with sparkling eyes and trim bodies. *No Smoking* signs were everywhere and the murals were of rolling, clear, unpolluted hills and blue skies. To me, the customers looked thin, haggard, pinched, angry, sweaty, resentful and tired as they gulped down vitamin pills with swallows of juice and compared mileage with other runners. They wore unmatched sweaty outfits that looked like they'd been stolen from a chain gang. They looked nervous, tense and ready to run like hell at the first challenge.

At the back of the room was an archway leading to the second half of the establishment. You had to push aside millions of crystal-clear strung beads that dangled from the arch and then you found yourself in a fairly typical Third Avenue–Upper Sixties place. Except that this was located on 56th Street just west of Broadway. It was smaller than the first room, darker, smoky, filled with bright young men and women dressed in designer health-nut outfits. Fashionable colors, more stylish, no sweatsuit types back here. This was a fun place, a let's pretend we're into the whole running-jogging health thing place. At least let's dress up to show we're wise to what's happening. People were drinking from heavy mugs of beer or slender stemmed wine glasses. They were chomping into thick, bloody hamburgers, with a side of French. They were smoking straight cigarettes or pot or hash. They were more relaxed, more comfortable and probably a lot more healthy than the occupants of the first section. At least, that was *my* opinion.

"Lots of show business people—musicians, actors, whatever—drop by after work. It's sort of an offbeat little place, not like Studio 54 or any of the flashy places where you go to be seen. Ah, here comes Henry. He's one of the people we want to see."

Henry looked as though he'd blundered into the wrong section: he had the tense, dead-eyed look of the long-distance runner. His lips were parted to catch the elusive oxygen. His fists were clenched against the muscle aches and pains of the wonderful sport of running. He was in the right section. He slid into the booth opposite us and immediately stuffed a thick cigar in his mouth and nearly asphyxiated himself and everyone near him with the first offensive blast of smoke.

"Ya mind?" he asked.

I minded. Very much. He squashed the stogy into the ashtray and shoved it back into his jacket pocket. He was dressed exactly as Bobby and I were: another one of the three stooges; triplets. Cute.

"Henry is co-owner of this section of the Jog-gon-Inn," Bobby explained. "Lynne works in my office," he told Henry by way of introduction. I kicked Jones in the shin, but with my old worn-out sneakers, I only hurt my own toes.

Henry had signaled for three beers and he smiled with pleasure when they arrived. Then he popped something into his mouth—one or two somethings—and swallowed them down with beer. He leaned his head back, closed his eyes, smiled as he felt whatever it was take hold.

"Ah. More like it. Friday nights, ya know. This is only the start. What, ten-thirty. I'll be going until maybe three, four A.M." He sat thinking that over for a moment; then as if performing for our amazement and amusement, Henry's hands worked under the table, out of our sight, and he ducked down and sniffed loudly, inhaling whatever he had sprinkled into his palm. He came up grinning and winking.

85

"So far, I love him," I told Bobby Jones.

"Lissen, you want something?" Henry began to gesture, pantomime broadly just in case we missed his meaning. "Hey, lissen, Jones, she's okay, isn't she? I mean, you guys are off duty, like this is all off the record, right?"

"She's okay," Bobby vouched for me.

Henry then offered us a hit of whatever we might desire: first hit on him; freebie just to get us into the mood of the place.

"No, no, we're fine," Bobby assured him and slurped some beer.

"No, no, we're terrific," I assured him and wrapped my hands around the beer mug. I hate beer.

Bobby led him finally to talk about Sanderalee Dawson.

"Sandy comes in here sort of regular like. Not every night, ya unnerstand, but she's in and out. She knows everybody, it's like a gang here, ya know, show types, crews, actors, technicians. No stars here, just working guys when it gets down to it."

"Does Sandy hang out with any particular group?"

He shrugged at me. "She don't stay very long, if you take my meaning."

"No. I *don't* take your meaning. *Tell me.*"

He checked eyes with Bobby Jones, then winked at me. "She comes for one thing or another, you know."

"No. *You* know. I'm a stranger here. Tell me."

"Hey, who is this girl, Bobby J? Policewoman or something? This is a friendly off-the-record just-for-information talk, right? You guys are not gonna come down on me or something?"

"No way," Bobby told him and signaled me to back off. I sipped the beer. Soapy water. Henry caught my expression.

"Hey, look, babe, I got the message. I'm gonna get you white wine like you never tasted. My own special." He got up, took away my mug of beer.

"Is *he* going to sign my Pavarotti?"

"No, ma'am. He's going to tell us the off-hours activities of Sanderalee. Just lean back and let me lead him on, babe."

"You got it, babe."

The wine was very good and I sipped it slowly. I have a very low tolerance.

I relaxed and Bobby relaxed and Henry confided. "Sandy's been coming here a long time. We've been here two, nearly three years, and she's been a regular. Even before she got so famous. See, she knows it's low-key here, no creeps, no sightseers. And it's close to home. So she stops by. Sometimes she leaves after just a look around. Sometimes she stays, smokes a little, snorts a little, whatever she wants. Sometimes she leaves with a friend."

"Any friend in particular?"

Henry winked at me—a preliminary signal: a confidence is coming. "Sometimes *old* friends, sometimes *new* friends."

"Sometimes *white* friends, sometimes *black* friends?"

"In here, it's all the same. No color. These people are show-biz."

"So she has gone off with white men?"

"Oh, that whole hate-whitey is just for the camera. Believe me, Sandy don't discriminate when it comes to men."

"Was she in here Tuesday night?"

"The night of the attack? Jesus, that was terrible. Hard to believe, ya know, what the beast done to her. No. She didn't come in Tuesday night."

"You seem positive about that. How come?"

"I am positive," he said. "We're closed on Tuesdays." End of that discussion.

Bobby Jones already had a long list of the regulars and a shorter list of those known to be friends of Sanderalee Dawson. He had a few people working on the list, checking out the names.

"Any particular place your customers go on Tuesday nights?"

"I haven't the vaguest," Henry told me. "Wherever they go, they're right back here Wednesday night in full force. They appreciate your old Jog-gon-Inn more than ever. Same thing on Monday nights 'cause we're closed Sundays."

Bobby went through a long series of questions that he had obviously covered already in a prior conversation/interview with Henry. No, there was no one special involved with Sanderalee; no, none of his regular customers seemed to have "disappeared" since the crime against Sanderalee. Yes, everyone discussed it; yes, everyone was upset, horrified by it. No, no one had any ideas at all.

"Well, I gotta go and spread my charms around. They expect it. Lissen, nice meeting you, little lady. Anything you want, you just ask Henry. Got it?"

"Just ask Henry. I got it."

After he left, Bobby asked me, "Sure you don't wanna snort, or pop or pill or smoke, babe?"

"Sure you don't wanna get yourself arrested, babe?"

Bobby's face lit up. "Ah, here's the man we're waiting for." He signaled to a slim, dark-haired man who was standing uncertainly, with strands of crystal beads dangling over his shoulders.

Alan Greco had a nice smile: gentle, sad, slightly quizzical. It went perfectly with his black liquid eyes and he looked directly at you when he spoke to you. He gave you his fullest attention; it was at once flattering and reassuring. He had a way of closing out the commotion and action taking place all around him. He created a small, private enclosure around himself and whomever he was speaking with. There was an instant, sympathetic rapport; a comfortable feeling; a feeling of familiarity.

I resisted, just barely, asking him what Pavarotti was really like. We were here to learn about Sanderalee. From the photographs he had taken of her, Alan Greco seemed to have penetrated deeply into many of the facets of her personality.

With Sanderalee Dawson, Alan Greco told us, working was more like playing. They communicated on a rare level; they were able to create a special, secret make-believe world just for the two of them. He was able to penetrate the stylized makeup, the high-fashion dead-flat expression. He was able to reach into the hidden fire, the deep, buried passion; to catch a thought as it surfaced and flashed from her eyes, touched her lips, was instantaneously registered by the position and tension of her body.

"When was the last time you were together with Sanderalee?"

"I haven't seen her for nearly a year." He shook his head, and there was a great sadness in his eyes now. "We had a falling out, I guess you'd call it. Sanderalee is a very...basically a very vulnerable woman. She has a large heart; she can be used very easily; she reacts emotionally, not intellectually. Which is not to attack her intelligence. She is very intelligent. But very easily led. We...abandoned...suspended our friendship over her trip to the Palestinian camps. She wanted me to come with her and photograph the whole thing. I told her I couldn't. I had an assignment for *Newsweek*."

"Did you, or were you just putting her off?"

"Both. I could have worked something out. But I tried to tell her to back off, to find out who was using her and why, to slow down, to inquire a little, not to just plunge in. But...she was very taken with the man who arranged the whole thing, this Regg Morris. For the last year or so, he has just about controlled every move she's made. It was all his idea, the PLO thing; the dancing with the guns overhead. My God, I'd never have taken those pictures. I considered them obscene. But you see, Sanderalee didn't have the vaguest idea of what she was getting into."

"Alan, do you have any idea who might have done this to Sanderalee? Any idea at all?"

He clasped his hands together and shook his head, then looked up. "Sanderalee is a very simple and, at the same time, very complex woman. She grew up feeling ugly and skinny and outcast. Undernourished, underloved, with those unbelievable green eyes. She was tormented for all the very things that have created her

89

beauty. Her environment was totally hostile to *her*, in particular."

This was very much in line with the information Wes Copeland had given me: Sanderalee's very differentness as a child, all that had made her a famous beauty later, caused her a childhood of torment.

"What you're trying to say, but are reluctant to say, is that Sanderalee needs the reassurance of many men. Even now."

He nodded and sighed. "Of many men."

"Strangers and friends alike?" Bobby Jones asked.

He nodded. "She has been known to be totally indiscreet. Sooner or later, she was almost...fated to meet the wrong man. Apparently, she ran into him last Tuesday night. Unfortunate choice of words: *ran* into him."

"Is that how she picked up men, Alan? Through running?"

"One of the ways. I cautioned her. I told her it was as dangerous as, say, hitchhiking. She didn't listen. And I haven't seen her in nearly a year. And now she is so wounded. I only hope she is not destroyed. Listen...you'll see her, won't you?"

"Yes, Alan. You want us to give her your love?"

"Oh yes, Lynne. Oh yes. Tell her...just tell her that. She'll know. And please, let me know how I can help. Maybe, when she's able to talk. She'd talk to me. I know she would."

"Yes. I think you're right. All right. When the time comes, we'll tell her you're waiting." I put the softcover book on the table and Alan Greco looked down, then up at me, surprised. His smile was modest, almost embarrassed. He signed his name and thanked me for asking.

I didn't have to ask him what Pavarotti was really like. It was all there: in Alan Greco's photographs.

12

When the telephone rang at five the next morning, I leaned over Bobby and became instantly alert.

"Lynne. Sanderalee is beginning to talk. It's very hard to understand and she's not making sense, but I thought you'd want to be here."

There was a controlled undertone of excitement in Lucy Capella's voice. That in itself was highly significant. Lucy Capella does not show emotion very often.

She is from the Bronx and it is rumored that her father was connected: a common rumor attaching to anyone with an Italian name. I was more interested in her own personal connections during her job interview. Lucy was a dropout nun who had gone into a religious order at age eighteen to escape a domineering father and an unsympathetic stepmother. Her own mother had jumped in front of a subway train at 34th Street and Sixth Avenue at age twenty-two as her solution to a miserable four-year-old marriage. Lucy's memory of the incident was hazy: a passerby had snatched the three-year-old Lucy from her mother's grasp, pulling her to safety. She remembers nothing more of the moment. Her retreat into the religious life was to avoid a forced marriage to a thirty-eight-year-old business associate of her father's.

The order she joined was actively involved in education and, once Lucy's intelligence was discovered, she was sent for a degree at Marymount. After teaching for a number of years, she was allowed to attend Fordham Law School. By the time she earned her law degree, her order was wearing street clothes, discussing priesthood for women, supporting publicly controversial causes. Since she was moving more and more "into the world," it was a natural progression for her to make a final break. Lucy spent a year or so in a transition community of former nuns and priests who had made similar decisions. Through consciousness-raising sessions Lucy perceived herself as a victim of male domination and she moved into an activist role. She wanted to use the law to avenge herself, her twenty-two-year-old mother, and other women for the wrongs inflicted on them by a sexist society.

That was what she told me in our initial interview. She also convinced me that her passion was tempered by judgment, self-control and a love of pure justice.

At thirty-three, she had the shining brightness of a clever twelve-year-old girl. She was small, compact, with a softness of voice and a gentle, quizzical manner that were sometimes mistaken by the defense for timidity or ineptitude. In actuality, she was a steely avenging angel in full pursuit when a case aroused her sense of justice, and she left behind her in many a courtroom an unexpectedly convicted defendant and a stunned, defeated defense attorney who had totally underestimated her.

She had volunteered to spend the midnight-to-eight shift at the bedside of Sanderalee Dawson. The assignment couldn't have been in better hands. Lucy Capella would remain alert, listening, watchful, expectant, ready and able to discern the slightest change in breathing pattern, bodily position or atmosphere within the room.

Lucy still dressed like a parochial schoolgirl. She greeted us in a plaid skirt, Peter Pan-collared white shirt, open navy blue cardigan sweater. On more than one occasion when she had ventured from the room for a five-minute break, she had been scolded by some nurse or administrator: Little girl, where are you going?

"She seemed restless earlier this evening, Lynne. It's logged in the case book at about six P.M. The police officer on duty heard some strange noises and she caught what sounded like 'Help me.' Then nothing at all, until a half hour ago, when I called you. She's quiet now, but I thought you'd want to come over."

The room was dreary-dark, restful, soundless except for Sanderalee's raspy breathing and an occasional echoing sound from down the hall. The hospital still hadn't come alive with the morning staff. Bobby stood quietly to one side, reading the hourly reports. I leaned over the bed and tried to see Sanderalee Dawson.

It was difficult to find the human being beneath the wrappings and trappings that were being used to preserve and restore her. Her reattached left hand, positioned on a pillow, was held firmly in place by a semi-cast halfway up her arm and clean white gauze down to the last joints. The fingers, swollen and shapeless, curled toward the palm and were motionless.

Sanderalee Dawson was located somewhere beneath all the swelling and distortion. Her jaws were wired shut into place so that the broken bones could knit properly. Her nose had been broken. Each breath seemed to cause her great effort and was accompanied by a whistling, wheezing sound. Her mouth was ripped naked down below the gum line. The lower teeth, thus exposed, seemed too long for a human being. Some of them were broken off and jagged. A dental problem to be dealt with later, along with the plastic surgery to create a new lower lip. There was a long way to go for Sanderalee.

"Has a doctor been in to see her since you've been here? Does anyone know that she's starting to come out of it?"

"Since I've been on duty, no doctor. The night nurse checks, but she just pops in and out every so often. I read the chart through. Earlier in the evening, Dr.

Cohen and Dr. Waverly, the microsurgeons, stopped by to check her hand. The police officer told me that Sanderalee seemed aware of them. She started to moan, to cry out. Sounded like 'Help me.' The doctors noted her condition on the chart and said it was a good sign: that little by little she'd be coming out of it from now on."

Sanderalee began moaning and Lucy leaned close to the bed and spoke softly and rhythmically. "It's all right, Sanderalee. We're here with you. You're not alone. We won't leave you. And Lynne is here too." Lucy motioned for me to go around to the other side of the bed. I did, and reached out for Sanderalee's right hand and applied a slight pressure. Her head rolled toward me.

"It's Lynne Jacobi, Sanderalee. From the District Attorney's office. I've been on your show a few times. Lynne." I got a sudden flash. "Your birthday twin, Sanderalee. April twenty-fourth Taurus. I'm here to help my astrological twin."

Lucy stared at me, puzzled, but there was a definite returning pressure from Sanderalee's hand in mine and I leaned closer to her face.

The only living aspect of her was her eyes: they burned and stared from behind swollen lids, making contact, registering an awareness. She was awake; she was listening; waiting.

"Sanderalee, I saw Alan Greco this evening."

Her hand tightened and relaxed: she understood what I told her.

"Alan sends you his love. He loves you very much and wants you to know he's just waiting for when you want him to come."

Slight pressure from her hand. Her eyes closed, then snapped open. She groaned and seemed suddenly terrified. Her hand struggled from mine. Lucy looked up sharply.

"Bobby, please wait outside," she said. Bobby, who had approached the bed, glanced at me, then back to Lucy, shrugged and left the room. Lucy whispered softly to me, "No men. They seem to frighten her. Even when the doctors come, she seems agitated."

I nodded. "Sanderalee? Do you know who I am? Lynne Jacobi, from the District Attorney's office." I took her hand again and felt the pressure. She was hearing me; understanding; but to what extent, I couldn't say.

"Hurts." The word was whispered through her wired jaws.

"Yes. We know it hurts. It will get better from here on. This is the worst it will be; it can only get better from now on."

That was what my mother used to tell me when I had strep throat.

"Help me. Please."

"Yes. That's why we're here. Lucy and I. No one will hurt you anymore. Can you talk to us a little, Sanderalee? Can you tell us what happened to you?"

Her hand pulled from mine; her eyes closed tightly. We could see her withdraw into herself. Deep into herself. Locking us out.

But again, the thin voice said, "Help me."

Lucy's fingers gently stroked Sanderalee's forehead; soothingly, hypnotically tapping and brushing.

"She's asleep again. That's how it's been since a few minutes before I called you. It's going to take time, Lynne. There is no way we'll be able to question her for days. We don't want to bring her back into the attack yet; not until she's stronger, and has a more definite idea of where she is, and that she's safe. God, we don't want to shove her back to the attack yet."

We heard a sound from between the locked jaws. I leaned my head down, my face close to hers. The odor of medication was powerful and sickening, mixed as it was with the remnants of fear and horror. If I were Sanderalee, I wouldn't be in any hurry to wake up and face this awful reality either.

"Regg Morris," she said in a thin, wavering voice. *Regg Morris.*

13

The Bureau office, at seven of a Saturday morning, had that standard municipal-building gray feeling. All the black rubber-topped grayish green metal desks were deserted; all the standard five-drawer file cabinets were locked. The large room had been swept and dusted by the middle-of-the-night crew of cleaning women who were apparently required as part of their union contract to remain invisible at all times.

My office was no different from the rest of my people's: it was just larger, with a window behind my desk that fronted on a slash of Foley Square. Just enough view to tell if it was raining, snowing or doing something wet: no sunshine could ever be detected because of the permanent arrangement of shadows. My desk had been dusted, my floor vacuumed, my wastebasket emptied, my memos neatly aligned along the edge of my desk blotter.

Call Glori Nichols. I had forgotten. To call, not the name. I had checked with Jhavi, since he knew everyone.

"Be very careful, Lynne," Jhavi had warned. "She's made of steel nails and she has her own reasons for doing things. Don't come on too cooperative with her. Let her work for whatever it is she wants and make sure your interests are protected."

Wonderful. I was about to get myself involved in a situation that required alert self-protection at all times.

I dug through the thick standup file in my bottom drawer and pulled out Lucy Capella's report headed *Regg Morris, Ph. D.* and subtitled *Ongoing Report.* Lucy, who seemed to have broken through the exhaustion barrier, was wide-awake, alert and very definite about her decision to continue on duty at Sanderalee's bedside. I felt pretty good about that. I count very heavily on Lucy. She would monitor and record the slightest sound, gesture, word or reaction from Sanderalee. She would catch what most others would miss.

Bobby Jones was on his way down to Regg Morris's home: a very large, expensive brownstone located on—check out Lucy's report: 44th Street between Third and Second avenues. I backtracked and read her report straight through:

> *Regg Morris, born July 12, 1935, in Doctor's Hospital, NYC. Mother: Eleanor Wesley Morris, age 30, occupation high school English teacher; Father: Alexander Sedgewick Morris, age 34, occupation lawyer/owner-operator of Morris Funeral Homes, Inc., 120th Street and Lexington Avenue.*
>
> *No previous births; no subsequent births.*
>
> *Education: First Baptist Church nursery school, 1939–40; Horace Mann 1940–52; Columbia University Teachers College—graduated with B.S. in Education, 1956; Emory University—Master's Degree in Education, 1958. President and Founder: Educational Research Center, Inc., established 1960; funded privately; specialized in studies re educational methods for minority children; 1961–62 Peace Corps volunteer (not specified); 1964: Ph. D. in Education, Berkeley, Calif. (thesis re: special educational needs of Third World children—wherever found); 1965–70: Educational Research Center, Inc., operating on grants from the UN; U.S. Federal Government; internships provided by both State and City of New York—graduate students from Columbia,*

CCNY, Brooklyn College on work-study grants; supervised by Dr. Regg Morris.

1974: Dr. Regg Morris founded and incorporated and is chief owner of the "Wider World School"; located at 344 East 44th Street: the first three floors of Dr. Morris's brownstone, which is also his legal residence.

School is staffed by young, energetic, well-educated, political-activist graduate students, who are—more or less—working under U.S. government grants and internships. This is an elite private school whose student body, by and large, is made up of the children of UN personnel from so-called Third World countries. Although provision is made for these children at the UN's own international school, more and more interest is being aroused by Dr. Morris's school. Some parents have withdrawn their children complaining that they did not send them for "indoctrination of a political nature"; but each vacancy is immediately filled from a long waiting list of potential students. This is a very expensive secondary school. Admittance rate to Ivy League colleges is high; however, it should be noted that such admittance is not based largely on the academic achievements of UN children; they are admitted through a special quota system, which is not publicly admitted. Although many of the graduates do score very high on the SATs, one bursar from Ivy League (who will not be quoted by name) stated to undersigned that "these kids are more prepared to engage in empty, repetitive political rhetoric than in historical fact. They are being indocrinated rather than educated." (Note: same complaint of parents who withdrew kids.)

For last several years, Dr. Regg Morris has been a regular on the "college lecture tour" scene. He earns somewhere between $20,000 and $40,000 on the lecture tour—exact figures not readily available.

He is unmarried; inherited his father's funeral business, of which he is a silent partner; net worth somewhere over one million dollars. Exact financial standing not known.

For last two years, it has been an open-secret—fact that

Dr. Regg Morris and Sanderalee Dawson are not only romantically involved but are in a kind of student/ teacher relationship. He is identified with Third World, PLO causes. They have traveled and vacationed together although they maintain separate living quarters in NYC. He is scrupulous about not bringing women to his brownstone, because of the school's being located there. Investigation re background continuing.

Lucy Capella,
Investigator

Besides Lucy's report, I had read about him in the newspapers; read articles he had written in various magazines; had seen him on the television talk shows, had listened to him on late-night, all-night radio shows; but still, I was not really prepared for the face-to-face presence of Regg Morris.

He towered over me and was a few inches taller than Bobby Jones. His handshake was firm, enveloping, a warm, two-handed, friendly, sincere greeting, which took enough time for him to get oriented to his surroundings.

He stood graciously beside the chair in front of my desk until I was seated behind my desk; waited until he saw I was settled, glanced at Bobby Jones, who was already slumped in one of my two visitor's chairs. He allowed himself a slow, sliding, taking-it-all-in glance around my office: there was nothing special to take his attention, although he did seem to note my framed law degree. He played with his Phi Beta Kappa key with long, slender fingers until he was sure both Bobby and I knew he had it. He sat straight and tall, his full attention now focused on me. The force of his stare was physical; it eliminated our surroundings; it created an intimacy that was at once startling and inappropriate and yet somehow comfortable and familiar. His black eyes were lover's eyes; they were one source of the tremendous power that emanated from him. His body, long and lean and covered by beautifully tailored clothing, was in the center of a highly magnetized field of

99

tension and energy: he was the most totally sexual person I had ever encountered. A little more time went by than I had intended: I was supposed to be establishing the ground rules for this meeting, not him.

"Dr. Morris, I want to thank you for agreeing to come to our office this morning. I hope it wasn't inconvenient for you?"

He smiled slowly and spread his hands. There was something mocking, cynical just beneath his soft-spoken words. "In the interests of justice, my convenience is secondary."

"Do you have any idea at all who might have assaulted Sanderalee Dawson? Do you have any suggestions or information that might aid us?"

He folded his fingers, stiffened the two index fingers straight out, and tapped them against his mouth for a moment. "I want to ask you a question first." I waited. "How many people are working on the crime against Ms. Dawson?"

Bobby Jones, on signal from me, answered, "I don't think that's relevant to anything you might be able to offer."

"*I* think it's *relevant* or I *wouldn't* have *asked*."

"Make your point, Dr. Morris."

The atmosphere, the almost game-playing atmosphere, abruptly changed: hardened, tightened. Morris dropped his hands and slid them on the arms of the wooden chair. He turned his face and glared at Bobby Jones, then turned back to me.

"My point, Ms. Jacobi: Sanderalee Dawson is a *black* woman who has been brutalized by a *white* man. Now, in the history of our great nation, there is nothing whatever unique about this. Black people have always been victimized and brutalized by white people. What I want to know is..."

"Are you here to make speeches or to assist us in our investigation?"

He took a slow breath and smiled; his eyes shot into mine again, but that particular connection had been broken and we both knew it.

100

"All right. Let's skip the obvious. Let's skip right over what we all three of us know of the history of race relations in our country. You are prosecutors: you know as much as anyone else. I am interested, as a very close friend of Sanderalee's, in the progress of the investigation. Is that allowable?"

"More than half of my entire staff is working on this case along with the PD personnel assigned. We are working around the clock and under a good deal of pressure. It is a high priority case. We are handling this case exactly—*exactly*—as we would any similarly vicious assault. We haven't gotten into the racial—or the *sexual*—politics involved."

"Oh yes, that's a new political field, isn't it? *Sexual politics.* Well, yes, I can see where that might take *you*, Ms. Jacobi. But you see, black women have not yet had the *luxury* to be involved in *sexual* politics. They're still involved in the injustices of racial politics."

"Dr. Morris," Bobby Jones said in his bell-clear accusatory voice, "where were you on Tuesday night, March sixth, from midnight until five A.M.?"

Regg Morris shook his head in an exaggerated motion, as though he were a swimmer trying to clear the water from his ear.

"Am I being asked for an *alibi?*" The laugh was incredulous. "Well, I've been accused of many things in my lifetime. Passing for a *white man* has never been one of them."

"No one is accusing you of anything, Dr. Morris. We're just asking you a very standard question. You don't have to answer, if you'd rather not. You can come back with an attorney, if you'd prefer. We can set up such an appointment for you at your convenience."

"I was *with* my attorney Tuesday night. We were in Atlanta, Georgia, attending a seminar at Emory University, between eight and ten P.M. We returned to New York via Delta Airlines—first class—always first class when it's business-deductible. We arrived at LaGuardia well after midnight, maybe twelve-thirty, twelve forty-five A.M. Shared a cab into Manhattan.

Dropped him off first—he lives in Kips Bay. Than I was driven home by the cabdriver. I would guess I arrived home—you know my address: I have an apartment on the top floor of my brownstone—I would guess at around one forty-five or two A.M. I'm not really sure. I took a shower and had a late-night snack. I put on my radio and went to bed. I listened to...I'm not too sure what talk show it was, but I heard my name mentioned in connection with educational testing methods. I'm sure you would be able to check out what show it was; what time my name was mentioned; my radio is set on WOR. At that point, after they discussed my views, I turned off the radio and went to sleep.

"My clock radio woke me up at seven on Wednesday morning. I heard the news then. About Sanderalee. I dressed and rushed to Roosevelt Hospital and learned she'd been taken to New York Hospital. I've spent as much time as possible at the hospital for the last week.

"That is my statement. Now suppose you tell me exactly why you asked me for a statement. By what stretch of the imagination are you probing the possibility of putting a black man into the picture?"

"This case is still wide open, Dr. Morris," Bobby Jones explained. "And will be until we can get some information from Ms. Dawson. The doorman has stated he took her up to her floor in the company of a white man, dressed in running clothes. We have no way of knowing whether or not there was another man waiting inside her apartment, in the apartment next door, or anywhere in the hallway, just waiting for her to return home. We don't know if this man was someone she knew; was afraid of; had a relationship with."

"Or in fact if he existed," I added.

"And if he existed, of course he'd be a *black man?*" Regg Morris smiled bitterly. "And I would be black man number one to question. My God, you people are marvelous. If she doesn't come around soon, you'll be dragging in every..."

"She *has* come around, Dr. Morris."

"*What?*"

He rose from his chair and leaned across the desk. "When? How is she? *What did she say?*"

"*She said your name. She said 'Regg Morris.' And that's all she said.*"

14

The hospital had made provision for the numbers of people involved in the waiting, guarding process. An intern cot had been set up in the tiny lounge room connecting with the private ICU where Sanderalee Dawson lay. Lucy Capella and I arranged a rotating on/off schedule between us and we informed the Police Department personnel that under no circumstances was a male officer to enter either room. We delegated their women officers to the outer, larger waiting room. That annoyed Chief of Detectives Jim Barrow and we had a few not too friendly phone conversations, but since I was already in residence, he reluctantly agreed to the arrangement. His people were stationed in the very pleasant, sunny "family waiting room" where VIP visitors of VIP patients did not have to observe any visiting hour regulations. It was beginning to look like a branch of Chicken Delight or Carvel. Each new shift came loaded with paper bags of fast food.

Also firmly established and sharing space with the police personnel were studio representatives; a few of Sanderalee's crewmen who dropped by with flowers and a kind word to be relayed; some surly looking, but nicely dressed, gentlemen who let it be known that they were PLO. They tried to tape poster-sized pictures of Sanderalee, dancing around their campfires, rifle overhead, to the wall, but were forbidden by hospital officials.

Outside the hospital, there were pickets from various Zionist organizations protesting the presence of PLO people inside the hospital; some PLO pickets protesting the Zionist pickets; and, of course, NYC cops keeping the two groups apart.

By late Saturday afternoon, Sanderalee had not come fully awake again, although she had stirred from time to time. The visitors cleaned up after themselves, although the greasy food smells lingered, and I remembered I was hungry. I'd have eaten anything anyone offered me, but no one offered. The visitors had left behind enough flowers to start a shop. The police personnel gathered up the cards from the various offerings and gave the flowers to a terminal-children's ward a few floors down.

During this time, Regg Morris and Bobby Jones moved around to other areas of the hospital where no one would recognize Regg: no interviews, no photographs, no assumptions, no guesses. He agreed fully with our suggestion. He stated he would wait "forever, or however long it took" to speak with Sanderalee. He would be present the next time she mentioned his name. Bobby contacted me on the hospital phone at regular intervals. At about eight o'clock that night, when all the sounds around the ICU had settled into a quiet, soothing, rhythmic humming of medical equipment, Lucy and I stood on one side of the bed watching the nurse perform the regularly prescribed rites upon Sanderalee: temperature, pulse; professional, competent fingertips touching along the swollen jaws, applying some clear semiliquid medication to the torn lip area; testing the shapeless, curled fingers for warmth. Then the nurse smiled and said, "Well. Hello. Are you with us again?"

Sanderalee's voice seemed to come from a deep, dark,

measureless place, the words rising heavily, laboriously.

"Please. Help. Me."

"You bet, sweetie. You are doing fine, just fine." The nurse dipped the edge of a washcloth into the pitcher of water, then carefully dabbed at Sanderalee's mouth. "Just suck on it a little bit. After a while, I'll give you a nice piece of ice and it will feel *so* good."

There was a loud sucking sound, then a moan and the nurse took the cloth away.

"Hand?" the far-off voice said.

"Well, I've got some good news for you," the nurse answered in a friendly, loud voice as though what she was saying was the most normal, natural thing in the world. "That hand of yours is doing just fine. Now, how about that? It's right back where it belongs."

"What? Where...it...belongs?"

"You bet, honey. You've got circulation going in those fingers, and a nice warmth and we're well past the danger point. Now, isn't that good news?"

It was obvious to everyone but the nurse that the patient hadn't the vaguest idea what she was talking about. Lucy and I waited impatiently as the cheerful nurse made her notations, and told us in her unnaturally loud hospital voice that she'd see us all later.

Lucy leaned forward. "Sanderalee. It's Lucy."

"Lucy?"

"You want that little bit of water again? On the cloth?"

Lucy held the washcloth, newly dipped, to Sanderalee's mouth and glanced at me. The sucking sounds were terrible. Her eyes were locked tight in concentration. Finally, eyes snapped open, looked at me thoughtfully.

"Lynne? Jacob?"

"Jacobi. Right. District Attorney."

"*Regg. Regg Morris.*"

Lucy started to say "Did *he*..." but caught herself before I interrupted.

"You want to *see* Regg Morris? Is that it, Sandera-lee?"

"Yes. *Must see Regg.*"

"Okay. I'll have him here in five minutes. You hang on and I'll get him."

"Oh please. Regg. Help me. Regg. Help me."

We had the Police Department personnel clear not only the family waiting room, but also the corridors. Not even the people at the nursing station were in a position to see Bobby Jones and Regg Morris enter the area of the ICU where Sanderalee Dawson lay waiting. Uniformed police then stood guard in the hallway to keep curious recuperating patients and their visitors away.

Regg Morris grabbed my arm for a few seconds as he looked down at Sanderalee. We had forgotten the effect of seeing her for the first time. He turned his face away, took a long, heavy breath. I could feel him steadying himself.

His voice was very low and controlled.

"Hey, Sanderalee? Hey, lady? Whatcha doing here, lazying away a fine Saturday night?"

"Regg? Regg? *Regg?*"

She struggled to rise. Lucy, standing on the opposite side of the bed, carefully held her shoulders. It wasn't much of a contest. Sanderalee could hardly hold her eyelids open.

"We got him for you, Sanderalee. You talk to him. It's okay now."

There were long streamers of tears running down Regg Morris's face. He smeared his cheeks with the back of his hand. Gently, he reached out and rested his fingertips on her brow. It seemed the only uninjured place.

He leaned toward her and whispered, "I'm here now, Sanderalee. No one, ever, will hurt you any more. Regg is here, baby. Don't you try to talk just yet. We got forever to talk. Gonna stay with you."

"*Regg. Listen. Listen.*"

106

She slipped away again. He turned to me, then looked at Lucy in a sudden panic.

"It's okay. She's in and out of coma still. It's the aftereffects of the concussion. This was the longest she's been awake. She knows you're here. She'll sleep easier now. You want to sit in this little room where Lynne and I..."

"I'm going to stay here. At her bedside. No one is going to move me anywhere else."

Lucy left, then came back with a chair, which she brought to him. "Dr. Morris, here. Sit down. You want anything at all, you let us know. Lynne and I are taking turns staying in the room with her."

I don't know if he even heard her. He stood, watching Sanderalee, his face a study of despair, his long fingers hovering above her restored hand, wanting to touch, afraid to touch.

"Lucy, come on in here for a minute. Bobby Jones just brought some coffee. Let's just leave them alone for now."

15

It was a tedious, uneventful weekend. Bobby and I spent a cold wet Sunday afternoon watching new bootleg movies on Jhavi's seven-foot Advent. Regg Morris left Sanderalee's side only for a quick trip home for a shower and change of clothing. He sat through the night and Lucy, resting next door, heard his soft voice humming, singing, whispering nonsense syllables whenever Sanderalee groaned or stirred.

Although it was absolutely coincidental, the minute I arrived at my office on Monday morning, a little after nine-thirty, at least two people commented on the fact that Bobby Jones and I were dressed alike: dark gray flannels, a shade deeper than sky blue wool knit turtlenecks, rough tweedy blazers. We hadn't shopped together or dressed together or discussed what we'd wear.

Arnold, one of the office legal secretary-assistants (we have two young law students who work part-time), tapped lightly on my door and entered. He had a collection of phone messages for me and a comment he considered important enough to whisper.

"Wait'll you see the *person* with Bobby Jones. She's a real knockout, Ms. Jacobi."

Bobby was at my door and with him was a young woman. He stepped aside to allow her to enter as he announced her name. "Ms. Glori Nichols."

She was the female version of Bobby Jones: wonderfully clearcut features, small straight nose, firm jawbone, huge light gray eyes with a fluttering of thick lashes; what could be called—what *was*—a cute chin. Wide upturned lips, deep dimples in her rosy cheeks; clear, healthy complexion. Her hair looked like a television commercial for shampoo: you could almost see smiling strangers ask how that shoulder-length, amber-honey, straight-cut gleaming hair could smell so delicious. You just knew she'd brush it back casually with long fingers—as she did while waiting for me to acknowledge her—grin hard enough to flash those dimples and show those perfect, square white teeth, and shrug: just lucky I guess.

She looked so *American*, without the slightest hint of any ethnics lurking in the background. She was tall, long-legged, with small but rounded breasts, slim of waistline, flat of hip and totally at ease with herself. She was accustomed to being the standard against which other people measured themselves. Her manner was self-assured, brisk, just this side of abrupt. What must it feel like to look into the mirror and see a Glori Nichols looking back?

"How do you do, Ms. Nichols. Seems I have about eight or six or something messages to get back to you, but I haven't had an opportunity."

Her handshake was timed for a sudden release, which left my hand hanging awkwardly in the air. "Is this a good time for you? Say, the next five minutes, just to set things up?"

She sat down and crossed her legs. Bobby, standing behind the chair, could not possibly miss my signals. He shrugged helplessly. Glori Nichols turned and gave him a quick once-over, then looked back at me. "My God. Was this by prearrangement?" She waved airily at us: I felt as though we were wearing matching clown suits. Bobby Jones remembered some telephone calls that had to be taken care of immediately. He closed the door, and Glori Nichols turned back to me and smiled.

"M-mm. He's yummy. Is he any good?"

"You'll never know."

What the hell was going on here? We were introduced three seconds ago and we're behaving as though we've been in the middle of an ongoing game.

I flipped through my appointment calendar without looking at it and shook my head. "I'm pretty tied up. I can't arrange for an appointment right now and..." My phone rang. I deliberately made an unimportant phone call sound classified and urgent. "As you can see," I told her.

"Tell you what," Glori Nichols told me. "How about if I just follow you around for a day or so. Just me—no crew, no staff. Just so I can get a *feel* for the sort of thing I'll be wanting to shoot. What point of view I want to develop."

I stood up. "What we haven't decided yet is *if* you're going to include me in your documentary. That's priority number one for discussion, and *that's* what I'm going to need time to decide."

Glori Nichols cocked her head to one side. She could get away with cocking her head; it made her look very inquisitive and bright. "Well, we apparently *are* missing signals somewhere along the line. I was under the impression that Jameson...*Jameson Whitney Hale*...the District Attorney..."

"I know the man."

"Yes. *I do, too.* I was under the impression that you and Jameson...Mr. Hale...had already discussed the preliminaries and that it was a matter of *when* I could arrange to..."

"Then you were under the *wrong* impression. The question is *whether* you *will* arrange..."

"But you see, I've been researching you. I've worked up a sort of preliminary background and I've decided you'd be perfect..."

"*I am perfect. In every way.* And every day, I just get more and more perfect. Talk to me next week, you'll see how much more perfect I am than I am today. Ms. Nichols, I don't have time for any of this crap right now."

Her voice switched to deep frozen steel; nice and smooth, no chipping along the edges. "*Then set a time.* Which will be mutually satisfactory to both of us."

"No time will be satisfactory to me. Maybe you're easier to satisfy than I am."

By now, she was standing, too, which was a disadvantage to me. I am five-foot-a-little-something-and-a-half and she, standing straight and marvelously indignant, was about eight feet tall. Whatever her height, five-seven or five-eight, it was perfect for *glaring down upon*. Which is the real reason that witnesses testify sitting down in an American courtroom: *glaring down upon* is very effective. I walked around my desk and sat down and glared *up* at her. Also effective.

"You want to discuss this with me on...say Wednesday, at say three o'clock?" she asked brightly.

"No."

"How about Friday...no. How about Thursday. Lunch? Four Seasons? Look, Ms Jacobi. I don't quite knew what set this whole thing off between us but it seems foolish. Very foolish. I am a professional documentarian—film producer. What I am working on—what Jameson...Whitney Hale... cleared and expressed enthusiasm for—is something that could be extremely helpful to you. I could arrange to have it shown sometime in the early fall. Strategically near election time. The exposure for you would be priceless. I'm sure I can answer any of your questions, relieve your mind of any doubts..."

"Would I have *final cut?*" It was what Jhavi had told me to ask. I wasn't quite sure what it meant, but it brought forth a strong reaction.

"*Final cut? You? Are you crazy?* This is my project, not yours. I'll be glad to sit and discuss my point of view, what the thrust of the documentary will be: why I have chosen my three subjects, what direction I will take. You'll get a feel for what we're doing as we do it. No tricks, no games, nothing derogatory to worry about. But *final cut?* Ha! That's ridiculous."

"I think we've just had our meeting. Ms. Nichols, I've got a heavy schedule today."

"I'll set up an appointment with you through Mr. Hale's office. At your convenience, of course." Her voice was flat and deadly.

"Mr. Hale, the *District Attorney*, is *not my secretary.*"

She glared down a little bit more, then did a great turn, her long honey-amber, shining hair flying around straight out from her shoulders.

Quite truthfully, I'm not exactly sure what the hell it was all about. Except for an intuitive warning. I'm not comfortable with the knowledge that someone has been researching me; backgrounding me; making decisions about me.

That's *my* job. That's the sort of thing *I* do. Regardless of any prearrangements with *Jameson*. That's *Whitney Hale*. The District Attorney. Jameson? What the hell was going on there?

16

Sanderalee Dawson was partially awake for longer periods of time. She was still existing most of the time in some deep, dark, far-down place. She was transferred from the ICU unit on Wednesday, March 14, and established in quarters just as secret, just as secure, but far more comfortable for the personnel assigned to protect her. It was a suite of three rooms with a large entrance hall furnished with a desk and chair for the uniformed police officer; a smartly modern sitting room for visitors and hopefully for the patient when she became strong enough to seek a little sunshine.

There was a convenience kitchenette sunk into one wall: a minuscule refrigerator, two-burner electric hot plate, cupboard with a small collection of china dishes and cups. A teapot; a coffeepot. Bare necessities.

The patient's room was large and cheerful. It looked like a fairly expensive hotel room, except for the hospital bed and the battered, injured woman, whose bandaged left hand rested on contoured pillows, whose face was turned from the light.

Jim Barrow and I had a meeting with Dr. Roger Fernow, an internist who was now in charge of Sanderalee Dawson's case. Although she was out of intensive care, she would still receive around-the-clock medical attention. He had conferred with all physicians who had worked on the case so far and they were all in agreement with Dr. Fernow's plan: he was assigning a female psychiatrist to spend some time each day with Sanderalee Dawson.

We met and spoke with Dr. Martha Chan. She was as fascinating as an ancient ivory figurine. Serene, tiny, beautiful, glowing, her voice was a soft wave of assurance. Her words, pure New York, which was good: which was what Sanderalee was used to. We were allowed to sit in on a meeting with Dr. Chan and Regg Morris.

"After spending a short period of time with Ms. Dawson, after speaking with the doctors, after listening to Ms. Jacobi here, and Ms. Lucy Capella, I feel very strongly, Dr. Morris, that you may be the connection that Sanderalee needs, to get her over the terrible reluctance to face the horror of the attack."

She turned to Barrow and me. "Now I know, from your point of view, what is important in all of this is determining as much as you can about her assailant. My point of view is quite different. My concern is assisting Sanderalee to deal with what has happened to her in the least painful way possible."

"You mean, if it'll be better for her to just forget the whole thing, to not answer any questions, that's *okay* with you?"

"Easy does it, Chief Barrow," Dr. Chan said with a smile. "I'm on your side, pal. I want to get the bastard who did this, maybe not as badly as you do, but pretty badly. Just in my case, time is not quite so important. What I am advising is that she not be pressed too much. Dr. Regg Morris here has the best chance with her. They are friends. She trusts him, can lean on him, confide in him."

Regg Morris's face was expressionless. He glanced away, stared through the window behind Dr. Chan's head. She reached out and tapped his clenched hands.

"Yes, we'll be *using* you. But not for a cruel reason. Sooner or later, she'll have to deal with it. Better sooner; here, in this environment, where we can all help her."

Regg Morris nodded.

"And Lucy Capella. I've noticed that Sanderalee seems to have great trust in Lucy. I understand it has been arranged for Lucy to be right near by, around the clock?"

Barrow looked at me. "You've got Capella doing round-the-clock time? How come you didn't tell me that?"

Barrow was getting a little edgy. He felt we were withholding things from him.

"It's in the report Bobby Jones dropped at your office last night. Read your reports, Jim. Yes, Dr. Chan. Lucy is set up in a connecting room on the other side of the bathroom. Sanderalee has a signal button directly to Lucy."

Regg Morris went upstairs to sit with Sanderalee for a while. Jim Barrow and I had a quick hospital-cafeteria supper. I checked upstairs with Lucy, who was settled into her own room, snug as a nun in a cell. She didn't require much: a few books, a radio, some knitting. She didn't even want a television. Sanderalee Dawson was in a deep sleep by the time Regg Morris offered me a ride home. His limousine was very large and very comfortable.

"Ms. Jacobi," he began as my doorman waited for me to emerge. "Lynne, when you catch this...beast, will you prosecute him *no matter what*? No...'crazy' pleas? No...'extenuating circumstances'? *I want to know.* Because if you people let him get off, I promise you...*he will be gotten.*"

His voice stretched tight with certainty and in the shadows, his face was set into something far deeper than anger or hatred or determination. There was something singular and primal and deadly in his expression.

I pressed his hand and said, "Regg. Go home. Go to sleep. You look wiped out with exhaustion."

"You haven't answered my question."

"What the hell do you expect me to say at this point? Let's get him. That's priority number one, all right?"

114

The doorman reached his hand for me and before I could turn and wave goodbye, Regg had slammed the back door and his driver had pulled the long black Mercedes into traffic.

At two-thirty in the morning, Lucy Capella woke me up. Her voice on the telephone was as shocking as cold water and as snappy and startling as crackling ice.

"Lynne, get up here as quickly as you can. I'll call Bobby. Lynne, get here right away. And bring a tape recorder."

17

Bobby and I met in the lobby of the hospital and didn't even compare possibilities. We were both trying to remember when, if ever, we'd heard Lucy Capella's voice that urgent, that commanding. When the elevator door slid open, Lucy was there. She grabbed us each by an arm, hurried us past the nurses' station where one very busy nurse glanced at us, then back to her work. Instead of taking us directly into the suite, Lucy whirled around, stepped into a phone booth, sat down and spoke to us.

"Now, listen. She's dozing but she'll come out of it as soon as I call her name. She's been talking to me all night. Since about just before midnight. When she finally fell asleep, it was the first chance I had to call you."

"Lucy, what . . . ?"

Lucy looked from me to Bobby Jones, then back to me. Her face was flushed, her eyes sparkling. "Oh, Mother Mary, if this doesn't knock you on your asses, nothing will."

Sanderalee's room was semi-dark, shadowy, mysterious. Lucy went to the bedside and quietly called to her. "Sanderalee? Are you awake?"

A cool, clear voice, stronger than we'd heard since the attack, responded. "Are you here? Lynne Jacobi? And her assistant? Bobby Jones? Have you told them anything?"

"Just to come over."

We moved closer to the bed. Her right hand held a filmy paisley-patterned chiffon scarf over her mouth and chin. It fluttered lightly as she spoke. Her eyes looked larger now; the swelling had receded and her lashes, as she slowly blinked, were long and thick. She looked and sounded alert and aware.

My God, what sort of exorcism had Sister Lucy performed? Sanderalee was not only back among the living, she seemed strong and certain and as she spoke, anger came through the words that were forced through her wired jaws.

"A miracle of restoration, isn't it?" Her right hand reached across her body, flat beneath the covers, the intravenous tubing pulling at her arm. With her index finger, she tapped lightly at the heavy bandages on her left hand, resting on a pillow. She wriggled the ends of the encased fingers slightly. 'This hand, they tell me, is warm. Almost human-body temperature. The fingers are able to move a little now. This hand might one day function, but they won't say to what extent: just that they are hopeful. Those three microsurgeons. The miracle team, I think *The New York Times* called them: Dr. Adam Waverly, Dr. Frank Esposito and Dr. David Cohen. They sound like a political ticket, don't they? The Wasp, the Italian and the Jew."

Her voice had a harsh and bitter sound and then she

116

was silent. Lucy's eyes locked on Sanderalee's as though they were holding a secret between them, for one brief instant deciding whether or not to share it with us.

"You've told them nothing?" she asked.

Lucy said, "Just that you want to make a statement."

I switched on the tape recorder. "Now, for the record, with Lynne and Bobby as witnesses, will you verify that this is, in fact, your true statement, as exact and accurate as you can remember, of the events of the evening of March fifth into March sixth, 1979?"

Lucy sounded as though she were conducting a swearing-in ceremony for a secret society: her voice was low and solemn and intense.

There was a deep sigh from Sanderalee. It was obvious that she was exhausted. "Yes, yes. This is my own true statement. Please. Let's get on with it. I want to tell you what he did to me that night. As exactly as I can."

18

Lucy Capella's voice droned on through the official identification: who she was, where she was, time of day, date, introduced Sanderalee Dawson, who was to make "a true statement about the occurrence at your apartment on date in question."

Sanderalee's voice was fragile in the beginning, but picked up in strength.

"On Tuesday night, after the show, I was still all keyed up. That happens sometimes, if it's been a tight show for some reason or other. Funny, I can't even remember the show that night—who was on or what we talked about."

After her driver brought her home, Sanderalee changed into her running clothes and set out toward Columbus Circle.

"It was really cold and windy up there. I had my blue angora scarf wrapped around my face. It's hard to breathe when it's that cold. The place was deserted. The junkies and dealers were probably down in the subways somewhere. So I ran up Central Park West, as far as...wait...up to...Sixty-fourth Street, and it was so cold that I turned around and headed back to the Circle. Then I slipped on a hunk of ice and turned my ankle. There, at Columbus Circle. Twisted it, it really hurt, because it was so cold. God, even my hands ached when I tried to massage it. And then...wait a minute, this gets mixed up. Was I at the Jog-gon-Inn? In a booth and he came up to me, this man, a runner, dressed in navy running clothes, and he said he'd seen me twist my ankle at the Circle."

Her voice was puzzled and she was trying very hard to put events into order. Concussion is a strange thing: it disturbs time-sequence memory. She was aware of something's being wrong; after a long pause, she caught her error.

"No. That must have been another time. Someone else. The Jog-gon-Inn is closed on Tuesday nights. I was on the bench at Columbus Circle, bent over, rubbing my ankle and he came over. He said that he'd cut through the transverse at Seventy-second and saw me turn back at Sixty-fourth Street and had been behind me all the time. Saw me slip and twist my foot. He told me to show him my ankle.

"He said he was a doctor and knew about these things. And then..."

She stopped speaking. Lucy's voice, soft, encouraging, urged her on.

118

Sanderalee spoke faster now; tension was growing in her voice, as she remembered what she didn't want to remember. The strain came through.

"We went up to my apartment because he said he was a doctor and knew about these things. I mean, what the hell? He seemed okay, you know? What was the difference, if he was or wasn't...so anyway, we went back to my apartment." She faltered again. "This is very hard for me, Lucy. This is. Pain. You see, it intensifies the pain. Right through all the dope they've given me, when I think about going back to my apartment, with him, I can see it all again, it all comes back over me, I...it's hard. Too hard."

Lucy stayed completely away from Sanderalee's growing panic. She led her carefully through the sequence as she remembered its happening. He had rubbed her ankle, manipulated it gently; the pain actually subsided. He really seemed to know what he was doing. She went to the bar to prepare something cold to drink; running makes you thirsty. Some Perrier. The lime. Some cheese. Her back was to him. She was talking to him, about what he wanted to drink, about how cold it was, about how wonderful her ankle felt. And when she turned to face him, she realized he hadn't said another word to her, after adjusting her ankle. The silence was a little frightening.

"He kept looking at me. So strangely. It was so...awful. Oh my God, Lucy, then he said something, so peculiar. It was awful. Wait. It's something very important, terrible but I can't quite...it's there but I..."

Her voice was suddenly very calm. Eerie. Coming from somewhere other than her own throat. It was a stranger's voice, flat and remote. It was almost an imitation.

"He said: *This is not my fault. I have no control over it. I really am sorry, but it has nothing to do with me.*"

There was dead silence now. Sanderalee was right. It was peculiar. It was awful. It was important. And it was very, very terrible.

The rest of her narrative was about as cruel a collection of horrors as I've heard in many years of listening to and acting upon horrors.

Her memory drifted, became vague and confused and then, suddenly, she recited with the needle-sharp clarity peculiar to victims of a sudden, unanticipated, vicious physical attack.

"And when he was choking me, it was with a very strange kind of pressure. Not just, not just his hands wrapped around my throat but, oh God, he was sort of pressing with just his fingertips. Pressure. That's it, he was using some hard pressure points and I think I blacked out, but only for a moment or so, but it was paralyzing, what he was doing to me, he hardly seemed to be exerting himself, it was so specialized, as if he was so positive of what he was doing...like...like a soldier or something."

She described the rape and then the act of sodomy in a dead, flat tone of voice: quickly, thoroughly, clinically.

And then, moments she could not recall exactly.

"We must have, somehow...there was so much blood ...wait, I know I was in the kitchen...no, but first, I tried to defend myself, in the living room. I hit him, stabbed at him with a small silver unicorn, I think I punctured him in the face...he... there was blood on his face and he became so furious at that, oh God. That made him more crazy, I... please...I...a drink of water, okay?"

The fact of his own wound seemed to have enraged her assailant. He slashed at her face with the side of his hand, first one side of her face and then the other, across her mouth. She could hear the cracking, breaking sound of shattered bones, could feel the rough edges of broken teeth, her lip, somehow she had bitten her lower lip. She felt not actual pain, but numbness; not actual terror, but disbelief.

"And then, I went into the kitchen. To call Mr. Doyle, old Timothy Doyle to help me. But first...wait ...no...wait..."

She could not remember whether he had grabbed the cleaver or she had attempted to strike him with it and then he had gotten it from her.

"And then I was just there, on the floor in the kitchen and the blood was, the telephone was swinging back and forth and oh God, my hand, the blood and I didn't know if he was still there, inside, if he'd come back to hurt me, to kill me. And then it was very quiet and then I felt the pain, my God, the pain then, then, voices and it was some men, was Timothy Doyle there? But he wouldn't let them hurt me. I don't really remember, I think Tim was there but then there was a younger man, another man he leaned in to me and tried to smother me, his mouth was on mine, I . . ."

Lucy gently, calmly explained: the young policeman had saved her life. Had sucked the thick bitten-off lip flesh from her throat and breathed for her. She didn't remember any of that.

"And then, drifting, I was floating. On drugs. That was the first thing I was aware of: I'm on something; somewhere and on something. A collection of faces, people in white, moving around me, talking from far off. Sudden pain, oh God, terrible, terrible. I tried to tell them, but my voice wouldn't travel, there was pain inside my mouth, my tongue was cut, the edges of my teeth were . . . broken; I couldn't tell them how much I hurt.

"And then, faces, looking down at me, leaning over. And then . . ." There was a silence, then a huge intake of breath and Sanderalee said, "And then *him. He* was there, and I thought, no, this is not true, he's . . . not here . . . he's in the next room, he's coming back into the kitchen. It got all mixed up, I couldn't seem to focus, but then I knew I was in the hospital. I *knew* that. I realized that. There were nurses and doctors and people all around me, and tubes attached to me. I couldn't move or speak, but I could see and listen and hear.

"*He* stood there, just looking down at me. It was *him*. He seemed to belong there, and I couldn't tell anyone.

I pretended not to see him. Oh, God, I didn't want him to know I had recognized him.

"So I just lay there, watching and waiting and trying to find out who he was, how he had gotten in there with me. He would come in and look at me, at my hand, and then ask the nurses questions, and then talk with the other doctors. I knew about my hand, I remembered seeing it...on the telephone receiver, back and forth and all the blood..."

There was an absolute silence in the room. Then Lucy's voice next, quietly asking, insisting: "Who was it, Sanderalee? Who did these terrible things to you?"

"The tall one, with the glasses. The surgeon who they told me did the most work reattaching my hand. He did this to me, beat me, hurt me, raped me, cut off my hand. All of it. He did all of it.

"Dr. David Cohen."

19

I informed my office that for the time being, Bobby Jones, Lucy Capella and I could be reached at my home number. Lucy had carefully checked out the fact that Dr. Esposito would be the attending surgeon to check on Sanderalee Dawson that day. She was satisfied that Sanderalee was being guarded by competent teams, from our office and from Barrow's office.

The three of us spent hours playing and replaying

the tape: each of us scribbling notes, questions, phrases on the long yellow legal pads of our profession.

At about one-thirty, Jameson Whitney Hale, Himself, called. To make an appointment for me with Glori Nichols. Honest to God, that was why he called.

"Mr. Hale, I'll be in the office either much later today or first thing in the morning to tell you why I do not think it would be wise for me to follow through on that matter."

"Lynne, I think possibly there has been a simple misunderstanding of aims, goals, whatever, which can be very easily clarified."

I had the distinct impression that Jameson—that is, Whitney Hale—was not alone in his office.

"Mr. Hale, I'm here with my Chief Investigator, Jones, and my super-special Investigator, Sister Lucy Capella. We are up to our eyebrows in something which may or may not be absolutely crucial to..." Caution prevailed. Jameson Whitney Hale may or may not be alone; may or may not be smitten—a perfect word to describe what may or may not be his relationship with that sensationally perfect All-American girl, Glori Nichols.

"We are all three of us trying to make heads or tails out of some evidence just uncovered on an investigation that has had us puzzled for a long time now."

I ignored the raised eyebrows, the set of sky blue and the set of black brown stares.

"I just think you ought to take a quiet moment out, *we* ought to take a quiet moment, perhaps in my office, perhaps over a drink, where you gir—...where you two top-professional women can compare notes and..."

Jameson Whitney Hale was definitely not alone; was definitely smitten; was behaving in a very uncharacteristic manner; would have to be protected from himself.

"Just ask the lady if she'll agree to give me *final cut*," I said, as though I knew exactly what was involved. Thank God for Jhavi. "That is all that's holding things up. There's no point in talking further with your

123

friend...with Ms. Nichols if she won't give me the *final cut*. It's a very simple request."

"Lynne, is there anything in particular I should know about what you're up to right now?"

"Not at this time, Mr. Hale. You'll be the first to know, as-soon-as, sir."

We agreed to "get back to each other."

"What the hell is 'the final cut'?" Bobby wanted to know.

"It's the last slice of pizza in the pie, Bobby. Why don't one of you super assistants call the local pieman. I'm starved."

20

Lucy Capella took her list of questions back to the hospital with her. She was to remain on the spot: at Sanderalee Dawson's beck and call.

We had decided that the most important concern, at the moment, was keeping Sanderalee absolutely silent about her accusation. She was to mention it to no one. If she hadn't already.

All three of us had exactly the same question: had she told any of this to Regg Morris?

My recollection of our last, brief conversation in his limo suggested that he had heard most of what was on the tape before we did. That would be for me to handle.

Bobby Jones was assigned to do a thorough background report on Dr. David Cohen: day of birth up to and including what the man was planning to have for breakfast tomorrow morning.

Bobby was more than a little reluctant. "Lynne, this is—to say the very least—ludicrous."

"What's ludicrous? Besides the whole thing? What *specifically* is ludicrous?"

"You know exactly what I mean. *Dr. David Cohen*, for God's sake. Look, she just happened to open her eyes and there he was, probably she was at a critical moment, some kind of crisis point, trying to grab on to reality, and she opened her eyes and there he was, looking down at her. So he just became incorporated into her nightmare, as a participant. As the perpetrator."

"Yes, that's a very sound hypothesis. However."

"However?"

"However, Sanderalee Dawson didn't open her eyes and look up at *you*, or at *Regg Morris,* or at any of the many doctors and hospital personnel who've been in and out of her room and say: *Him.* That's the man who did it."

"She might have. Isn't that the point? She could just as easily have picked someone—anyone—else, in her confused frame of mind. And incorporated him..."

"You just said all that part, about how she inadvertently incorporated Dr. David Cohen into the nightmare."

"So?"

"So, nothing. So the fact *is* she didn't pick out you or Regg Morris or Dr. Esposito or Dr. Waverly or Jose Peppino, the orderly, or Thomas Clark, the physical therapist, or George Whatsisname, the respiratory guy. She *did* pick out *David Cohen.*"

"How about this, Lynne? How about I establish an airtight, chip-proof alibi for David Cohen. Before I start on one of my famous back-to-the-womb investigations."

"You got something better to do with your time, old Bobby Jones?"

"Yes. For instance, trying to come up with a more likely perpetrator-candidate."

125

"You know, or should know, my opinion of the air-tight, chip-proof a-fucking-number-one alibi. A perfect defense. Except not necessarily. Bring me a man who was a guest speaker in front of three hundred people between the hours of eight and ten of a certain night, at which time he has been accused of strangling some-one a hundred miles away. Give me a priest and a minister and a rabbi and a virgin, who'll all swear the subject never left their combined sights during the questioned time. Then, *maybe*, I'll say he has the perfect alibi. That he, *personally*, didn't commit the crime. Barring the possibility that he himself committed the crime alleged, while his clone was having dinner and making sure he was being seen by all of the above. Barring the possibility that he personally *hired* an as-sassin. Barring any and all physical evidence that may connect with him: I might say hell, yes, this guy's alibi is pretty near perfect. But just for the holy-hell of it, let's do a background on him anyway. What have we got to lose?"

"Lynne."

"Bobby, come on. This is all early law school stuff. You give me David Cohen from the day of his birth, through every publicly available fact of his life. Just for the holy-hell of it, okay?"

"Yes, ma'am. You want me to spend my time that way, I will. But for God's sake, just between you and me and little Jhavi next door, can you really, truly even begin to conceive of such a possibility? That this emi-nent, world-famous microsurgeon, the very man who reattached the severed hand...that this man could possibly, by any stretch of the imagination, have been involved in the attack on Sanderalee?"

"Bobby, I have a very tiny funny feeling about you on this. You, personally, have come upon many very strange and very totally weird situations on this job. Things never dreamed of in Lincoln, Nebraska. But you are digging your heels in on this. You are abso-lutely rejecting the slightest possibility, in spite of the fact that our complainant is adamant. Granted her very

126

precarious mental and emotional state as of right now, she seems to me unshakable, *as of right now*, on her ID of David Cohen. Right off the top of your head, Bobby Jones, what's your problem?"

He stalked to the window, shoved the drapes aside, ignoring the fall of dust that I'd meant to vacuum but hadn't. Then he jammed his hands in the pockets of his jacket and marched over to where I was sitting, watching him do battle with himself.

"Lynne. No doctor could have done a thing like this."

"You want me to quote you chapter and verse of atrocities committed by physicians? Ever hear of Auschwitz?"

"Okay. Okay." He jammed his fists deeper, threw his head back and regarded the ceiling for a moment, as if there were words printed up there for him to recite. I knew exactly what he was going to say. And he said it.

"Jewish doctors don't do things like this!"

I leaped up and began applauding.

"Terrific. Absolutely wonderful, Bobby Gentile. You've caught on to the secrets of my race; of my species; of the setaside group of humans who are immune to behavior performed by any other group of humans."

"No, Lynne, what I mean is..."

"I know, darling. Some of your best friends...and in fact your best lover is a Jew. Well, Nebraska, let me tell you something you might have forgotten. Something I will never have the luxury of forgetting. That nice Brooklyn College boy, the sweet-natured, obedient, doting only son of hard-working, self-sacrificing parents, that *really* nice Jewish boy, nineteen years old, blew up the airplane his parents were on. And blew up my parents along with his own; and I think...I'm not sure of the numbers, but he also blew away ninety-something other people."

Bobby Jones sighed and spread his hands helplessly and said, "Dr. David Cohen, from day one up to and including what he plans to have for breakfast tomorrow morning. You want it, I'll get it."

But reluctantly. That was the one major flaw in Bobby Jones, his reluctance to approach an investigation totally with the born prosecutor's point of view: that anyone, at all, can do anything, at all; is *capable* of committing the most unimaginable acts, given a set of circumstances—emotional, physical, personal, mental, environmental, whatever.

Most of us manage to muddle through life avoiding the combination of motives, circumstances and opportunities that could make monsters of us. In fact, most of us, given a strong motive, in an ideal situation in which to commit atrocious crimes, would not.

But many of us would; a great many of us would. This is where Bobby Jones and I part company. His approach tends to be that of devil's advocate to my accuser-general.

So now, we had to find out about Dr. David Cohen. At least, one of us was taking the open-ended point of view.

21

The first two significant pieces of information re Dr. David Cohen were one, he resided on East 69th Street, between Fifth and Madison Avenues; two, he was a runner.

Of course, any number of people lived in that area, and probably four New Yorkers in six were runners. But *he* was the particular New Yorker who Sanderalee

Dawson claimed had told her he had crossed from Fifth Avenue to Central Park West via the 72nd Street transverse. Which would be a logical cut-through for David Cohen, if he wanted to cut through the park. For whatever reason.

Dr. David Cohen was called by his emergency service at 5:05 A.M., Wednesday, March 7, 1979, and asked to report to New York Hospital re possible microsurgery. He was at home at the time of the call and apparently had been sleeping. Which meant nothing, one way or the other.

Sanderalee Dawson, prodded further, gently, persuasively by Lucy Capella, stated she was sure—she thought—that during the course of the terrible struggle she jabbed/stabbed her assailant. She guessed with her silver unicorn. She wasn't totally sure of any of this. It was a passing impression. But yes; she might have stabbed him; jabbed him; scratched him. It was hard to say. There were blank periods; blackouts. Only one thing remained positive: it was him—David Cohen.

Carefully, arrangements were made through the doctor in charge of the case, Dr. Roger Fernow. He was told a believable story by ex-Sister Lucy, whom no one could credit with a lie and who therefore was our most perfect liar: it seems that Sanderalee had developed some kind of aversion to the doctors involved in the rejoining of her hand. Apparently they recalled to her the terror of the event. Could it possibly be arranged, at least for the next few days, that she be attended by Dr. Fernow, at the instruction of the surgeons? So that this hysteria she had developed would not interfere with the information she was now giving to Lucy? No problem, my dear. Is it true you were a teaching nun once? My, my. You must have quite an interesting life story.

Dr. Martha Chan had a quiet visit with Sanderalee. Good old Dr. Chan, sweet face crinkled, told Lucy Capella, "It seems you've replaced me as confidante-in-chief. If something unexpected develops, call me."

Dr. Cohen's life story, as researched by Bobby Jones,

wasn't particularly interesting; certainly not incredible.

> *David Leonard Cohen: born 3/12/42, Doctor's Hospital, Man. Mother: Edna Rubin Cohen, housewife, business partner; Father: Samuel E. Cohen, manufacturer woolen goods, business partner w/wife; weight: 7 lbs. 6 ounces; length: 21"; normal delivery; no previous births.*
>
> *Education: attended Dalton School, 1947–55; Bronx HS of Science, 1955–59; Cornell Univ., 1959–61; Berkeley, 1961–63; Columbia School of Physicians and Surgeons, 1963–67. Interned: Columbia Presbyterian; resident: LI Jewish Hospital. Married: Melissa Wise; OR nurse, Columbia Presbyterian Hosp., March 12, 1970; Beth Sholom, Manhattan. Wife deceased: April 10, 1974 — accident (autopsy/inquest report requested).*
>
> *Dr. David Cohen returned to Col. Pres. Hosp.—further training orthopedics; studied NY Hosp. Joint Diseases—spec. training orthopedic surgery; studied one year clinic—Switzerland—orthopedic surgery/plastic surgery. Taught Col. School of Physicians and Surgeons—specialty, ortho. surgery; worked in Veterans Hosp.—Wash., D.C., and New York City; also in Los Angeles: specialized treating victims of severe disfiguring trauma—i.e., burn victims; disfiguring limb injuries.*
>
> *1977: teamed up with Drs. Esposito and Waverly— participant in new microsurgery. Taught techniques at Columbia. Dr. Cohen is one of the very few specialists in the world doing this type of surgery; patients are referred to him and his team from all over the world.*
>
> *Dr. David Cohen has run in the Boston and NYC Marathons.*
>
> *Dr. David Cohen was rejected for military service because of a physical condition—not specified (note: will check out— B.J.).*

The rest of the report contained standard information: his financial standing (no outstanding debts; pays bills on time); has driver's license; owns 1978 Mercedes SL 450; Dr. Cohen has resided at current address, 48 East 69th Street, tenth floor, for past nine years. Good reputation; nothing derogatory noted.

> *Dr. David Cohen has never instituted nor been involved in any lawsuit.*
>
> *Dr. David Cohen has never been arrested; never fined for any violation; never—as far as can be ascertained—been committed to a mental institution, or received psychiatric therapy.*
>
> *Dr. David Cohen owns a summer cottage in East Hampton; he plays tennis; jogs/runs. Good health; average build and appearance. Dr. David Cohen has a "normal, active social life"; he has been known to date a number of women, generally professional women—doctors, nurses, etc.*

"What do they do on their dates, Bobby Jones, hug and kiss in the old-fashioned way, or what?"

"You want I should find that out for you, Boss-Lynne, you just say the word and I'll find out for you."

I flipped through the report.

"What happened to his wife? Melissa Wise?"

"I'm getting the synopsis of the inquest in about"— he consulted his wristwatch—"one hour. When are you going to interview the good doctor?"

"Soon. And unless he was sleeping that night with a couple of very wakeful bedmates, actually he has no verifiable alibi."

"Yeah, but then neither do I," Bobby Jones pointed out.

"Yeah, but then Sanderalee Dawson hasn't fingered *you*," I reminded him. "What physical condition kept him from military service?"

"I'll have that by tomorrow the latest."

"Maybe a Jekyll-Hyde syndrome?"

"Undoubtedly."

"Good. I would like that very much. Except of course Jews don't have the old J-H syndrome, which everyone knows comes from eating pork."

"Every day I learn something new from you, Lynne."

"I hope so. My job is to teach. Now get lost, Nebraska."

Lucy Capella reported that Sanderalee had, indeed, told Regg Morris most of what she had told us. I had an appointment with Regg for late in the afternoon, the aim of which was to seek his cooperation. We wanted to maintain a silence for as long as possible. If that was at all possible.

Bobby Jones returned with a synopsis of the inquest report; the full minutes would be forthcoming in a day or so. What we had was intriguing to say the least; suspicious to say the most.

On April 10, 1974, at 11:00 P.M., Mrs. Melissa Wise Cohen, wife of Dr. David Cohen, fell or jumped from the balcony of their residence on the tenth floor at 48 East 69th Street. She was clad in a nightgown; no evidence that she had been drinking. Died of massive internal injuries and listed as DOA on arrival at Emergency, NY Hospital.

According to Dr. Cohen, his wife had suffered for many years from manic-depressive syndrome. She was being treated by lithium therapy and had been stable for at least three years. Mrs. Cohen was an OR nurse of extremely competent reputation. Dr. Cohen states that his wife had stopped all medication for a period of about two months. On the evening of her death, he reports she was just beginning to enter what he recognized as a "high swing." During this time, she tended to behave in a highly irrational, overexcited manner. Dr. Cohen states he and his wife had been watching TV news in their bedroom when his wife rose from bed, began talking about a vacation they were planning. She became very exuberant (note: typical behavior of a "high swing personality"); she "danced" through the living room, describing what clothes she would wear

132

on the forthcoming trip to Mexico. Dr. Cohen states his wife went onto the balcony. He asked her to come back inside; it was raining lightly; she would get wet. States his wife began "to dance about," turning her face up to the rain; states that as he approached his wife, to restrain her, she somehow pulled herself to a sitting position on the railing, facing him, her back to the street; that she suddenly thrust her arms over her head and as he dove for her, she toppled backward and fell, landing in front of the building.

She was dead on impact. If one injury hadn't killed her, another had. Any one of at least four of the massive injuries could have caused death.

Her psychiatrist, a Dr. Calendar, testified. His testimony was not included in the synopsis.

Finding of the inquest: death by accident.

"What do you think about this, Bobby J?"

"What am I supposed to think about it? A kind of strange way to go, I guess."

"Did she jump or was she pushed? What was that old song? You remember a song like that?" Funny theme for a folk song; funny way to die.

"Her parents still alive?"

Bobby Jones dug into his notebook, flipped through, held up the address. "I have an appointment with them tomorrow morning at eleven A.M. They live in Forest Hills. They own a bakery on Queens Boulevard. Want to come with me?"

"Yes. It might be interesting to meet with someone who has less than a kind word to say about the good doctor Cohen."

"What makes you think they won't vouch for him? That they won't tell you what a saint he was for putting up with their nutty daughter?"

"Oh. Just a feeling. How about this Dr. Calendar? What the hell kind of doctor is he, letting her go off medication when she was still swinging up and down?"

"That gentleman is coming in to the office tomorrow morning at ten A.M. Kind of strange: he actually *offered* to come here, rather than have me talk with him at his office at the hospital."

"The plot thickens, Dr. Watson."

"And leads where, Ms. Sherlock?"

"Who the hell knows? Listen, I'm having the Honorable Regg Morris in this afternoon. I'd kind of like you to sit in on it. Sanderalee made her accusations to him before she told us. That's why he was so damned edgy with me that night he dropped me off. I'm a little worried about him. About his tendency to talk very loud to whoever—whomever?—will listen. Particularly media people. We've got to impress upon him the importance of keeping big mouths locked shut."

"He looks like the unimpressionable type, but I'll back you up all I can."

The phone rang and the office secretary popped his sweet young head in the door and told me, "Lynne, it was him. The District Attorney. Mr. Hale. He wanted to know if you can come up to his office right away. Something about a TV documentary. I said what you told me to say: that I'd see if I could find you and get back to him right away."

"Tell him you couldn't find me. Can you do that?"

"Absolutely."

"Good boy. Bobby, get out of here and get me those minutes from the inquest. I want a line on this psychiatrist, Dr. Calendar."

"I'm on my way. Just one more thing, Lynne."

"Yes, Bobby?"

"Wanna have at it?"

"Bobby Jones, is that what they teach you in Nebraska? That's a hell of a way to talk to your boss."

22

This meeting with Regg Morris was different from our previous encounters. Instead of magnetism, he gave off repellent rays. He was wary, watchful, hostile, suspicious and judgmental. What he wanted to know, basically, was what I intended to do with the accusation made by Sanderalee Dawson.

"We are conducting an intensive investigation into all aspects and possibilities of the case," I told him.

"We are conducting an intensive investigation," he repeated, mimicking my words. He shook his head and his laugh was very unpleasant. Finally, he looked directly across the desk at me. His black, angry eyes sought to impale me.

"And to what *end* is this intensive investigation into all aspects and possibilities being conducted, Ms. Jacobi?"

"To the ends of justice," I said, somewhat pompously. We were both having a highly dramatic moment. I have been known, on occasion, to rise to other people's dramatic moments.

"To the ends of justice. Um. Very, very impressive. Now let's just examine what we have here. What we have here is one terribly injured, just-about-destroyed young black woman. A black woman in her prime: the prime of her ability, the prime of her power to influence, the prime of her political awareness, the prime of her activism. Cut off and destroyed: mutilated; violated; her effectiveness obliterated. By one man. One *white* man. Whom she has now *positively* identified to you, the representative of the established power, the organization to whom a black woman must appeal. For justice, as you said. For justice. And here we sit, you and I, and your 'main man' here, my blond, blue-eyed friend, a paradigm of the American male."

Coolly, Bobby Jones ducked his head and said, "Thank you, Dr. Morris. Very kind of you."

"Yes, very kind of me, indeed." His eyes slid back to mine. There was a tightening, tensing of the large muscles across his shoulders, a stiffening of his body. He softened his voice even more; a good, effective technique. Bobby and I did exactly what he intended for us to do. We strained to hear him.

"So here we sit. And the accused, whom Sanderalee Dawson has *positively* identified, whom she has pointed out to you as the man who assaulted her so viciously, where is he, Ms. Jacobi? Where is he?" Regg Morris looked all around the room. He lifted the corner of a folder from my desk; he ducked his head under the desk. "Is he here? Is he incarcerated somewhere? Is he locked up so that Sanderalee Dawson—and all women like her—are safe from his attack?"

"Dr. Morris, this is all very entertaining and dramatic, but it is all very premature. The reason I asked you here today was to brief you on where our investigation stands at this moment. And to elicit your cooperation so that nothing impedes or interferes with this investigation in any way. We are working toward the ends you want to serve: justice. We are doing it in our own way. Dr. David Cohen is under investigation. Now, all that I am going to tell you from here on is confidential. If you reveal anything you hear in this office, you might very well jeopardize a case we are working to build. I'm asking for your cooperation at this point. That's why I asked you to come to my office this afternoon."

We sat poised, watching each other. There are some

situations where, to establish dominance, you force the other guy to make the first move, blink the first blink, lick the dry lip. There are other situations where you establish who's in charge by taking the initiative: deciding to break the contest, deciding when it is to end. Games. Games. More of life's little games.

I stood up and turned my back on Dr. Regg Morris and looked out toward the street. All I could see was a portion of the brick wall of the building next door: pale gray light; dampish. Two-three-four. Turn; smile; sit down; speak.

"Dr. Morris, you'll agree that on the face of it, we have a rather delicate situation."

A grudging nod; more an inclination of his head. An agreement to listen for a while.

"We *are*, I assure you, taking Ms. Dawson's accusation very, very seriously. But you can understand that an accusation, without backup proof, without any solid physical evidence, is very fragile. I couldn't even begin to think about taking this to a Grand Jury at this point. What we are doing—what my people are doing—is backtracking. We are researching into every aspect of the accused's life that might shed some light on what kind of person he is. We know his public credentials. He is world-famous for the techniques he has developed in a very specialized field of surgery. We are looking for the other side of the coin: the unexpected side of the personality. Maybe he is a Dr. Jekyll—Mr. Hyde. That would be one explanation."

"And in the meantime? Where is this…eminent… healer?"

"He is pursuing his daily rounds: whatever that entails."

I explained that provisions had been made to keep him from Sanderalee.

"Now, I want to ask you some questions that might help us in evaluating Sanderalee's accusation." Immediately, the tense, hostile, adversary expression; a raising of his chin, a squinting of his eyelids so that the black-light shone at me like twin beams. "When, what

137

day, at about what time, did she first speak to you about Dr. Cohen? Under what circumstances?"

He spoke carefully in a measured manner. He had spent a night with her when she was in the ICU. Even before we had any idea that she was lucid for more than a minute or two at a time, she was confiding in Regg Morris.

"At first, she talked in disconnected sentences. She moved in and out of time. The very first words to me were 'He's here. The man who did this to me. He's been in and out of this room.' That was what terrified her; that was why she kept asking you to get me to her side."

"All right. We are aware of the time lapses and the confusion. We'll be dealing with that for weeks, to some degree or other. Now, at what point did she identify *Dr. Cohen?* What, exactly, as accurately as you can recall, did she say about him?"

"'*He did this to me. That man. The tall one with the thinning hair.*' That's what she said. On the day she was moved from the ICU to her present room. She asked me who he was."

"Who was he?" Bobby Jones repeated. "What did you tell her?"

Regg Morris slid down low in his chair. His chin resting on his chest, he glanced slowly to his right and focused on Bobby Jones.

"I told her I would find out and I did."

"What did you find out? How did you check on him?"

A brief, unfriendly smile. "I have methods of gathering information, Ms. Jacobi. I am not without resources. I promised her she would be safe with Ms. Capella on guard. I checked out this....doctor. And came back to Sanderalee and identified him to her."

"What information did you give her?"

"His name. Where he lived. What his job was. What he had done for her...once she was in the hospital."

"And she said? When you told her the man is Dr. David Cohen, of such-and-such an address, et cetera?"

He didn't bother to look toward Bobby Jones anymore. He directed his words to me.

"She said, 'I'm pretty sure he's the man who did this to me.'"

We both pounced on this. "She said, 'I'm pretty sure'?"

"That's what the lady said. *At that point.* 'I'm pretty sure.'"

Bobby caught my signal and leaned back. "And your reaction was?"

Regg Morris came up straight in his chair and glared at me. "And my reaction *was?* My reaction was, *girl,* I wanted to get that muthuhfucker and rip off his goddamn balls, that's what my reaction was!"

I let the silence build for a moment in the shattered air, then leaned forward and went for my deadly voice. It sounded like I meant business.

"Listen carefully. You call me *girl.* Then I'm gonna have to call you *boy.* And then there we'll be: a *sexist* and a *racist,* sitting here wasting time. I don't have time to waste, do you?"

His grin was swift and dazzling: a showing of perfectly shaped, neat white teeth. He shook his head at himself, sucked in his breath and raised his hands, palms turned out. A gesture.

"Mea culpa. Forgive me. I became carried away and slipped into the scene. I am very close to Sanderalee and I feel, to a very great extent, not only my anger but her pain. Answer to your question: my reaction was a feeling of tremendous anger. And some bewilderment. Not terribly different from your initial feeling. Your continuing feeling, possibly."

"And what did Sanderalee tell you about her initial encounter with...the man who attacked her?"

"That she was running and twisted her ankle. That he had apparently been running behind her and witnessed this. That he approached her at Columbus Circle; told her he was a doctor; offered to help with the ankle. Told her he knew how to manipulate it so that

139

the injury wouldn't cause swelling. Told her that sort of thing."

"*He told her he was a doctor?*"

"Yes."

"When did Sanderalee say that to you? *Before* or *after* you identified *Dr. David Cohen?*"

Regg Morris shook his head from side to side and said, "Games again? All right. I'm not too clear of the sequence myself. She said; I said; she asked; I answered. This is *particularly* difficult for you, isn't it, Ms. Jacobi?"

"What is particularly difficult for me, Dr. Morris?"

"He is the standard mother-in-law's dream catch, isn't he?" He hesitated and then decided to impress us a little. "Except I'm not too sure what his late wife's mother might have to say about him, are you?"

"No, but I'm going to find out. And I warn you to back off and not interfere in our investigation." He did a "hands off" gesture with his shoulders, shrugging, his hands open and empty. "Now, get back to what you said before. About it being *particularly difficult* for *me.* What does that mean?"

As if I didn't know. I knew. Oh yeah. I knew where this was leading.

"The stereotype prize catch for the Jewish-American-Princess: the Jewish-American-Doctor. Not that you fit the former description, Ms. Jacobi. You're not the princess type."

"What does that mean?" Bobby Jones asked, getting lost somewhere along the line.

"You find Dr. David Cohen's religion significant in some way? To *my* handling of this investigation?"

"Yes, I consider Dr. David Cohen's religion significant. In *every* way. Given Sanderalee Dawson's recent involvement with the destitute peoples of the Palestinian refugee camps. Yes, I find it significant that the man who *destroyed* her, *physically and possibly emotionally*, is a *Jew.*"

"Did you mention to Sanderalee, when you provided

her with background information, that Dr. Cohen was Jewish?"

Regg Morris smiled without pleasure. "It would hardly be necessary, would it? With a name like *David Cohen?* Would you find it necessary to mention the fact that I was *black* in introducing me to someone?"

"If he were *blind* and it was *relevant, yes.*" I shot it at him. It stopped him cold. He awarded me his broad, wonderfully warm smile and a nod of approval. I was quick, he gave me that much.

"And when you identified Dr. David Cohen for Sanderalee Dawson, did you make any suggestions to her? As to why this man might have taken it upon himself to assault her? Did you suggest any political motives? Did you suggest that he knew who she was and that the crime against her was not random, but calculated against *her, specifically*, for reasons other than what appear on the surface?"

"You are accusing me of telling Sanderalee Dawson that what happened to her happened for political reasons? And that I then offered proof to her along the way? That I provided her with a Jew-doctor, all made-to-order? Is this what you are now saying?" He drew himself up in rage. Quite frankly, he was more than just a little frightening.

A soft answer turneth away wrath. I learned that in high school. It was printed neatly on a card tacked over the blackboard in the English-comp. room along with other quotations of worldly wisdom.

I answered softly: "We are trying to establish what the facts are in this matter, Dr. Morris. You're the one who has introduced an entirely new slant on this case."

He stood up so violently that he knocked over the chair in front of my desk. Bobby Jones started to move toward him. He thought Dr. Regg Morris was going to have at me. He wasn't; it just seemed that way. Morris whirled around, uprighted the chair with a thud and faced me, standing very straight and very stiff and with a very righteous expression on his handsome face.

"I think, Ms. Jacobi, that Sanderalee Dawson will

be well within her rights to demand that another prosecutor handle this case. One perhaps with a less *vested* interest."

"Uh-huh. And my vested interest is?"

He leaned forward and his eyes tried to pin me to my chair. "We have got us the culprit, lady. And he is a bright-eyed and bushy-tailed *Jew-doctor* and we're gonna check him out good and see where he fits into the *Zionist* scheme of things, you got that? And we're going to find out who you get *your* orders from. What part of the international Jew-conspiracy gives you your instructions."

I leaned way back in my chair.

"*Shalom*, Dr. Morris. In Zionist-talk, it means go fuck yourself."

23

I stopped at the hospital for a quick conference with Lucy Capella. Sanderalee was asleep. There was sensation in her fingertips and motion to the second joint; her hand was pink and warm. Her jaws, though they would be wired for many weeks, no longer ached and the swelling had subsided considerably. Of course, there was the horror of her ripped mouth. Sans lower lip and with broken teeth, she did not look very pleasant. However, she took enough interest in herself to ask to see a plastic surgeon and she had taken to draping her lower face with filmy chiffon scarves whenever she had visitors.

"Some dental surgeons are scheduled to take a look either today or tomorrow," Lucy told me. "Sanderalee is very confident of what they can accomplish. She's in good spirits and a lot more relaxed since we made that tape."

I discussed the meeting with Regg Morris. "I'm not sure how we can keep him out, Lucy. But I'm pretty sure we're going to have to. At this point, I am getting very worried."

"About what? About what Sanderalee told us?"

"About what Regg Morris may have told Sanderalee. Look, just for the sake of argument, let's say the assailant picked her up in the park or at Columbus Circle or wherever. They proceeded to her apartment. The man goes bonkers and attacks her. She wakes up and *thinks* one of the faces looking down at her is the guy who did it. Let's say she honestly doesn't remember very much of the conversation that took place with her assailant that night. Regg Morris checks out the guy she thinks she recognizes and tells her he's a doctor. Let's say he then 'helps her' to remember talking with her assailant that night. And in order to tighten her resolve, he leads her a little. Like 'Didn't that guy tell you he was a doctor?' That sort of thing. So that she'd feel a little stronger, a little tougher when she tells us about him. After all, you don't accuse an eminent microsurgeon of this kind of brutality every day. You need some sort of a lead-in."

"If only she had mentioned that her assailant told her he was a doctor. At some time prior to when Regg Morris spoke to her." Lucy was on my line of thinking exactly.

"I'm assigning reinterviews with every person who had any contact with her, from the first people on the scene—Doyle and the two patrolmen, the ambulance medics, the people at the emergency room. And the key question will be: did she mention the word 'doctor' at any time. Maybe she groaned the word and they just

143

assumed it was a logical thing. That she was injured and asking for a doctor. Maybe it was so logical that no one really noticed that she said it. And maybe zeroing in on even one single groan that sounded like 'doctor' would..." I threw my hands up. "Would I don't know what."

Lucy said it for me. "Would reassure you a little that the word 'doctor' as assailant wasn't put into Sanderalee's head by her good friend, Regg Morris." Lucy stretched her neck and massaged it lightly. "A little peculiar, though, the whole sequence. She twisted her ankle while running on a cold and lonely night. No one around but a doctor, who just happens to be running in back of her, sees what happened, offers help." Lucy raised her eyebrows. "Lynne? Come on."

"You don't believe in terrifically good luck coupled with terrifically bad luck? She's running; twists her foot; only person in vicinity is very competent doctor; they are right near her apartment; he helps her home; he massages her aching ankle. Then, instead of accepting a nice drink, he proceeds to rape, sodomize and dismember her. What is this 'Lynne, come on'? You find this all hard to believe?"

Lucy's dark eyes were steady on mine and she spoke slowly. "I find anything at all in the whole world believable. Maybe not likely, but believable. I'm thinking in terms of a jury. But let's put that aside, Lynne. Was Sanderalee in the habit of picking up men and taking them home with her?"

I shrugged. "It would not strain the limits of credulity."

"That means yes?"

"That means yes."

"Then why the big story—of the running and the twisted ankle and the doctor just happening along? Why not just the truth—if it is the truth—a casual pickup that went wrong?"

"I think when we figure that out, we'll know a great deal more than we do now. I do sense the fine manipulative hand of Regg Morris in some of this. Let's say that yes, our good Dr. Cohen is indeed a lunatic-monster and did in fact do what Sanderalee says he did. Maybe Regg felt she should offer a few upfront statements as to how come Sanderalee brought a total stranger home with her. Listen, Lucy, I'm not in the answering position yet." I dug my notebook out and jotted a reminder to myself, reading as I wrote it down. "Ask Tim Doyle if he noticed Sanderalee limping when she came back with unidentified male. Also, ask hospital personnel if anyone examined her ankle and noted any swelling." Lucy seemed about to say something, changed her mind, thought it over and started again.

"Lucy? What?"

She hesitated. "I think...it would be a good idea to consider...at this point...having her declared a material witness and hold her in protective custody. That way, no Regg Morris. No outside influence."

We did indeed think alike. "But not just yet. It might backfire. I have to see how Regg is going to conduct himself. We'll have to start shortening his visits. 'She's in therapy.' 'She's resting.' That kind of thing. Get that Dr. Fernow to go along with you. He's a real police buff; tell him it's an important part of the case and he'll see to it that Sanderalee has ten sponge baths a day. Let's just keep putting Regg Morris off for now. And when he does visit with her, you stay in the room. No secret whispered conferences."

"Lynne, what do you think?"

"I'm not sure. It's a farout possibility. Crazy. But possible. In the last three years there have been nine dismemberment murders in New York City. At least two of them fit a similar pattern: rape, sodomy, beating, partial dismemberment. The others we can cancel: male torsos, obvious gang rubouts, drug-related scare-murders. But there are two cases in Manhattan where the women were seen entering their apartments with a 'white male,' no further description. He doesn't leave prints. He doesn't leave anything of himself behind. Except for the corpses."

"Maybe this time he left a not-quite dead victim. Surely he must have thought she was dead or dying."

"Which would account—if by some chance it was the good Dr. Cohen—for his telling her he was a doctor. What difference would it make what he told her? If he was planning to kill her?"

"If he did it."

"Right, Lucy. If he did it."

If he did it. Could he have done it?

Dr. David Cohen?

24

"I know Dr. David Cohen as a teaching colleague since for many years we were both on the staff at Columbia. And of course his wife was my patient, but that had very little to do with him."

Dr. Irving Calendar was a pompous jerk. He had shaved the remaining hair on his head to make it appear that his state of baldness was his option rather than nature's. As he spoke, reacting to a pre-set inner time clock, he periodically reached his right hand behind his head and slowly, lovingly brushed his fingers along the shaved edge of his neck.

"I used to be a Freudian," he told us. "But I realized a few years ago that the therapy of the future was preventive medication. Instead of seeing maybe six, seven patients a day for the famous fifty-minute hour, I can now deal with four, maybe five patients an *hour*.

That's twenty-four, thirty patients a day. At fifty to sixty bucks a throw."

"That is remarkable, Dr. Calendar. How many patients does that multiply up to per week?"

He shrugged at me and pulled his wide lips into a smile, then gave his neck the old feel.

"Depends. There are days when I just don't schedule myself. Days when I devote myself *to* myself." He pressed his hard flat stomach and flexed his hard wide shoulders. "*Tennis.* That's my game."

It sounded like his raison d'être. It was said with tight but passionate emphasis.

"Another thing about this type of therapy is that it doesn't leave me drained. They make no emotional demands on me. My patients. They come; I check their reaction to dosage: good, bad, effective, not effective; high, low, stable. I have each one keep a journal. I give them a coded notebook I have printed up especially for this kind of notekeeping."

"So your patient just shows you a notebook and that's it?"

"I *evaluate* what's been going on, medication-wise. And make whatever adjustment, if any, is necessary. And decide when the next visit should be. Maybe two weeks, maybe four. The patient is reassured by the visit. We don't get involved with their emotional hang-ups or past lives. After all, it is the current day-by-day life we have to deal with, not mama and the toidy potty and papa and the primal scene."

"Are many of you former Freudians crossing over?" Bobby Jones asked.

Another gentle shrug; another brush of the stubble; another smile. "The smart ones are."

Dr. Calendar had treated Mrs. Melissa Wise Cohen for depression. It had been a lifelong syndrome with her. She had tried conventional therapies and found none that helped. Regardless of what was going on in her life, when her biological time clock messed up her blood chemistry, she hit bottom. The fact that there was no precipitating cause for the depression, the cyclical nature of it, and the degree of total despair she suffered during it were right up Dr. Calendar's alley.

"Very typical type of case and the most likely to respond to medication therapy. An almost casebook demonstration of clinical depression."

"And what about the other side of the syndrome, Dr. Calendar? What was Mrs. Cohen like when she entered the manic period?"

Dr. Calendar moved around in his chair. He studied his fingertips as they made contact with each other, gently tapping. "Mrs. Cohen was not a *manic-depressive*. She was a flatout *depressive*. Her high cycle was well within normal bounds. To the best of my knowledge, she never experienced a manic state."

I quickly scanned the minutes of the inquest, which Bobby Jones had given me an hour before Dr. Calendar arrived.

"I'm quoting from the inquest into the death of Mrs. Cohen. Question: Would 'dancing around exuberantly on a balcony, despite rain, and seating oneself precariously on the edge of a metal railing and waving her arms up in the air without regard for consequences while in a state of great hilarity'—would that kind of behavior be fairly typical of a person during a 'manic state'? That question was put to you, Dr. Calendar, and your response was 'That just about sums up the kinds of activities of a person in a manic state.' Question: If during this surge of manic behavior, a person toppled over backward from a great height, how would you categorize her death? Your answer: *Accidental*."

Dr. Calendar nodded and contemplated his fingertips.

"Dr. Calendar, if you never treated Mrs. Cohen for manic behavior, if her case was clinical depression, how do you explain this alleged outburst of mania during which she was so careless of her own safety that she inadvertently toppled off the railing of her balcony, ten stories from the sidewalk?"

"I never said that *she* was manic. I never said that it was my opinion that *Mrs. Cohen, in particular*, had behaved the way you just described. I never said, in so many words, that *her* behavior caused *her* to die an *accidental* death."

"That was the finding of the inquest: *death by accident*. Based largely on your opinion." I came around my desk and leaned against the arm of my couch. I was elevated a good six inches from his face. My heart was thumping. Jesus. Maybe.

"How *would* you characterize Mrs. Cohen's death?"

Say *murder*. Say murder-most-foul. At the hands of her schizo husband who every now and then, in between performing surgical miracles, killed women. *Say murder*.

"*Suicide*," Dr. Calendar said. "No question in the world about that. Melissa Cohen killed herself. Committed suicide."

I lifted the minutes of the inquest and flipped the pages at him. "There is not one single word about suicide in these minutes. You never even suggested suicide."

"I know. I was in a bit of a bind."

He had bright, round, clear monkey eyes: light brown and jumpy, hopping from side to side, never seeming to stay on any one object for very long. The minute you made eye contact with him, you lost it: the eyes slid away. Nutty. The psychiatrist began to look very nutty with jumping monkey eyes that seemed to be trying to steal a look at my forehead but blinked rapidly when caught trying to focus. This guy was suddenly very agitated. He tickled the back of his neck, then locked his hand on the armrest and pulled himself up in his chair.

"This was five years ago. Yes, five years ago. My program was still being funded by a government grant. We weren't *exactly* experimental, yet we were in a transition period. A period of trying out new drug therapies. At government expense."

"Doesn't that constitute 'experimental'?" Bobby Jones asked. "Trying out new drug therapies sounds experimental."

The round eyes darted to Bobby, then found something interesting on the wall and seemed to be reading words very quickly. Then he spoke. "Semantics. Actually, every time you tell a patient to take an aspirin, in a sense, it's experimental. Will the aspirin help? Will it harm? Will it cause some previously unsuspected reaction, some totally new freak of chemical combinations?"

Bobby and I looked at each other. This guy might be a loon but there had to be a reason for what he had done and it was self-serving. No wonder he hadn't wanted it known that people from the D.A.'s office were questioning him.

"Dr. Calendar, return to Melissa Cohen. What kind of medication was she taking? At the time of her death?"

He gave us a rundown of Melissa Cohen's experience with antidepression medication. For a period of some nine months, when she entered the program, she had done very well on one particular medication. Then she developed unpleasant side effects: dry mouth, sore chapped lips, sore throat, sweats, trembling hands. Dr. Calendar checked all this information in his coded little notebook labeled "Melissa Cohen," which he had thoughtfully brought along with him.

"We switched medications for about the same period of time, a little longer, perhaps a year, with similar results. The depression was controlled but she developed side effects after a while: insomnia, blurred vision, nausea." His eyes darted from Bobby to me to Bobby to me to the wall to his fingers to me to Bobby. "These are very esoteric drugs we're talking about. These are not pills that give a high of any kind. The depressive who is doing well on the recommended dosage has no inclination to escalate. There is no high. There is actually no particular mental-emotional response. Not even a feeling of well-being. Just a feeling of being able, capable of handling whatever comes along in a normal, intelligent manner.

"Now, Melissa Cohen seems to have had difficulty

with all the various medications we tried after a period of time, after having first used them successfully without side effects. This happens. On an individual basis, this happens. The last medication I gave her was *lithium*. It was part of a *test program* that she agreed to enter. It was a testing of the uses of lithium."

"Isn't lithium used, basically, for manic-depressives?"

He blinked approval at me for my small bit of knowledge. It was gleaned from a reading of an article in the Sunday *New York Times Magazine*.

"Exactly. That has been its initial use. It has had a great success. Now, we are trying it for patients with just the depressive symptoms."

"Which meant," Bobby said—he had read the same article—"that in effect, Mrs. Cohen was receiving a medication that she actually didn't need."

Dr. Calendar nodded brusquely at our wisdom.

"So that," I continued, "when it was determined at the inquest that she had been on lithium for a time, it was *assumed* that she was manic-depressive because that was the drug being used for that illness at the time. And no one bothered to explain why she was getting lithium?"

"You got it."

"Why not? Why wasn't this explained?"

It was quite simple, actually. Dr. Calendar's program was government-funded and was coming up for review. How the hell would it look if it was officially recorded that one of his depressives, on lithium, had had an uncontrolled depressive cycle and killed herself? It would be easier to accept the theory of a careless moment during a modified high. Accidents do happen to people, even to those not on medication.

"And where did Dr. Cohen fit into all this? What did he tell you about that night?"

"That his wife was despondent. She had been off her medication for nearly two months. She..."

"Why? Why was she off medication?"

"Ms. Jacobi, we have been noticing there are pa-

151

tients, in some numbers, who come to resent their therapy. We've heard of diabetics who refuse insulin; patients with high blood pressure who won't take their medication. Ulcer patients who don't follow preventive instructions. Some people are very high-strung, very independent, very resentful of having to take medication on a regular basis for the rest of their lives. Mrs. Cohen, as far as I could determine, rebelled against taking medication. She hadn't come to see me for nearly two months. Apparently she was fully into the depressive cycle that night; too deep even to want to seek help. That's when it happens with depressives: the suicides."

"Why was she still carried as being on your program? If she'd been off the medication, how could her suicide affect your funding?"

His eyes raced back and forth. If you ever look a monkey dead in the eye, you will notice he immediately gets a shifty, guilty look. That's how Dr. Calendar looked.

"Well, you see, *statistically*, she was carried on my program. We work with computer readouts. It's the numbers that count."

"Uh. And did Dr. Cohen ask you to go along with his story of accidental death—caused by his wife's unbridled hilarity?"

Ah. He had us there. He steadied himself. "I in no way perjured myself. You can read over the transcript very carefully, line for line. I never flatly stated, because I was never flatly asked, what I thought happened to Mrs. Cohen. The questions were always framed hypothetically."

He was right, they were.

"What was Dr. Cohen's purpose in telling this story about her manic behavior and accidental falling off the balcony? Why didn't he just tell what happened?"

"You'd have to ask Dr. Cohen that. My guess would be, to save face perhaps. Doesn't sound too good: doctor's wife kills herself. My God, we're accused of enough things as it is, what with all this damned malpractice litigation they seem to be teaching all the new young lawyers. A regular separate profession."

Bobby Jones and I fish-eyed him. He became very fidgety and began to talk rapidly. Nothing like a good, double-barreled fish-stare to unnerve a witness.

"Well, you know what I mean. It's an age of litigation, isn't it? Anyway, perhaps Dr. Cohen wanted to protect Mrs. Cohen's family, her parents. It's hard enough to lose a child without bearing the burden of suicide. Accidental death is more acceptable. There, perhaps his motive was altruistic as well as self-serving. Ask him. He'll probably tell you."

"Dr. Calendar," Bobby asked, "at any time did Mrs. Cohen tell you that she was having marital difficulties? That she and her husband..."

He held up his nice pink hands and stopped Bobby Jones right there. "Oh, hold on now. Remember what I told you. This is not *talk* therapy. I never inquire into my patients' private lives. That has nothing to do with me. All I ask about is their reaction to medication. I do not get drawn into those tangled webs anymore." He sighed deeply, a very happy man. "Thank God."

Part Three

The Case

25

From the outside, the pseudo-Tudor attached house in Forest Hills was deceptive. You'd guess the rooms inside would be tiny and claustrophobic, but the Wise home was cheerful and bright and spacious. It was the meticulous home of people whose children have grown and gone. There were collections of family photographs on the mantel of the corner fireplace, in modern plastic frames on end tables and cocktail tables: wherever a picture could be placed, there were family faces.

Mrs. Rita Wise was what is called a handsome woman: large-boned, broad intelligent forehead, clean-cut features, strong wide mouth, head held high, penetrating amber eyes. She had thick, wiry hair cut short and touching her cheeks in silver and black curls. She introduced us to her husband, who was a tall, thin, bland and nervous man, and when we settled on their couch, he deferred to her.

She had prepared tea, but offered coffee if we'd prefer. She had set out a plate of homemade coffee cake, and seed cake, and prune cake. We commented on the wonderful tastes and asked if these were sold in their shop or if they were special for their own home. They were from the shop; all baking done on premises.

Mrs. Wise watched us closely. We had hardly come to drink her tea and devour her cake.

"So, you are from the District Attorney's office," she said, the question implicit in her remark.

Bobby Jones, who had made the initial contact with them, took the lead. "Yes, Mrs. Wise. As I told you in our phone conversation, there is a matter we wanted to discuss with you, in the strictest confidence."

She shrugged and gestured about the room. "There is no one here but Martin and me." The amber eyes narrowed. "So? What is this about?"

"About David Cohen," Bobby Jones said.

Mrs. Wise inhaled; her breath caught momentarily and then she coughed. Mr. Wise reached for her hand; squeezed it. As he did so, her arm turned slightly and I caught a glimpse of the blue numbers tattooed on her arm. It accounted for some of the terrible sadness in her eyes.

"But all that, it was years ago," Mr. Wise said. "It was finished with a long time ago."

"This is about something else," I said cautiously. "But what we wanted to know from you was what your experience had been with David Cohen. I read the minutes of the inquest into your daughter's death. You weren't given an opportunity to say anything. There is...a matter...a current matter pending, and it would be helpful to us if we could hear from you. Can you tell us, confidentially, it will go no further, one way or the other, what you know of David Cohen's character, personality, whatever you can tell us."

Mrs. Wise stood up and went to the fireplace and carefully lifted a framed photograph, which she handed to me without looking at it.

"That is a picture of our daughter Melissa. It was taken when she graduated from Mount Sinai. She was a wonderful girl; bright, intelligent, she loved being a nurse. She loved helping people. She was not a great beauty, but she was a good girl. A fine girl."

The picture showed a strong, determined young woman: pride; confidence; strong resemblance to her mother. I admired the picture, showed it to Bobby and

158

then handed it back to Mrs. Wise, who took it without looking at it.

"*Dr. David Cohen murdered my daughter in cold blood.* He beat her and then threw her from their balcony and then said she 'fell' from happiness or whatever he said at the time. That she was 'hilarious,' I think was what he said. And fell accidentally, when she was discussing their trip to Mexico. They planned no trip to Mexico. She did not dance to their balcony and fall over. She was planning to leave him. And so he beat her and then threw her over the balcony."

It was said in a dead-flat tone of voice: a voice of certainty, not open to question as to its accuracy. I glanced at her husband; he met my eye and nodded. It was knowledge they had shared between them for years: it was indisputable.

Of course there was no proof. How could there be proof? They had been alone in their apartment. David was a doctor; he would be sure to come up with a clever explanation.

"He seemed to be so wonderful a husband for our daughter, this doctor," Mrs. Wise said; monotone; emotionless. "But you see, there was something wrong with David; something not quite right. Something... missing. I...know things about people. I have had experience of people. It is something in the eyes. David Cohen had that something, but what could you tell a young girl? 'I don't like his eyes, they frighten me'?"

I picked up a large hunk of cake and took a big bite. I had the excited feeling of hearing something terrible; something true.

"Did your daughter ever tell you anything disturbing about her husband, Mrs. Wise?" Bobby asked.

She shrugged. "She was not a complainer. She knew life is not perfect; that sometimes things are difficult. Melissa was a fine girl; she did not want to...burden us. My son had been in an accident with an automobile and he was in the hospital for a year. Thank God he recovered and is fine, but she would not tell us things were wrong. But I knew Melissa. And David had a 'look.'"

"What kind of look?" I asked.

Again, the shrug. A strange look; a look you could see if you knew about people; a look that disturbed both the father and the mother.

Mrs. Wise stared down at her large hands and twisted her fingers around her wrist and stared at the blue number and did not look at anyone as she spoke.

"He had the look of cruelty. A kind of coldness, a remoteness—is that the word? Remote from feeling." She dropped her hand and her light, beautiful amber eyes, filled with knowledge, with awful knowledge, fixed steadily on me. "Just once, when she came alone, she was stiff." Mrs. Wise's shoulders stiffened in illustration, and she shuddered. "Stiff and I asked her what? What is it? There are times when it is good to talk of things, it is not to be disloyal. She was a very loyal girl, Melissa; we taught her that, that family must stick together, must care for each other, that is all there is, yes, Martin?"

Martin Wise nodded; he kept his face down; he clenched his hands and nodded.

"So this one time she said to me, 'Mama, there is something about David that frightens me.' And she told me that sometimes, when she wakes at night from her sleep, David is standing there by the side of the bed and looking down at her. Just staring at her and that she jumps up and says, What? What is it? What is wrong? And she says he doesn't answer. She puts on the light and he just watches her and she said his face...his face..."

She stopped speaking and unexpectedly, Mr. Wise said, "She said his face is the face of a stranger; of a man I do not know and he frightens me."

Mrs. Wise nodded and reached for her husband's hand. "Yes. That was what she told me. And she said that in the morning, when she spoke to David about it, he said she must have dreamed it, that it had never happened. That she was being foolish."

160

"Did he ever strike her, that you know about?" I asked, almost knowing the answer.

"Yes," the mother told me. "Yes. During the night; during one of those strange times when she woke up and found him there. It was like a stranger, she said. Punched her; punched her. And she didn't go to work in the morning, she was black and blue and sore and he told her again, no, that she dreamed it, that she walked in her sleep and did it to herself."

"You said she planned to leave him. Tell us about that."

Mrs. Wise nodded and slowly, twisting her narrow gold wedding ring, reaching back for the memory, she began telling us.

"Shortly before Melissa...died. A week maybe before, I'm not sure. David came late from the hospital; hours later than he had said and she was worried. Usually he would call and say he was detained, something had come up. But this night, he did not call and she was worried and she called to find out if he was there. Maybe there had been an accident. Her brother had had an accident and we didn't know for hours. Not for hours." She turned her face away from us and was silent for a moment. Her husband reached and held her hand, pressed it. Mrs. Wise looked up and her face was painfully sad with remembering awful things.

"But that is another matter, and that turned out well. But Melissa called the hospital and they told her, no, David was not detained, maybe did he have a meeting and she said yes, probably that was it, a meeting of some kind and he forgot to tell her. And then, David came home, hours, hours late and she had waited up for him. And she told me he had that...that middle-of-the-night look on his face. The look of the stranger. And she asked him where he'd been, what had happened, and she said he didn't answer, he just ignored her, he went and took a shower and got into bed. And the next morning, she tried to talk to him and he became very angry. And started saying things like 'What's happening to you, Melissa? Something's going on with you that is very strange.' That kind of thing. And so she made up her mind to leave him. And it was maybe two or three days later, after she told me this, that Melissa...that she was killed."

"We know about the medication Melissa had been taking," Mr. Wise told us in a very soft and gentle voice. "She learned about that kind of help when she went into nursing and she was careful about medication. She would never have let herself get that depressed without taking the medication. And she never was what David described. Hilarious. What a terrible word. And he used it so easily."

"David lies very easily. It is part of his nature. He is like a beast who kills and then moves on and continues with his life."

They knew no one else who might verify what they had learned about David Cohen; only their daughter, and she was dead.

"His family?" I asked and both parents sighed; shook their heads.

"They would tell you nothing. They are very...superior people? They think they are; that David married a 'baker's daughter.' You can see how people like that, in the business world and both of them successful, they saw Melissa as the 'baker's daughter.' We know, they let us know in the way people have. Ach, people. So foolish; so foolish."

It was at that point that Martin Wise surprised us; even his wife seemed surprised by the sudden energy with which he leaped from the couch and went to the pictures on the fireplace mantel.

"You see these people," he said in a hoarse and shaking voice, "these are parents and brothers and sisters and cousins; these are children and grandparents, all these people were family."

He grabbed one group photograph: the faded sepia, the faces barely discernible. This was indeed a family: grandparents and parents and children, dressed in a different time, their faces innocent of their approaching fate.

162

"*Murdered*. Every single one of the people you see in this photograph, murdered. *And no one paid. No one.* Still, they are walking around, the murderers of my family, of my wife's family."

Mrs. Wise's face was frozen, her chin raised, her teeth clenched, her body rigid and straight.

Mr. Wise took the picture of their daughter, Melissa, from her hands and looked at it, then turned to face me and Bobby Jones.

"And then, this one. This girl. This beautiful girl who was born here, who we raised with love and with care in this safe place. Who could imagine such a thing? Who could have thought such a thing?" He put the photograph back on the mantel carefully, then he leaned close to us.

"David Cohen murdered our daughter. We don't know why you are asking us questions about him, but we want you to know this. He is a murderer." He took a long breath and then exhaled in a terrible sobbing voice and said, in a chant, "Get him. Please. Get him. Get him. Get him."

26

Dr. David Cohen, seated across the desk from me, indeed resembled that mythical prize catch of my mother's generation's dreams: a nice Jewish boy all grown up into a reliable, steady, good-income doctor. In the clever, cool, vaguely remote expression of his thin, high-foreheaded face, one could still see glimpses of the class smart boy: the pain-in-the-ass kid who was ready to answer the question before the hapless teacher had a chance to finish posing it. There was nothing really memorable about his face. In fact, he brought back my mother's early admonition: you marry a man not too handsome, this way you don't have to worry about other girls they should try to take him away. Thank you, Mother.

He had the barely discernible smugness of the highly skilled professional who wasn't very interested in anything outside his specialty. A certain coldness: an innate aura of cleanliness that went beyond the scrubbed sterility of a surgeon.

His only remarkable physical distinction was his long, elegantly beautiful hands. I can't recall ever seeing either a pianist or a surgeon with short, stubby or unpleasant fingers. I wondered if the condition of one's hands was a precipitating factor in making a specialty decision. I wondered what would happen to a brilliant young doctor who wanted to be a surgeon but who had dwarfishly small, scrungey, unbeautiful hands. I wanted to ask Dr. Cohen about that, but I was sure he would consider it frivolous and he was clearly not a frivolous man.

Bobby Jones had set up the appointment by telephone and it was just by good luck that Dr. Cohen had a free half-hour or so that he could spare. He appreciated the fact that Lucy Capella, who was joining us for the meeting, was available to give him a lift to our office and would also provide him with a ride back to the hospital at the conclusion of what, I had assured him, would be a brief meeting.

He sat and studied me expectantly, having glanced around the room with a disinterested air. The only thing that caught his attention was the tape recorder that was on my desk.

"Dr. Cohen, I want to inform you that as of this moment"—I had clicked the machine on—"this conversation is being recorded as part of an ongoing investigation into the assault on Ms. Sanderalee Dawson. I want to inform you, and advise you, that you have a right to have an attorney present with you at all times. That you do not have to answer my questions. That you may discontinue this meeting at any time."

For which I thank you, members of the Supreme Court. And wish you a similar situation and wish I could see you operate from that moment on.

Dr. Cohen's expression barely changed but there was an intensity, a narrowing of his eyes, a movement of his head. He leaned forward and sounded not exactly wary but just a bit puzzled.

"Is that a customary statement? It seems just a bit strange to me under the circumstances of my being here. Ms. Capella told me you wanted an update on the condition of Sanderalee Dawson. Have I need of an attorney to bring you people up to date?"

He seemed to direct his questions more to Bobby Jones, the only male present. I corrected that tendency once and for all.

"Dr. Cohen, you are here at my request as the Bureau Chief of the Squad responsible for the investigation into the assault on Sanderalee Dawson."

He focused on me now: a total, emotionless waiting.

Looking at him, what I was about to say seemed ludicrous. I concentrated on what we had heard on the tape from Sanderalee's tortured voice. Hit it, no explanations, for God's sake, no qualifying excuses, which is what I had been about to do: Hey, doctor, you're going to think this is really crazy, but you know what this lady said about you? Forget it, Lynne.

"Dr. Cohen, for the past two days you have not visited or tended Ms. Dawson. This has been at the explicit request of the patient."

"Yes. I was told that."

"What you have not been told is that Ms. Dawson has been conscious and lucid for several days now. And she has been telling us—the members of my staff and myself—as best she can recall, the events of the night of her attack." Deep breath; match his careful atten-

165

tion; find his light gray eyes behind his sparkling glasses. Remember what his dead wife's parents said about him: he is a murderer.

He inclined his head politely if impatiently.

"Yes? And?"

"Dr. Cohen, Ms. Dawson has identified you as her assailant."

The statement hung in the silence. There was no reaction from anyone. The four of us just sat, waiting for something to happen; for someone to react. I had an insane, scary moment when I thought I was going to laugh. For God's sake: laugh.

"Dr. Cohen?"

He asked me, "Am I supposed to say something about that? What would you like me to say about that?"

Say: Yes, I did it. I am a murderous lunatic and I hacked and I raped and I beat and I then put her all together again.

"It was a serious detailed accusation, doctor. I have here a typed version of what Ms. Dawson stated on tape. In order to bring you fully up to date, so that you'll know exactly what we're talking about, I'm going to give you the typed statement. Would you like some time to read it?"

He reached for the stack of papers and flipped through them quickly. No expression; nothing. Clinical; noncommittal.

"Would you like a cup of coffee, Dr. Cohen?" Bobby Jones hovered over the hotpot. Dr. Cohen shook his head. He was immersed in the typed report.

I had said all the official things into the tape recorder: time of day; Dr. Cohen is now reading statement of Sanderalee Dawson; interrogation will resume when he is finished.

I watched him intently. A tall man, nearly six feet, sitting tall in the chair before me, adjusting the papers slightly to avoid a shadow; scanning, reading very quickly. A speed-reader; going back, double-checking. He fingered a small gold pencil or pen, whatever, and seemed about to make a note or two on the copy given

166

him, but instead he touched the gold instrument to his lips momentarily. Finally, he leaned forward and placed the report on my desk, removed his glasses, gently rubbed his eyelids with his long and probably soothingly cool fingertips. He studied his glasses, breathed on them, wiped them with a clean white handkerchief, then looked at me and shrugged.

"So? Where does that leave me? What is my status here, in this office, as of this moment?"

"You have no official status. At this point. An accusation has been made against you. We are trying to clarify that accusation and to evaluate it. With your help and cooperation if possible."

I had turned the tape recorder on. Dr. Cohen stared at it for a moment, then looked back at me. No expression. I glanced at Lucy and then at Bobby Jones. Was this significant? No expression. What did that tell us? Anything?

"Dr. Cohen." Bobby Jones waited until the doctor turned in his chair, watched Bobby come to the desk and sit next to him. "What is your immediate reaction to what you've just read?"

A slight shrug. "This woman has been in and out of coma. She hadn't been speaking rationally as far as I knew. I haven't heard her make one complete statement. This"—he nodded to the report—"seems to me astonishingly complete and consistent, given the woman's medical condition. I would like to hear the tape itself. I'm curious as to the actual sound and continuity of her voice as she relates this . . . sequence of events."

"As to the accusation itself, Dr. Cohen?"

"I am in no way responsible for what Ms. Dawson said or asserted. I would point out, of course, that I was among the first people that this woman saw as she hovered in and out of consciousness. I would suggest you speak to Dr. Chan. I believe Martha Chan has been handling the psychiatric end of this?"

"Dr. Cohen, in this situation I am obliged to ask you certain questions."

He turned back to me and regarded me as a teacher

167

would regard a not particularly clever student who had just asked him if the correct procedure was being followed. "Yes, I can understand that."

"And you are here voluntarily, and have been advised of your status as of the moment, and of your rights?"

"Yes, I understand. Ask me what questions you feel necessary."

No, he did not know Sanderalee Dawson personally.

Yes, he had seen her on television.

No, he did not, at any time, in any way, harm, injure, attack, defile or attempt to murder Sanderalee Dawson.

No, he was not politically active. Every four years, he voted for the President.

No, he had never been a political activist.

"Are you active in any religious organizations, Dr. Cohen?"

"No. I'm a Yom Kippur Jew. Once a year obligation to ancestors; parents; the Holocaust. Conscience. Superstition. You know."

I nodded. I knew. Bobby Jones looked puzzled. Lucy Capella looked serious and intent.

"Are you a Zionist in your beliefs?"

"I believe in the state of Israel and the right of Jews to their own country. Does that make me a Zionist?"

"I mean actively, in any way. Do you belong to, or donate to, any Zionist organizations?"

He smiled. "My mother, before her stroke, was a very active fund raiser for ORT. She still hits me up pretty good every year. That's the extent of my 'Zionist commitment.'"

. Dr. Cohen stopped speaking and carefully looked at each of us in turn. He seemed to close in upon himself by the time he faced me.

"Are you serious about all this?"

"Yes, I'm very serious about all this."

"In that case," Dr. Cohen said quietly, "I think I would be well-advised to return with my attorney at a mutually agreed upon time."

"I don't think that would be a bad idea at all."

Hell, in his position, I'd be sitting with my lawyer's hand over my mouth.

"A couple of quick questions, Dr. Cohen, if you don't mind?" Sister Lucy smiled so sweetly, even I wanted to lean forward and pat her head. Dr. Cohen turned and nearly smiled at her.

"Dr. Cohen, if you don't mind? I see you have a rather large Band-Aid on your left cheek. Mind telling me what happened? Accident or what?"

He touched the edges of the flesh-colored bandage with the tip of his index finger, barely tracing the shape of it.

"I slipped on a discarded yogurt container in my classroom one day and hit the edge of my cheek on the corner of my desk. Metal corner. Metal and flesh; bad combination."

"At Columbia, Dr. Cohen? That's where you teach, isn't it? Specialized microsurgery classes?"

"That's where I teach, yes."

"Was it a serious wound? Many stitches?"

He didn't answer. He was busy gathering himself together, leaning over to pick up his attaché case; adjusting his handkerchief in his pocket neatly; refitting his glasses.

"When did this happen, Dr. Cohen? Recently?"

Lucy sounded concerned: poor man; wounded on the job.

His mouth opened, then his lips clamped together and he shook his head. "If you feel this is significant in some way, Ms. Capella, then perhaps we'd better discuss it when my attorney is present."

"Dr. Cohen, I would suggest you try to recall, to the best of your ability, your activities on the night in question—up to when you were summoned to New York Hospital."

I stood up and walked with him toward the door; looked up at him and asked pleasantly, "Dr. Cohen, how come you were rejected for military service?"

There was no taking this man by surprise, that was

169

what surprised me. His calmness; his readiness for questions from any direction.

He turned and looked down at me; far down from his height to mine. He leaned over and hiked up his trouser leg, then lifted his right foot and showed me his shoe.

"Observe, Ms. Jacobi. Didn't your research go this far or are you just testing my recall? As the result of childhood polio—I was of the unfortunate generation before Salk—this leg is two inches shorter than my left leg."

"Not even noticeable, Dr. Cohen. Not particularly handicapping either, is it? You do pretty well in the marathons."

"Yes," he said vaguely. "I suppose you will want to know that. Yes."

I saw the look that had been described to me by his inlaws: a cold, angry, cruel expression fastened on me, and then he turned and walked out of the office.

27

I had hoped to slip out of my office undiscovered but the District Attorney obviously had a spy planted in my office. He would be a damn fool not to: I had a couple situated in his office.

"Lynne," he said, "why don't you tell me what's been happening?"

It took me a half-hour to update Jameson Whitney Hale. He sat quietly, his face somber and thoughtful.

"When's your next meeting with Dr. Cohen?"

"At two P.M. tomorrow, he'll appear at my office with his attorney."

"What are your thoughts in this matter, Lynne?" He watched me closely, trying to penetrate, trying to catch me out should I try to hold back on him.

"If Sanderalee sticks with her story, I don't feel I'll have much choice but to bring it to the Grand Jury. What I'm trying to do, of course, is to come up with more than just her word."

"Your doorman witness, Mr. Timothy-whatsis?"

"Doyle. Mr. Doyle. Mr. Doyle sat in my outer office, on the bench next to Dr. Cohen when Lucy Capella left him for a moment to announce his presence." I spread my arms. "Nothing."

"Nothing. Too bad. He seemed a good strong witness. Had he actually witnessed anything."

"Actually, he studied the doctor from the knees on down. Which wouldn't be too good an ID at best. But the shorter leg—it does fit in with the 'special running shoe' that Mr. Doyle insists on."

"And Dr. Cohen's suggestion that you ask that psychiatrist, Dr. Chan, for an evaluation of Sanderalee Dawson's statement?"

"Lucy will speak to her tomorrow A.M. Lucy also hit on something that Bobby Jones is going to follow up. The Band-Aid on Cohen's left cheek. Sanderalee stated she thinks she stabbed-jabbed-whatever her assailant with that unicorn statue. With the horn. It shouldn't be too difficult to find out—visually—if Cohen had any abrasion or Band-Aid or whatever on his cheek on the morning of the attack. Bobby is going to check out the TV news tapes."

"Have you briefed Jim Barrow, Lynne? Are you keeping up to date on all this?"

"I was intending to; meaning, of course, no, I haven't been right upfront with Jim. But I called him for a meeting just before you asked me to come up here. Want to sit in on it? I was going to Jim's office, but if you'd rather, I'm sure he'll come over here."

171

"No, I think not at this point. I do think that search warrants are in order: Dr. Cohen's residence; his place out in the Hamptons; his office at Columbia Presbyterian; his office at New York Hospital."

"In the works. I figured I'd ask Chief Barrow to assign people for the searches. Just so he won't feel too left out. With my people on the scene, of course."

"Well, you have a busy schedule and I don't want to keep you, Lynne. Just be sure you keep me updated." The District Attorney stood and seemed about to escort me from his office, but his hesitation was totally expected. I just wondered when he would slip it in.

"Lynne, about this television documentary thing. With Glori Nichols. I think I should tell you something."

"Oh, please, Mr. Hale. Not an intimate confidence."

Ordinarily, I wouldn't get away with a crack like that. My heart felt like lead. Jameson Whitney Hale smiled and waved away my suggestion as foolish rather than showing an angry reaction to a presumptuous remark.

"Lynne, when, and if—but probably *when* is the operative word—I announce for the Senate, Glori...Ms. Nichols will be my public relations director. She is good at what she does; she is a strong professional. And we have also discussed your future position."

"Really? How interesting."

The District Attorney switched to careful New Englandese, which is sharp, clipped, precise and demanding. "What *is* it with you, Lynne? Do you have something personal against Glori? Since I will be working rather closely with her in the future and since I will be backing you when I make my public declaration and since there must be a certain cohesiveness among the people I am associated with, I think we should clear things up. What's it all about?"

I shrugged.

Suddenly, he sounded fatherly. Amused and fatherly. He almost put an arm around me: good old Dad.

"Lynne, is it just one of those 'woman-things'?"

Oh shit. How the hell do you answer a question like that: one of those *woman-things*. Visions of long intimate conversations between ethereal creatures, drifting along early morning beaches in the clean fresh air, discussing such *woman-things* as feminine hygiene, flashed through my brain.

"There seems to be a rather complex if unstated incompatibility of personalities, Mr. Hale. I'm not at all sure what Ms. Nichols has in mind. But I couldn't possibly allow her to intrude with a camera crew on any of the workings of my office. That would be ludicrous to say the least. And foolish and possibly dangerous professionally. I hardly imagine you'd sanction an 'open-office' policy."

"What she has in mind," he explained to me, "isn't an intrusion on any of the confidential spheres of your job, Lynne. She described it to me as a sort of cinéma-vérité with accent on the overall scope of your job. You'd be seen in conference with your staff and visiting the scene of a crime, talking to witnesses. No actual sound, of course. Possibly checking with your people in the field, that sort of thing. What she wants to show is a *woman in charge* of men in a traditionally male-dominated occupation. I should think, given your background, you'd be delighted to cooperate. It would be a marvelous opportunity to show you as a very accomplished, experienced, professional prosecutor. She'd bring in your background in the narrative. Voice-over, I think she called it."

Oh, Whitney Hale, you are learning all about television. How wonderful.

"And she'd be showing that you are totally qualified and capable of assuming the demands of the office of District Attorney. You could not possibly buy that kind of publicity, Lynne."

Just what I needed: Glori Nichols' stamp of approval. What I had worked for for fourteen years.

"But she won't give me any kind of editorial assurance, Mr. Hale. What if things don't turn out the way you're describing? What if something backfires and she's got it on film or tape or whatever? What if it would make a better story for *her* if I were to screw up on something? Rather than to succeed. Have you considered that possibility, sir? *Her* goal is a *story*."

The District Attorney sighed and shook his head and showed his sadness and disappointment.

"Oh Lynne, Lynne. I think sometimes that we—all of us—are so constantly exposed to the suspicious, the double-talk, the devious, that we look for the devils behind every spoken word and in every suggestion offered."

"Which, I believe, is the natural function of a prosecutor."

"Lynne, her purpose in this film is not to 'do you in' somehow, but to praise you, to show you as one of three women of great strength and achievement and ability and determination. Women who have held their own during the years when they—you—were substantially alone, without the backing of a women's movement. Real heroines: those of you who had the fortitude and determination to act on your own. Will you meet with her and discuss this?"

Real heroines. Now I was a heroine from yesteryear. Terrific.

"Do I have a choice?"

Jameson Whitney Hale did not answer. He just kept staring at me. His look suggested disappointment but at the same time confidence. Lynne would come through somehow; she always had; she always would.

"All right, as soon as I have a free moment. But I'm going to be very tied up for a while on the Dawson case."

"Lynne. The Dawson case." He came and stood beside me, his hand on my shoulder, gently pushing me to the door. "This could be a tremendously important case for you. In the public eye: a total media event. It could be the *very* thing that would put you over."

Now, that was not *my* Jameson Whitney Hale speaking. It was *her* Jameson Whitney Hale. Definitely, this man was smitten.

174

"Find a moment within the next day or two," he advised me with a smile. A cold, positive, assured smile.

"Yes, sir. I will do just that."

Like hell I would.

28

It had been a long and unpleasant and exhausting session with Chief of Detectives Jim Barrow and several of his top people. I went alone and sat feeling physically and emotionally small, surrounded by his staff of six-foot detectives with wounded faces. It wasn't that I had been withholding anything from Barrow; it was just that I hadn't been sharing fully. I was alone in a room filled with offended giants of delicate sensibility.

It took an hour to update them and during all that time, I did most of the talking and Jim and his henchmen stared and glanced at each other at statements they apparently considered significant.

Finally, I confronted one of his top investigators, a huge red-headed, green-eyed movie-extra type who had been listening intently and I hoped evaluating professionally.

"Well, Detective Kasinski, what do you think?"

"About what?" he asked. True detective style: answer a question with a question.

"About everything you've heard in this room tonight. Tell me candidly, without looking at your boss, Chief Barrow, or your partner over there. C'mon, eyes on me.

You've focused on me for one solid hour: now talk. *I'm* soliciting opinions. Give me yours. Quick. Top-of-your-head!"

Detective Kasinski fish-eyed me: large bright glazed green eyes unblinking and steady.

"The consensus is, Chief Jacobi," Jim Barrow said in what sounded to my tired head like a semi-whine, "that this has not been exactly a wide-open, totally cooperative investigation. And the general feeling is that we might have avoided certain things and accomplished other things had we been let in on 'your' investigation earlier."

I was going to ask Barrow: How did you do that? How did you arrive at a consensus right before my very eyes? But I was too tired for games. I was remembering my boss, newly smitten and involving me in *his* games with his television lady. I was remembering the expression on Mr. Wise's face when he kept repeating over and over to us, about his son-in-law, David Cohen: get-him; get-him; get-him.

I leaned back in the uncomfortable chair that had been provided for me, stretched my legs out without finding any place to rest them; sat slumped and drained and looked across Jim Barrow's desk and said quietly, directly to him, excluding the members of his staff who were placed strategically about the office, "Stop fucking with me, Jim. I'm too tired even to be kissed."

It embarrassed him, as I had intended. I knew my Jim Barrow: his foul and energetically creative mouth was closed in the presence of a woman. He glanced around at his men and somehow, wordlessly, transmitted a signal and they filed out quietly, politely. Coffee appeared in a short time: hot, fresh from the bakery around the corner and served with paper trays of warm Danish pastry.

"You do look tired, Lynnie. Look," Jim back-pedaled a little; all his points had been scored; now we were to be pals again. "Look, Lynne, we've been doing all the background stuff and you've been right front and center with the main characters. My guys are a little edgy.

This is a big headline case; updated on TV every night; rerun during Sanderalee's time slot."

"And my pretty little face has been seen and not handsome Mr. Kasinski's or Kelly or whatsisname, the handsome football-player type who works with Moscowitz? C'mon, Jim." I pulled myself up straight and took a good bite of Danish. Some kind of little nuts; a tiny piece of sharp shell cut directly into my gums. I fingered it out and examined it. "Thank you very much. Any more shells or hidden tortures?"

Jim relented a little; good-pal Jim approach. "You know how these younger guys are, Lynne. They watch all the damn silly cop shows and even though they know life isn't like that, I guess they all fantasize a little. Case ending with closeup on handsome young cop who modestly shrugs it all off: all in a day's work and what's the boss got lined up next, for Pete's sake?"

His men had all been assigned and had all been working hard at their assignments, to do background investigations and to interrogate all the various names who were connected in any way to Sanderalee Dawson. They had compiled a thick, fairly neat volume of interviews and comments and statistics and data. Might come in handy someday if Sanderalee ever wanted to write a book called *People Who Knew Me*.

They were feeling a little left out. My people were visible and easily spotted at the heart of the case. My people were assigned close contact with the victim and daily contact with those people immediately involved with her. Jim's prima donnas had been toiling in the unglamorous places.

"Okay, your people do the search of Dr. Cohen's apartment, office at Columbia, office at New York Hospital."

"What about his cottage out at East Hampton?"

I stared blankly and Jim Barrow winked at me. "*Gotcha.* Don't look upset, Lynne, you've had a lot on your mind. Okay, any hints, clues, suggestions, instructions as to what my gentlemen will be looking for?" He grinned and gestured toward the door. "You want to brief the troops or will you defer to the old soldier here?"

"How's about you and me go out to the cottage at East Hampton, Jim, just you and me together and... search around a little, huh? Hey, Jim. I'm tired. Very tired. Give me one of your silent but non-hostile types to drive me home, okay? I've had a lousy day; I anticipate a sleepless night and a rotten tomorrow."

"Sounds like a buildup to a television commercial: take one search warrant and a half, and feel better in the morning. So, Lynne, what do you think? The doctor a nut? He do all this?"

It was a genuine question: we never exchanged "Oh-my-God, could this possibly be's." Both Barrow and I knew anything could possibly be.

I shrugged. "Listen to my tapes; study my notes. Could I have your whatsisname—Henry? Hendrison—sit in tomorrow when Dr. Cohen and company come to my office?"

"Hendrikson, Sam. You got him. Lynne, did he do this? This David Cohen of the international reputation?"

"Ask Sanderalee Dawson, pal, don't ask me. I wasn't there."

Bobby Jones didn't answer his phone so I went next door to accept Jhavi's invitation to share their newest bootleg movie. My cat was already at their apartment; he preferred Harley's cooking to mine. I relaxed and scrunched down into the depths of their marvelous sofa. Jake Jacobi came and cuddled on top of me: he was so damn heavy I could hardly breathe, but I guess I could breathe enough because I fell asleep and when I opened my eyes, I was covered with a cashmere blanket. The background sounds from the movie on the huge Advent had been turned down very low.

Jhavi's fingertips tickled my forehead and he held out the telephone and he whispered quietly, directly into the phone. "Shall I tell him to just blast off, my darling, or do you want to speak to the voice of the Midwest?"

We had brought my phone into their apartment on the extra-long extension cord. I didn't snap instantly, adrenally awake as I did when set off by a loud ring. I stretched and yawned and reached for Bobby Jones.

"Lynne, listen. I might be on to something important. What time tomorrow are we seeing the doctor and his lawyer?"

"The doctor? And his lawyer? And his Indian chief?"

"Lynne? Are you awake or what?" Bobby Jones was certainly awake...what? annoyed with me? about what?

"What time is it, Bobby? What are we talking about? I called you when I got home from Barrow's office. Talk about your offended stars. My God, Bobby, it seems we have been stomping all over Jim Barrow's best fellers. Hey, where were *you?* Out on the town?"

He was all-businesslike is *how* he was anyway, wherever he had been.

"Lynne, I have—I *will* have a freeze-frame from the news conference held the day of the attack. At a news-briefing session after the team of surgeons rejoined Sanderalee's hand: David Cohen had a small, round Band-Aid patch on his left cheek, Lynne. I'm having the picture blown up and I'll bring it in in the morning. Lynne, are you following me?"

"To the ends of the earth. Where are you now?"

"I'm at home and I just got here and I've been out trying to get the information we needed. I think I've got it."

He sounded: how? Remote? Distracted? Annoyed? Excited? Impersonal? What? What?

"Bobby? Everything okay? You sound...kind of...funny?"

Silence; not more than a split second. A professional judgment: this man has something to hide. A personal

179

judgment: whatever it is, I don't want to know. I said goodbye.

What gives? I wondered. A warning? From Bobby? Suddenly I felt very cold.

29

Some investigations have a life of their own: an almost biological rhythm or tempo. They are slow-paced and steady and are accomplished through meticulous researching and digging and sorting and sifting and evaluation of facts to prove or disprove the theory with which we begin. These are the somewhat leisurely, somewhat boring and arduous but somehow reassuring cases that are self-contained within the agency assigned. There is no outside monitoring or speculation or accusation or implication. Time is not particularly a factor. Accuracy and the ability to present a tight and binding case against the accused are all-important. We have the luxury of moving in one direction, compiling data, examining it and striking it all if necessary and starting again from another premise entirely.

That is the ideal type of investigation: unpublicized until such time as, equipped with substantial evidence, we bring the culprit into court. To the public, it seems that, as if by magic, we have uncovered dark foul deeds of criminal activity. Our false starts and wrong assumptions are unknown and unavailable for public discussion. If we have in fact done our job properly, there is a strong possibility that the accused, in the light of the evidence and upon sensible advice from counsel, will cop a plea: make a deal: bargain with us. Then, we can get on with the business of our office at a minimum cost to the taxpayers.

And then there is another type of investigation that gets away from you almost immediately by the very nature of the people involved. If we had any doubts at all as to the pressures to be applied in the Sanderalee Dawson investigation, reality came upon us in full force in the form of what is known as a "blind item" on Page Six of the *New York Post*. This is the page set aside for all kinds of interesting, unsubstantiated and titillating bits of gossip and innuendo.

> What's the story on the internationally renowned Israeli doctor who has been barred from Sanderalee Dawson's hospital room? Have they previously met under very different circumstances? Is the truth more horrible than we can imagine? If so, who's sitting on it and why?????

Every second, third and fourth phone call into my Bureau was an inquiry based on the Page Six item.

Chief Jim Barrow called: he was upset because as his men arrived with search warrants in hand at Dr. David Cohen's apartment, at his office at Columbia Presbyterian and at his office at New York Hospital, there were mobs of newspeople, equipped with questions, cameras, microphones.

"Even, for God's sake, out at East Hampton, Lynne. My guys called me to tell me that reporters from the little rinky-dinky local newspapers had been tipped. What's the story on all this crap?"

"What's the story, Chief Barrow? Okay: here's the story. You've been complaining that your men were left

181

out of everything, so I called the tip in to Page Six. Then I disguised my voice as a member of the lunatic fringe and spent all morning calling the news media. I've been telling everyone that Jim Barrow's guys are on the job. That this is the opportunity they've all been waiting for: these are really handsome guys, very photogenic. Jim, what the hell do you want from me?"

By the time Dr. David Cohen and his attorney, Jerry Ashkenazi, arrived for our 2:00 P.M. appointment, things had gotten hectic indeed.

Dr. Cohen's attorney looked very agitated. He was a heavyset man of about forty with a thick dark brown toupee that was set slightly at an angle veering toward his left eyebrow. He had pudgy, thick hands, which he used to grasp his client's wrist in what I guess he considered a reassuring gesture. However, the impression I got was that he was hanging on to David Cohen for dear life.

They had been accosted in the lobby of our building by the hungry hordes of media-land. They had had questions screamed at them, accusations shouted at them, demands for explanations, statements and unhindered photo opportunities. In effect, our office represented a safe-house and we assured them of a secret, reporter-proof exit at the end of our conference.

Jerry Ashkenazi was not a criminal lawyer. He had been intimidated by events from the time he got up in the morning and received a phone call from David Cohen to the effect that three men with a search warrant were seeking access to his apartment.

"Is this how these things are generally done, Mrs. Jacobi?" Mr. Ashkenazi demanded to know. He missed the signal that went around the room: from me to Bobby Jones to Lucy Capella to Jim Barrow's man, Sam Hendrikson. What we have here, friends, is a man in over his head. Let's hope, for his sake, he realizes this fact very soon. Or that he doesn't and lets his client talk and talk and talk.

Dr. David Cohen did not miss the signal. Dr. David Cohen did not miss very much. He sat straight in his chair, not leaning back, yet not looking tense. Just alert and slightly wary. And slightly angry-but-controlled.

"Is it customary," Dr. Cohen asked me, "for people with a search warrant to show up unannounced at seven o'clock in the morning?"

"It's as good a time as any. They were on the first shift. Did they also advise you about your offices and your cottage out at East Hampton?"

Dr. Cohen nodded. "Yes. If there was any specific item you wanted, it might have been easier to just ask me. They were going through my things like marauders."

His attorney leaned forward, pressing Dr. Cohen's wrist in what looked like a death-grip. "Easy, David, easy. Let me talk, let me make the complaint."

He proceeded to tell me that Barrow's men were going through David's apartment like marauders and that if they'd only said what it was they wanted, it would have made matters easier. He asked about ten questions relative to search-and-seizure procedure: what were they allowed to take? who had the receipts for items taken? why were they taking these things? where were they being taken off to? why? when would they be returned? if some tests were to be run, by whom and toward what end?

This guy was asking us to educate him.

"My advice to you, Mr. Ashkenazi, and no offense intended, is that you should confer with someone on your staff who is familiar with criminal procedure."

"Criminal procedure? Criminal procedure?" He stood up and looked around, shook his head and then sat down again. "What criminal procedure? Do you know the kind of man we are talking about here? Do you know the reputation of this man? Do you know the things David Cohen has accomplished? My specialty is defending against malpractice suits. This is what my firm does, that is what my partners and I do. If I thought for one minute that Dr. David Cohen—that this eminent microsurgeon, world famous, a pioneer in this technique—if I thought for one split second that he

183

should be represented by a—God-forbid—criminal lawyer, then a criminal lawyer would be sitting here next to him and not me. But just tell me, please, since I am not familiar with the procedure, under the search warrant, what are you people entitled to anyway?"

A really ludicrous thought flashed through my brain: what if, by some unexpected and terrible miracle, Dr. David Cohen felt called upon, right now in the presence of all here assembled, to confess to the crime that was alleged against him. Would it be thrown out because he did not have proper legal representation to advise him of his rights?

We led Dr. David Cohen carefully according to a prearranged plan we had discussed before he and his attorney arrived.

Lucy was good at the possibly incriminating areas. Her questions sounded more like sincere requests for information that might one day be helpful to her: *e.g.*, Dr. Cohen, you're a runner. From your apartment, where do you generally run? Goodness, do you risk the 72nd Street transverse? Ah, that would make a good run: from your apartment on 69th and Fifth, up to 72nd, across the park, down Central Park West to Central Park South to Fifth Avenue and 59th and up to 69th Street. At night, Dr. Cohen? Goodness, have you ever encountered any muggers? Well, you must be one of the very few New Yorkers who can make that claim.

"I've come to the conclusion that how you present yourself makes a difference," Dr. Cohen explained to Lucy, who nodded, taking advice and instruction very nicely.

"You know, Dr. Cohen, I think you're right about how you present yourself, the kind of aura of self-confidence one gives off."

He nodded at Lucy. They were on the same wavelength and she straightened up slightly, held her head high, showing her own confidence.

"When I was in...social work, I used to go into very dangerous neighborhoods. You know, where violence was just an ordinary fact of daily life. And yet, I was never attacked or anything. And it wasn't that I was known particularly, that I was treated with respect because of who I was or why I was there. I agree with you, I think it's a matter of self-confidence and being able to radiate that kind of confidence."

Bobby Jones' eyebrows asked me the question: What the hell's this all about? We going to start exchanging "element of danger" stories or something? I winked and nodded slightly in Lucy's direction.

Dr. Cohen was agreeing with Lucy. Although he looked somewhat breakable with his long slender arms and legs and slim build, he told Lucy, "Yes. I maintain there is a trick to it. I'm not about to give up favorite areas of the city to the 'street elements.' They are not all that stupid. They can sense who is not your perfect victim."

"And that's got to come from inside, I think," Lucy said. "From somehow knowing you can take care of yourself and then being able to sort of give off... what, rays of your own confidence?"

It sat there for a moment, not going anywhere, not taking off in any particular direction.

Sam Hendrikson got into it. Sam is the kind of man who can pass in the crowd and become whatever everyone else in the crowd is: he is a chameleon, a nonentity with hornrimmed glasses and a quiet self-effacing manner. When he asks a question, he seems slightly afraid of revealing his own stupidity.

"Yes, but Lucy, you were trained in self-defense, weren't you?"

"Oh, come on, Sam. Plenty of people take all kinds of classes but once they're out of the gym, it's a total washout unless they have that something extra special. Confidence. Right, Dr. Cohen?"

"Did you take up any self-defense techniques anywhere, Dr. Cohen? Well, I don't imagine you're called upon to go into the so-called dangerous neighborhoods. You hardly make house calls in your specialty."

Dr. Cohen slowly leaned back in his chair and regarded Lucy and then turned his attention to Sam. "Are you asking me if I'm a specialist in karate or kung fu or any of the other empty-handed combat techniques? Such as were probably exercised on Ms. Dawson in inflicting the various injuries on her face. Is that what you're asking me?"

Jerry Ashkenazi pulled out a handkerchief and waved it in front of him before he blew his nose.

"Hold on here, hold on now. David, don't answer any of this. You're not required to answer this."

And then, poor man, he honked his nose and leaned over and asked in an audible whisper, "David, you know this kind of stuff? Kung fu and all?"

Had he ever heard of the Jog-gon-Inn? No.

Had he been out running on Tuesday, March 6, 1979? He really could not say with any certainty.

Could he account for his time during the twenty-four-hour period immediately preceding the phone call that summoned him to New York Hospital for emergency surgery on Sanderalee Dawson?

"I will have to check my appointment diary," Dr. Cohen said. And then, directly to me, "Or you people can check it, since I assume it is now in your possession."

"Are you serious about all this?" Dr. Cohen's attorney kept asking us.

"Mr. Ashkenazi, an accusation has been made against Dr. Cohen. We are talking about an extremely serious felony charge against your client. It would seem to me, Mr. Ashkenazi, that it would be in your client's best interest—no matter what—to cooperate as fully as possible."

"No matter what? No matter what? My God, what are you saying? Do you know this man's reputation?"

"It is not his professional reputation that is at issue here."

Dr. Cohen began quieting his attorney; comforting him; reassuring him. *Counseling* him.

Bobby Jones.

"Dr. Cohen, when we asked you yesterday about the

Band-Aid on your left cheek, you told us you had a cut as the result of slipping and hitting your face against the metal edge of your desk. Could you be more specific about that, please?"

He gave some more details; it had happened about eight days ago. The "when" could be clarified by a check on what day he had taught class at Columbia. There were some forty-one or forty-two physicians present: witnesses to the event.

"One of them accompanied me to the Emergency Room on the first floor, where two stitches were taken in my cheek. You can get all the details: everything is a matter of record."

"Dr. Cohen, had you previously had a cut or injury or abrasion or blemish on your left cheek?"

"Previously? What previously?" his attorney asked.

"On the day that you did surgery to reattach Sanderalee Dawson's severed hand," Bobby Jones asked, "did you have a Band-Aid on your left cheek?"

David Cohen blinked, glanced at me, smiled tightly and shrugged.

"Did I? A cut from shaving or ... I haven't the faintest idea. Ms. Jacobi, is this significant?"

"What are you getting at here, Mrs. Jacobi?" his attorney asked. "Are you serious about all this? Are you *really* serious?"

Bobby Jones held up the 8x10 enlargement of a stop-frame from the news conference held in the last afternoon after the surgery on Sanderalee's hand. It was a blurry picture, hazy and soft-focus, but Dr. David Cohen's face was clearly identifiable and there, on his left cheek, was a Band-Aid.

Bobby identified the enlargement and Jerry Ashkenazi took it, leaned it toward the light on my desk, offered it to Dr. Cohen, who glanced at it and then at me.

"Well, then, there you are. You hardly needed to ask me a question to which you already had an answer."

"There is an old saying among lawyers, Dr. Cohen: never ask a question to which you don't already have the answer. At least not in a courtroom. Could you tell us, please, what injury, or whatever, was beneath this Band-Aid on your left cheek?"

"I haven't the faintest idea," Dr. Cohen said. Which, given his position, was a very wise answer. Although not the answer that I was beginning to believe we already had.

"What's the significance of this Band-Aid on the cheek?" Mr. Ashkenazi finally asked.

We told him: Sanderalee Dawson stabbed her assailant on the left cheek with a silver unicorn.

"And you think that the cut or whatever on David's cheek that day was..." He shook his head and grabbed his client's forearm and pressed it very hard. Dr. Cohen remained expressionless.

Jerry Ashkenazi was very pale.

"Mrs. Jacobi, I think my client has answered just about all the questions it is feasible for him to answer at this time." And then, to his client, in a worried-but-don't-worry-about-it voice, "David, you'll come to my office and we'll talk." And then to me, "Mrs. Jacobi, will you people please provide us with a way of getting out of this place? I'm not about to let Dr. Cohen go through that mob of crazy people down there. What are they doing there? What do they want from Dr. Cohen?"

I signaled Bobby Jones for an escort and then I told Jerry Ashkenazi, and more particularly Dr. David Cohen, "You'd better get used to mobs of crazy people. They're going to be with you for quite a while."

About ten minutes later, I was alone in my office, having dispatched my staff to their appointed rounds. The tap at the door was tentative and so was the expression on Jerry Ashkenazi's face as I waved him on in.

"We're waiting for a car," he said, gesturing over his shoulder. "Your man went to get a car and we're going to go out through the garage, I think he said."

"Good. That's fine."

He looked around the room quickly, then approached
188

my desk and leaned toward me, his fingertips resting on the desk blotter.

"Mrs. Jacobi," he started. I corrected him: there had been just about one "Mrs. Jacobi" too much. "I'm sorry: *Ms*. Jacobi. Please. I wanted to tell you this: off the record. Just for your information I wanted to tell you this. This is a very valuable, decent, wonderfully gifted man who has saved more lives, put together more broken lives than you can believe. Please, Mrs....Ms. Jacobi. Be very careful. Think about who it is that is trying to make you do this terrible thing. Think what their motives are. Don't let them make a sacrificial lamb of David. Please, think about this. Don't let *them* do this. Don't let *them* get to you."

"*Them?* The ubiquitous *them*, Mr. Ashkenazi? *We* are *them*; *they* are *them*. I don't give a damn who is out to get whom. What I want is to get the indictment and the conviction of the bastard who raped and sodomized and beat up Sanderalee Dawson. And then cut off her left hand. And if he just happens to be a wonderful and decent and valuable and gifted man most of the time, well that just isn't my concern."

"But look where it's coming from, the accusation. Look what he's trying to make of it, for God's sake."

Somewhere along the line, he had lost me.

"You don't know what I'm talking about? Ah, that's it, I can see that now. While we were in here, while we were talking in here in your office, that man, that PLO schwartze-pig, was on that afternoon TV news show, talk show, whatever, on Channel Five, I think."

"Whom are you taling about?"

Of course I knew and when this very agitated man said Regg Morris, I was not surprised at all. Only shocked.

"He said, here, I'm reading it from the last *Post*, he said, here, read it yourself, he's trying to make this into a black-Jewish confrontation thing. He's accusing you, as a Jew, of covering up for a Jew because Sanderalee Dawson is a black woman."

Mr. Ashkenazi was shaking from anger and anguish. I took the newspaper from him and told him to go home.

And, on impulse, off-the-record, I told him to call a good criminal lawyer. His client had need.

30

It was not a good weekend. Bobby Jones turned sulky on Friday night and when we returned to my apartment after a very long, exhausting evening of overtime consultations with staff members, this was not what I needed.

"Why don't you go home, Bobby? You look tired. Or something." No answer. "Well, which is it, BJ? Tired? Or is it *something?*"

"Let's just sit quietly for a while, Lynne, all right? It's been a long day."

"Spoken like a husband, Bobby." I shoved his feet off my coffee table. "C'mon, get going, pal. I don't need moody and I don't need hurt and I don't need secretive and I don't need sly glances and I don't need any of this."

"What *do* you need, Lynne? Have you any idea what you *really* need?"

His face even looks beautiful when moody; when angry. Borders on petulant, but a manly petulance. The fallen lock of hair just touching the brow, the golden eyebrows lowered over the clear midwestern eyes, the tension along his neck and shoulders, through his torso, along his perfectly proportioned arms and strong freckled hands, and down along his hard and slender thighs.

He put his feet back on my coffee table and fixed his clever blue eyes on my tired face and in a practiced, interrogator's voice he asked me: "When were you going to tell me about your plan to run for District Attorney?"

It was totally unexpected. Lynne, how long have you been having an affair with old Mr. Timothy Doyle? why have you been stalking Jim Barrow? why have you been seen lurking in the playground behind the local grammar school? Lynne, what are you up to with that dynamic devil, Regg Morris?

I turned it over carefully, absorbing the shock of the unexpected. We lawyers do that: do not answer in haste, do not follow up a surprise question with a surprise answer. Hesitate, evaluate. And then attack. Calmly and professionally. My God, we're turning my living room into a courtroom.

"Where were you last night when I called you, Bobby Jones?"

His feet came from the coffee table again; his jaw moved side to side as he ground his teeth, searching for his own careful reply: question or answer? attack or retreat? truth or lie?

Terrific. I had unknowingly made a connection. And then I held up my hand, because connections once made come quickly, clearly, and accurately.

"You spent a little time with the lady television biggie, the lady with the honey-colored hair. And she kindly provided you with not only a stop-frame clip of Dr. David, she also gave you a little bit of information about the Lady Lynne. And you've been walking around all day wondering when I was going to read your mind and offer you, *offer* you, as though I *owed* you, an explanation of my future plans."

"As they pertain to *me*, personally, damned right."

"They do *not* pertain to you, personally or impersonally or any other goddamn way, Bobby. My professional life, my career plans are mine."

"No hitching my wagon to a star, is that it?"

I whirled around, trying for a regal anger, for grace, for dramatic effect and hit my shins on the goddamn coffee table and had to hop, hunched over and gasping. Midwestern gentleman to the core, Bobby leaped up, came to my rescue, helped me to a chair. I sank down, hugged my leg: God, it hurt. Tears sprang from my eyes: of pain, exhaustion, anger. And regret. A small, sad, and unwanted regret. He is so beautiful; even when he's angry.

His hands were strong and gentle on my leg and then he lifted me lightly, strongly, and carried me in to my bed and propped me up with pillows and offered to bring me hot cocoa but there was that glass-hardness in his eyes. It was not a hot cocoa moment.

"Okay, Bobby. *First*, it is not definite. It depends totally on Jameson-the-Whitney-Hale's being nominated for the Senate."

"My information is that he has it pretty well tied up."

"Oh, fuck your information. And fuck your informant." We were making progress in this wonderful conversation. "Number two, in the event, and I certainly hope it comes to pass, that I do get the interim appointment, the hearty-Hale will endorse and support me all the way to the hilt. As will his political organizations and associations. It is all still tentative, Bobby. And somewhat dependent on this damn Sanderalee Dawson case not lousing me up. It would be to my definite, personal advantage to get at least an indictment prior to the primaries. It would be perfect to get a guilty plea. It would be maybe even better to go to trial and get a conviction."

"I was *wondering* about a few things in this case, Lynne. Now, it makes a little more sense."

"*What?*"

"Why we aren't out looking for other possibles. Why we are moving in one tight little circle: prove David Cohen did it."

"Bobby, for God's sake, Sanderalee Dawson has fingered him. The *victim* has pointed right into his face and...ah, the hell, Bobby. That's it. That's all. You don't like the way I'm handling this case, tell you what. You take off in any direction you want. Play devil's advocate. That'll strengthen my case. You raise the questions and I'll find the answers. Fair enough?"

He stood absolutely still and said quietly, "Lynne, do you *really* believe David Cohen did it? Committed this terrible assault on Sanderalee Dawson?"

"Yes. Yes, Bobby, I *really* do. *I really believe David Cohen did it.* And I intend to make a case against him."

"He didn't do it."

"Flat out, just like that, the hell with what the victim said?"

"The victim has got her head screwed on upside down. The victim was in and out of coma. The victim is easily led; she's highly suggestible; easily influenced. I think she *thinks* Cohen is her assailant."

"But you don't."

"Lynne, there are some people who just *cannot, under any circumstances,* commit certain crimes. A micro-surgeon could not, under any circumstances, cut off a woman's hand with a meat cleaver."

"Bobby, what about Mr. and Mrs. Wise? What about the things they told us about your Dr. Cohen?"

"He's not *my* Dr. Cohen, Lynne. For God's sake, be objective. You're a lawyer. Pick them apart: parents of a dead girl; grief-stricken; unaccepting. Lynne, no matter what they said, none of it is material to the case at hand. You're viewing them emotionally."

"They provided the one negative word we hadn't found before. A personality flaw—that's all it would take. An inexplicable personality flaw. Jim Barrow's checking out the murder that was committed around the time of Melissa's death. It might fit, Bobby."

"Now he's a multi-murderer. Lynne, you're losing objectivity. Look, in the tape, do you remember that Sanderalee said something about...at first, she thought she'd met him at the Jog-gon-Inn? Well, maybe this *was* a guy she met there. It was a cold night. He was bundled up. Maybe it was a guy who resembles David Cohen."

"Prove it. Find him."

"I'm damned well going to try. Don't rush this case, Lynne. You know, you haven't answered my question. Where does Lynne the District Attorney leave me?"

"It has nothing to do with you." He was glaring down at me now and I was glaring up and my neck hurt and my shinbone hurt and now my eyes were beginning to hurt. "Listen, Bobby, so you won't say I didn't tell you right at the start. If—*when* I make the move..."

He cut in. "Bureau Chief will become vacant."

That shut both of us up for a moment. He fixed me with such intensity that I almost lost the sense of what I was about to say. Almost; not quite.

I shook my head slowly. "Bobby, it took me nearly twelve years to secure the position of Bureau Chief for a woman. You don't really think I'd let it slip away after all that planning and plotting and hard work, do you?"

"Lucy? You'd give it to *Lucy Capella?*" He sounded incredulous.

"You're damn right. After all, I owe..."

I stopped not quite short enough and we both knew it. "After all, Lucy is totally qualified. She's waited a long time and..."

"No, why don't you back up a little bit, Lynne. 'After all, I owe,' I believe was what you were saying. As in 'I owe Lucy...' what? After all, 'I owe Lucy' *what?*"

I stood up and moved around a little bit; his eyes kept a tight hard focus on me. I could feel their glare between my shoulder blades. Finally, I turned to face him, took a deep breath. Here goes nothing; or something; or everything.

"After all, the position of Chief Investigator should have gone to Lucy Capella two years ago. Instead of to you."

"Based on what? seniority?"

We both knew that wasn't what I meant.

194

"Based on *ability; competency; qualifications; suitability;* and," I added softly, "seniority."

With each word I had spoken, Bobby's eyes became harder, colder, darker, bluer; his jawline worked as he clenched his teeth, trying to contain his anger. He turned his head slightly as though dazed by what I had just said. "Well. Hey, just let me think about all that for a second, all right?

"Bobby..."

He waved a hand in my direction, walked over to the window, pushed aside the drapes, spun away from the window and turned to confront me head-on.

"Do you mind telling me *why* you promoted me to a position that you feel I wasn't competent, qualified, suitable for? What was the first thing Lucy had that I don't have? Ah, yes. Ability. With my *lack* of ability and all those other specifications..."

"Hold it, Bobby, I didn't say you *didn't* have all of those qualifications. I just said...that Lucy would actually have been more qualified. Would have been the more logical choice."

"But I'm better in bed."

"You're not that good." I said it too quickly; it was the obvious rejoinder and I am known for obvious rejoinders. I sat down on the edge of the bed. "Bobby, I didn't mean that, you know I didn't. We just seem to be sparring and it seemed a good shot at you. The main reason I didn't appoint Lucy was that I felt it just wouldn't wash too well: two women in the two top spots. You can see for yourself how paranoid that is: you can have twenty-five top men and never give a thought to appointing a twenty-sixth man. But one top woman: I felt it the better side of discretion to appoint a man."

"Okay, you had to appoint a man. Why me? Why not...Sullivan? Troy? Russo? Why not...why me?"

"Listen, Bobby, you've had the job for two years now. You've worked into it pretty well. But if you want total honesty, I could have, *professionally*, made a better choice. *Lucy.*"

"Oh, let's have total honesty, Lynne. I've always ad
mired you for total honesty."

"Bobby, both Lucy and I have spent our entire law
careers as prosecutors. Do you think I was born wanting
to be a prosecutor? After law school, I surveyed the
field open to me. It was very, very narrow and the
further on I looked, the more it narrowed down. It was
a pragmatic decision on my part to build my career the
way I did. I had no guarantees, God, I had no smallest
hope at all that it would one day open up for a woman
the way it has. It's too late for me to make any changes
in direction now. I've developed my expertise and I
intend to cash in on it. I've nowhere else to go profes
sionally. I'm going to stick with what I know. And I
know how to be a prosecutor. It's not the same for you.
You can still go any way you want to go. It's always
been that way for you. That's probably why you're
not..."

"I love the way you always manage to get those last
few words out *before* you bite your lip, Lynne."

"Okay, Bobby. You're *not* a *good prosecutor.* You
don't have the *killer's instinct.* You aren't totally will
ing to believe the worst possible thing about a human
being. You constantly look for mitigating circumstan
ces. You are never willing to suspend every single
emotion, every single feeling, other than an intense
desire to nail the perpetrator to the cross." I made a
funny sound, intended to be a laugh; sounded more like
I was choking. "That's a hell of a terrible thing to say
about someone, isn't it, Bobby? That you've never been
purely, cleanly vicious or vindictive enough to be a top-
flight prosecutor."

"That isn't what you're saying. What you're con
demning are my professional qualifications for my job.'

"Have it your own way. Whatever you choose to believe. You've done a good job as my Chief Investigator.
But not... not as good a job as..."

"As Lucy Capella would have done? No, don't say a
word, Lynne. Don't say anything at all. I've got the
message. So that when you become the District Attor-

ney, and you've appointed Lucy Capella as Bureau Chief, she will of course appoint her own Chief Investigator, and that will leave me...?" He spread his arms wide.

"With a whole big wide-open world of law out there, Bobby. You've got all the options that I never had." And then I had a most unfortunate flash and spoke impulsively. "Ever think of entertainment law, Bobby? Why don't you ask your TV lady pal about her world of opportunities?"

That was a low blow and Bobby Jones' cowboy-killer eyes tightened and focused on me: I was the Indian.

"You mean hitch my wagon to another *rising lady-star?*" he said softly. "Uh-uh. I've already done that. *It isn't worth it.*"

And then he left and I kept falling asleep and then waking up and recalling the conversation verbatim. It is an unfortunate ability of mine. Among other unfortunate abilities. Like throwing away people I don't really want to throw away.

Oh, damn it, Bobby Jones. Damn you.

Part Four

Grand Jury

31

At 10:00 A.M. on Saturday morning in the Crown Heights section of Brooklyn, a policeman, disguised as an elderly Hasidic Jew on his way to temple, was confronted and robbed at gunpoint and then shot in the chin. His backup team, another "Hasidic Jew" and a "mailman," then engaged the assailant in a wild shootout during which some sixteen or eighteen shots were exchanged. At the end of the proceedings, the second "Hasidic Jew" backup cop had been hit dead-center but was uninjured due to his bulletproof vest. The "mailman" cop had been shot in the right foot, either by direct hit or as a result of a ricochet.

The culprit was dead, having sustained a total of eight direct hits scattered throughout the body: face, stomach, heart, lungs, et cetera, et cetera. It was determined by the Medical Examiner that the culprit, who was five feet eight inches tall and weighed approximately one hundred and sixty pounds, had been, in life, a thirteen-year-old, three-months-pregnant black female.

Semantics is a very important part of the public relations announcements offered by the Police Department. If anyone has ever wondered about the stilted, peculiar manner in which policemen describe events, it is because they are rigorously instructed to beware of certain sensitive areas of language. Never identify a black—regardless of age—as a boy or a girl. When referring to culprit by name, it is *Mister* or *Miss*. Beware such words as arrogant uppity nigger, colored guy, PR. Black is the word; Hispanic covers the requirement as needed. Thus, the announcement that a thirteen-year-old black female, the posthumously identified perpetrator of a series of similar assaults on previous Saturdays, had been shot and killed by stakeout police officers after an exchange of shots. Detailed descriptions of the actions and injuries of all concerned would be made a matter of public record as soon as possible.

The policeman who had been robbed and shot in the chin—not a serious wound—was interviewed for the TV news from his hospital bed, his wife and children at his side. He described the events as they had occurred and then, in a pain-killer daze, he described the culprit as "a very big black-female youthette." The department rushed public relations people onto the scene and it was left to fancy Freddie Mandell, Commissioner of the careful explanation, to describe the dead assailant:

> Miss Jewel Brown; age thirteen years; no known address; background of six foster homes; appeared in Family Court total of eight times on charges ranging from petit larceny to armed robbery to drug pushing to prostitution. Each time released to different foster family; last "family" has not seen Miss Brown for nearly five months. Never reported missing. By anyone. Miss Jewel Brown had been "turned out" at age eleven by a neighborhood pimp; thrown out by her then current foster family; arrested; released; sent away once or twice during her short life.

What he didn't reveal was that sewn into the lining of her jacket was the school photo of an eight-year-old child, female, with a bright, smiling, hopeful expression; third-grade parochial-school photo of lucky Jewel Brown, placed with a strict but loving Catholic foster mother, who died of cancer within the year. On the

202

back of the photo, in small and irregular print, was Jewel Brown's total written comment about her life. Undated, the comments were as follows:

Jewel is a pretty girl and good in reading.
Jewel is too fat and too big.
Jewel can hit real hard.
Jewel can fuck all she wants to.
Jewel got a gun and a man.
Fuck Jewel and kill her dead.
Big. Ugly. Dead. Jewel.

In the black community of Crown Heights, it was put out immediately that the men who shot Jewel Brown were, *in fact*, Hasidic Jews who had been permitted by the police to carry guns with which to shoot black children on the streets of Brooklyn.

The dead female—young woman—girl—child, who had been a homeless, vagrant, unwanted, unloved, uncared-for nonentity, was posthumously, and with an overwhelming love and anger and righteous indignation, adopted by *her* "community": a community that had previously all but ignored her existence. Funds were raised so that her funeral would be more costly than any amounts spent on her existence from time of birth to time of death. A copy of the picture of the third-grader appeared from somewhere, blown up to poster-size and mounted on a placard. The child-face was radiant with innocence and hope and expectation, unaware of her own plunging future and eight-bullet end. There was literally a wailing and crying on the streets as more and more Jewel Brown posters appeared and were displayed and exhibited side by side with blowups of the shot-dead Jewel as she lay face down in her own blood on the sidewalk where she had fallen.

There was a growing, tightening, solidifying racial grouping, which, by late afternoon, early evening, had traveled from Brooklyn across the bridges and over the borough lines until the entire city was put—unofficially—on riot alert. With the darkness came the first

sporadic wave of fires; within hours, the acts of destruc
tion escalated until long-established, solidly neighbor
hood shops on the Upper West Side, black-owned as
well as white-owned, were ripped open, looted, des
poiled by the wave of emotion and hysteria and anger
and frustration as well as the exciting possibilities of
opportunity that had spread from the poster-waving
procession in Crown Heights.

All Police Department and Fire Department days off
and vacations were canceled and both departments
were automatically put on an overtime basis. The of
ficial policy that Saturday night was to contain, rather
than control; do not engage directly; do not provoke. In
cop-parlance: let 'em have their fucking free color TVs
the welfare 'ud give it to 'em anyway, nothing to lose
my balls over.

On Sunday, Regg Morris appeared as one of the
guests on a half-hour, midday live *Black Voice* television program. His passion and anger, his pity and
heartbreak were marvelously controlled and genuine
To a point. The point being in his declaration that the
"murder of Jewel Brown, black-child, black-girl-child
is part and parcel, all of a line with the white establishment's plan for the annihilation of the peoples of
the Third World."

As he made his accusations, he held up the poster
of the bright-eyed third-grader and described the child
as though she had never grown up and acted out her
own rage and anger and violence and destruction. If
you didn't know better, you'd swear that Jewel Brown
had stood, an unarmed eight-year-old, before the on-
slaught of the white man's guns.

Regg Morris was careful not to put to rest the story
that the Hasidim-police were, *in fact*, Hasidic Jews.
When his host, rather shaken by Morris's insinuation,
interjected the fact of the police decoys, he was met
with one of Regg's best, coldest stares, the exasperated
shrug of well-tailored shoulders and then the comment.
"Well, you believe what they *tell* you to believe, I'll
believe what *I* believe."

204

Before the half-hour was over, Regg Morris issued a warning, neither veiled nor disguised: the days when the Jewish power structure can take to the streets and, with perfect protection, security and official backing, in cold blood, murder black women and black girl-children is over. Be warned. Regg Morris faced directly into the cameras and asked, his voice acid and deadly, "And where is the *Jewish assailant* of Sanderalee Dawson? Where is the *Zionist-lunatic* who has so far succeeded in silencing the voice, but never the spirit, of the newly acknowledged and universally loved spokeswoman of the Palestinian people's plight and of the plight of the peoples of the Third World?"

Thus saying, Regg Morris departed. Even I had trouble listening to the followup guests: civic leaders, black, white, Jew and Gentile; Police Department spokesmen; Hasidic spokesmen (Jews carry guns under their prayer shawls? Well, I ask you? The man is mad. Dangerous and mad).

Street rallies were held in various strategic parks, well covered by the media and well attended by both blacks and whites in an attempt to cool things down. Eventually, everything served to heat things up to boiling.

The clergy, both black and white, demanded an investigation and an explanation: Why was it necessary to pump eight bullets into this child's helpless body? Will the officers involved face Grand Jury proceedings? Would the matter be, as always, whitewashed, glossed-over, filed away as this child Jewel Brown is "filed away" in her grave as just another incidence of police overkill?

The clergy did state that no actual Hasidic Jew had been involved in the shooting: they were "decoy cops" and that of course was another problem. The question of entrapment was examined rather broadly at the open-air rallies.

"Why aren't medicated darts of some kind used in instances such as this terrible thing? Wouldn't that be better than shooting eight deadly bullets into the body of a helpless child? Such darts are used to subdue wild animals, with much success and no harm."

This question was asked by a well-meaning but luckless young white minister from a wealthy, liberal, politically activist Upper East Side church. His suggestion was greeted with fury by the black clergy, who were in no mood for an unfortunate choice of words. A black child had been placed in the same category as a wild animal. That's how they see us, ultimately, isn't it? Wild animals!

The suggestion caused a predictable breakdown in further communication among groups who were basically in sympathy with one another.

The street violence Sunday night involved more than the burning and looting and destruction of property.

The Jewish Defense League took to the streets and were joined by a large group of sturdy young men who called themselves "Concerned Citizens of Little Italy." It wasn't long before they all found opportunities to display their concern in face-to-face, baseball-bat-and-brick to chain-and-knife confrontations.

Whites were assaulted randomly and brutally wherever encountered by roving black street gangs in the theater district and around Times Square. Subways were declared unsafe in the off-hours and there was a distinct shortage of taxicabs in troubled areas.

Earlier in the evening, the Mayor tried a face-to-face visit with various groups of people. However, his being an argumentative rather than a pacifying personality, he quickly alienated even people who agreed with him. His chief aides, reinforced by the Police Commissioner, prevailed upon his good sense and all breathed easier when he finally consented to return to his office.

The orders to the Police Department were carefully changed but rigid in one respect: take control but *do not provoke*. Which is a pretty good order to issue from a wide antique desk and on contemplation of "trouble spots" that are identified by the color of the pin stuck in the map. But the city was determined, and rightfully so, in my opinion, to contain the situation without calling in the National Guard, which had been put on standby at the order of the Governor.

The first "round-up" types of arrest were being made in what previously had been considered the more stable sections of the city. Cheering the police on, with clenched fists of anger rather than support aimed in the general direction of the looters, were the heartsick black merchants who, within a matter of hours, had seen their small, expensive, stylish and highly mortgaged little shops swept away in the arms of grinning youths who were not only surprised but furious to find themselves, empty-handed, shoved into police wagons.

In Crown Heights, arrests were made selectively among the busted skulls and the skull-busters. Black and white together, youths were snatched, spun around, frisked, disarmed and shoved yelling, all-in-together, on top of each other or sideways or any other way, into the wagon or up the steps of the precinct. Young blacks deprived of the pointed, deadly looking Afro-combs demanded that the Jews be deprived of their yarmulkes: "They got long pins in their hats, man, can split your throat open." The young Jewish Defense Leaguers, who did indeed sport the longest, thickest, sharpest hatpins ever seen, swore their religion was being interfered with and yelled First Amendment.

Young attorneys from activist organizations and middle-aged sorrowful-looking family lawyers as well as district leaders, black and white, reporters, photographers, cameramen, all met and mixed in whirling arguments, pleas, threats, demands, confrontations, pushing, shoving, knocking-down and knocking-over action. It was hard to know who was actually in custody and who was there to speak on behalf of those confined. The only absolute police instruction was not to have blacks and whites cohabit: no murder within the precinct house, things were tough enough.

The only people who had sense enough to maintain a low, quiet profile, to make remote observations on

207

the rolling anger all around them, were the professional thieves who had been caught in the general net and hoped to get tossed out with the rest of them when things quieted down.

32

We were remote from all the street action, members of my Squad and I, although we kept up to date via telephone, radio and television. We had spent the entire weekend putting together—or examining—the case against Dr. David Cohen. The District Attorney had instructed me to prepare the case for Grand Jury presentation "as soon as possible."

By late Sunday afternoon, what we had, more or less, made us decide to charge Dr. David Cohen with attempted murder, atrocious assault, dismemberment, assault with a deadly weapon, rape, sodomy, and whatever else might stick. To this end, we had assembled:

> *Sanderalee Dawson's detailed accusation;*
> *Statement by Timothy Doyle that the running shoes we had confiscated under our search warrant were "similar to" the shoes he had seen on the feet of the man who had accompanied the plaintiff on the night of the attack;*
> *Statement by Timothy Doyle that to the best of his recollection Sanderalee Dawson was not limping on the night of the attack;*

> Lab report to the effect that a tiny, almost microscopic thread of blue mohair found on the sleeve of one of David Cohen's navy blue running suits was very similar to the mohair [angora] with which Sanderalee's scarf was knit (they gave a complicated point-by-point system of comparison); possible but not conclusive one way or the other;
>
> Lab report to the effect that all three of Dr. Cohen's navy blue miracle-fabric running suits had recently been laundered; detergent used: Tide. Two of the suits were taken from his apartment; one from his cottage in East Hampton; no trace of blood found on any of the three;
>
> Lab report to the effect that there were no traces of blood on any of the six (three pairs) of custom-made running shoes (two pairs from apartment; one pair from East Hampton);
>
> Further examination of these shoes indicated that a special built-up arch and hidden elevation was constructed in the right shoe (to compensate for Dr. Cohen's polio-shortened leg); as with the running suits, it would appear that the meticulous doctor was in the habit of rotating his running shoes; Note: Sam Hendrikson has contacted manufacturer of these special orthopedically designed running shoes for further information.

There was one other possibly significant piece of information provided by Jim Barrow's man. Sam had visited the microsurgery class taught by Dr. David Cohen and his report was very interesting.

"Out of a total of fourteen people interviewed relative to Dr. Cohen's account of how he received the injury to his left cheek, four stated, unequivocally, that they had actually seen the accident and the injury occur. Three did not see anything; they arrived as Dr. Cohen, clutching a handkerchief to his face, was rushed to the Emergency Room.

"But seven of the 'witnesses to the event' stated that on careful consideration they had *not actually seen* the accident, which appeared to have occurred right before their eyes. These witnesses are very intelligent and analytical young physicians and, in sum, what each of them stated to the undersigned is as follows (note—individual signed statements of these three attached hereto):

"Dr. Cohen entered the room very quickly as the class settled in. Usually, he was already at his desk, preparing his notes for the lecture. On the date in question, however, he entered rapidly, his right profile to the class. As he reached the desk, Dr. Cohen appeared to have slipped. There was a thudding sound at the corner of his desk and it was the distinct impression of at least seven of these witnesses that the 'thud' was caused by Dr. Cohen's slapping the desk with the flat of his hand rather than with the side of his face. Dr. Cohen disappeared for a moment, under the desk; general commotion and concern; he emerged, hand to left side of face. Blood was squirting; he pulled out a handkerchief and held it to the wound. Two of the witnesses closest to Dr. Cohen's desk stated it appeared to them that the handkerchief already had bloodstains on it.

"Dr. Cohen, holding handkerchief to face, kicked out at a flattened yogurt container and stated loudly, 'I slipped on this damn garbage and hit my face on the edge of this damn desk. Look, the metal edge is exposed. I guess I'd better get this seen to.' Someone suggested tetanus shots. One of the witnesses examined the desk edge, which did in fact have a rough metal edge exposed. It appeared to have been pried in some manner.

"Dr. Cohen was escorted by several students, including one of these seven, and at the ER he repeated that he had slipped on yogurt container, hit face on exposed metal desk edge. He was given t.a.t. shots; two stitches in cheek; class canceled for that day.

"On careful consideration, each of the seven witnesses whose reports are attached herewith state that in some peculiar way, they felt that Dr. Cohen had 'stage-managed' the accident. He was immediately taken at his *word, and the students proceeded to repeat to each other and to people who asked about the incident later exactly what he had called out to his audience, in almost his identical words. It was the impression—without any substantial grounds—of at least two of Cohen's students that when he entered the lecture room, he already had a wound on his face, newly opened. They reiterate this is a 'feeling.' Careful investigation failed to discover anyone, at all, who remembered seeing Dr. Cohen at any time prior to the 'accident' that is described above.*

"Efforts continuing.

"Det. Sam Hendrikson, Shield 340432"

All of which gave us something to think about, but wasn't really of too much use if Dr. Cohen would be able to match us, witness for witness, with people who would verify his version of the wounding of his cheek.

Motive of each of the skeptics would have to be examined and they would have to be squeaky clean with no score to settle against Cohen.

From the laboratory came the information that a small—less than a quarter-inch—thread of blue mohair had turned up adhering to the sleeve of Dr. David Cohen's running jacket. Now that would seem conclusive, establishing his presence in her apartment, right?

Not necessarily.

I asked Bobby Jones, who seemed very willing to defend David Cohen against the guilty appearance of the mohair thread on his running jacket.

It took Bobby about three minutes to alienate everyone in the room. It wasn't that his argument would hold up, necessarily. It was that he presented it so willingly.

"The mohair thread? Why, Dr. David Cohen arrived at the hospital on the night of the crime and had close physical contact with Sanderalee Dawson, who had, on her own word, been wearing a mohair hat and scarf that night. Some small threads of mohair had very likely adhered to some part of her—her hair, most likely. During his initial physical examination of her,

211

which was not done under sterile conditions, the thread attached itself to Dr. Cohen. To his sleeve, his arm, his head, his neck, whatever. After ten hours of surgery, he returned to his apartment and the practically invisible mohair thread was still on his clothing. He might have hung up his running jacket, or brushed against it, or whatever; the mohair thread floated onto the sleeve of his jacket. A perfectly innocent transference of the dreaded mohair thread."

"Transferring the goddamn mohair thread innocently to his goddamn jacket. Goddamn it, Bobby Jones. I mean, yes, that's possible, but my God."

"But Lynne, that's what we're doing here, right? Examining every possible angle, evaluating what you have to bring to the Grand Jury?"

"I hardly think I'll offer them your 'innocent mohair thread theory.' I rather think I'll go with my own 'guilty mohair thread theory.' Which I consider more likely. *Much more likely.*"

The one area that caused problems—more among the men of my Squad than among the women—was the very basic question: why had Sanderalee Dawson invited Dr. David Cohen, a.k.a. the culprit, to her apartment in the first place? Her explanation was unlikely: she had turned her ankle; he claimed to be a doctor and offered to massage it. Her explanation was downright silly.

"A pickup," Sheila Kennedy, one year out of Fordham Law School, said abruptly. "Two adults meeting and mutually agreeing to return to her apartment. So what?"

"So it sounds like soliciting," Sam Hendrikson volunteered.

"We won't go into the old clichés about 'prostitutes can be raped,' shall we?"

Ms. Kennedy took offense at that immediately. "Really, Lynne. Are you suggesting that Sanderalee was out prostituting herself?"

"What Sanderalee actually said," Bobby Jones said carefully, "was that she thought she recognized the

212

runner. She thought she knew him from the Jog-gon-Inn. Alan Greco told us that Sanderalee often brought 'runners' home with her."

"It's a given that she invited a man into her home," I said. "No one alleges that he forced his way into her apartment. And no one is accusing Sanderalee Dawson of good judgment. That's all beside the point."

"And at what point does sexual intercourse become rape?" one of our young law students asked rhetorically. "When the lady says no."

"When the lady says no *prior to penetration* and the gentleman proceeds either through physical force, fear or coercion. Sanderalee had a perfect right to invite anyone she wanted up to her apartment. She had a perfect right to allow him certain expectations of a sexual nature. We are not evaluating her common sense, her morals, her wisdom or her promiscuity. Even if he hadn't beaten her, but merely forced her through threat or coercion, she has a right to charge him with rape."

"*Even if she asked for it?*" Sam Hendrikson inquired.

I took one deep breath and pressed my hand over my eyes. "Yes, if you mean that by her actions prior to the sexual act, by her invitation to her apartment, by her general and specific behavior, she led him to believe she was interested in him as a sexual partner. According to Sanderalee, the man had her sit down, he manipulated her ankle exactly as he said he would. He told her he was a doctor and did in fact work some kind of adjustment on her ankle. She was getting ready for some kind of sociability: she was in the process of pouring out Perrier when he assaulted her from behind, without warning. Christ, maybe if he'd just waited, sipped his Perrier and listened to some music, it might have turned into a night of love. But he didn't. What he did was what he apparently had in mind all along: he viciously beat and physically subdued her. He raped her through the use of superior physical force, fear, coercion. He half killed her. All of which was hardly necessary, given the rather pleasant circumstances in which he found himself."

"Which means," Sheila Kennedy said solemnly, "that this kind of sexual assault was what he needed; was what he apparently had in mind from the first encounter."

"We don't have to get into David Cohen's mind. We just have to describe his actions. His motives are loony-tunes as far as we're concerned. We leave that to the shrinks."

Which covered the rape charge. For about the tenth time that day. During the endless discussion and argument and reviewing we went over the other potential charges. Again, again, again: the sodomy, the felonious assault by some version of open-handed karate-type blows; the assault with a deadly weapon; assault with intent to kill; the mutilation-dismemberment.

Someone raised a question about the fact that when Sanderalee was found on the kitchen floor, she was wearing her running pants and a sweater. Her bra and bikini underpants were found tossed on the living room floor. In her state of shock, had she been capable of partially dressing herself? Would she be able to recall doing so? No big deal, just a little peculiar, but something we would have to prepare for: against a defense attorney's questions. Stick to the facts: if you don't remember, Sanderalee, then you don't remember—period.

Finally, "I don't anticipate any problems with the Grand Jury on any of this, really. Given the extent of the injuries inflicted on her; given the ferocity of the assault. There will be one or two questions relative to her judgment. Remember, Alan Greco told us, Bobby, that he'd been afraid of just this kind of thing happening. He said she'd apparently picked up the wrong guy. That it hadn't surprised him. I will grant to the Grand Jury that Sanderalee showed very bad judgment. We've got until trial date to handle this case—to defend Sanderalee's honor and to cop out on her judgment. Which led to her being raped, sodomized, beaten, mutilated. At the trial, we'll let the good Dr. Cohen's attorney question Sanderalee's motives in extending what is, in effect, a street-corner invitation to a stranger."

"Or to a stranger she thinks she recognizes. From having seen him around the Jog-gon-Inn," Bobby Jones added, his eyes fixed on me intently.

And then, when we had all decided to call it a day, a weekend, there was a phone call about our good Lucy Capella, who, I wish sometimes, was not all that damned good.

Not only had the city reached the boiling point, not only were people robbing, looting, hitting, hurting, shooting, pillaging and just plain messing up, but now good strong reliable Lucy Capella was not to be available, when she was most needed.

Lucy and her damned stray dogs.

33

Lucy Capella had been on her way back to New York Hospital from her day off at her small rented home in Queens when, in the glare of flashing headlights, she saw a large, bone-thin, terrified, injured dog cringing against the wall of an underpass on Grand Central Parkway.

As God does occasionally watch over her own, this abandoned dog had been waiting for rescue by Lucy Capella, who had never in her entire life refused a needy human—infant or crone—or any animal in any stage of distress.

She pulled over as best she could in the not-too-heavy late Sunday afternoon traffic, set up her ever-handy blinker lights, yellow and red, managed to cajole the wounded creature into the back of her station wagon—which was fully equipped with all kinds of benign animal lures: old bones, dry feed, catnip for the kitties, cookies, smelly old dog blankets and pillows. The animal once safely installed in the nestlike arrangement, our Lucy had yet to achieve personal safety. She was sideswiped by an angry motorist who had appointments to keep and would not grant Lucy the twenty seconds or so required for her to safely collect her blinker lights and enter her vehicle.

She managed to get into the station wagon, call in the license number of her hit-and-runner, request ambulances for herself and her new dog.

When a local emergency ambulance arrived, Lucy steadfastly refused, as only our iron-and-steel little nun could, to ride in the ambulance without the injured dog, who had in fact thrown itself into her arms and growled weak but serious threats to anyone who tried to separate them. It might actually have been Lucy herself faking the growl, but it sounded real enough to cause a problem. She insisted the medical entourage first deliver the dog to the Animal Medical Center on the East Side of Manhattan at Sixty-second Street and then double back with her to the hospital in Queens that had human jurisdiction.

Lucy's left leg and right arm had been fractured and she had two black eyes and a scraped chin, yet the first thing she extracted from me at her bedside was a promise to check on the progress of Ambrose at the animal hospital. *Ambrose?* The wonderful wounded starveling had been so named in honor of the ambulance attendant who had finally given in, said what the hell, let's either take both of them to the Emergency Room at the animal hospital or the ER at the people hospital; we can't stay here arguing forever: neither this lady nor this dog is gonna give.

The animal hospital, somewhat impressed by Ambrose's arrival in a people ambulance, accepted him immediately but refused Lucy, who was then returned to Queens.

I was able to assure Lucy that Ambrose was not only going to survive, he was going to prevail. He had been featured on the late news and would be an early-edition front-page *Daily News* dog with adopters lining up. The story was receiving a great deal of play: it was a welcome change of pace from all the riot, destruction and terror stories that had been confronting us for the last few days. Some public relations hack from City Hall even put out a line that his Honor, the Argumentative Mayor, was interested in adopting Ambrose. They were that desperate for a good word re City Hall.

Lucy did not have a care in the world. Her friends from the old lapsed-priests-and-nuns commune, who had been cat/dog sitting her own collection of pets while she'd been on extended duty at New York Hospital with Sanderalee, would not only continue, but would also take care of her when she returned from the hospital.

So I left Lucy warm and cozy and reassured: encased in casts, bruises and a nice resolve to get that monster who sideswiped her.

I took advantage of having a driver and, before going home, paid a quick visit to New York Hospital. Sanderalee was sitting in "Lucy's room," half-heartedly reading a magazine. As soon as she heard me approach, her head ducked down and she adjusted a filmy veil, which she had attached to a couple of hair clips to float over her face. Actually, it was quite attractive and almost looked like a glamorous new style—as long as you didn't see beneath the veil. Sanderalee favored soft lights and distances. She dropped the magazine as she stood up, her right hand touching first the veil and then the heavy cast in which her left hand rested.

She had heard about Lucy's accident.

"I didn't know Lucy was a Miss Molly. A professional kindheart," she said in a peculiar tone. "I suppose every now and then, one of the collectors of the...maimed and the ugly and the...unwanted pays a price for her

217

charity." She walked across the room and stood with her back to me for a moment. Somewhere, she had lost me. I couldn't quite figure her attitude. I had thought she and Lucy were friends. "She is all right though isn't she?" The question was asked coldly.

I assured her that Lucy would be fine; it would be a matter of time and healing.

Sanderalee turned and raised her face toward me. Her green eyes glowing from the top of the veil seemed very deep and steady but her voice revealed her restlessness.

"When can I get out of here? I'm sick of this place Lynne. When is something going to happen?"

"*When* you get out of here isn't up to me, Sanderalee. That's up to the doctors. You know that. They're amazed at your progress. It's good that you're anxious to get out. I'm a great believer in a person's pushing herself. The question is, where will you go? Have you given that much thought?"

"I've given it 'much thought.' I have a place. I don't care to discuss it right now."

"But not back to your apartment?"

She drew her shoulders up, pressed her arms close to her body to suppress a shudder and shook her head. "Never. Never."

"That would be my reaction, too. Look. I'm preparing the case for the Grand Jury and..."

Her body hunched forward as though she'd received a blow to the stomach. She shook her head and there was a soft moan coming from her clenched mouth. "Not me, though, Lynne. Not me...I won't have to...Lucy told me that you'd go ahead without me...that I won't have to..."

Of course, it would have been much better for her to appear before the Grand Jury: the living proof of the damages inflicted on her.

"No, Sanderalee. It's okay. I'll make the presentation myself. I have your tape. I have all the medical documents to show them. You won't have to appear."

She sat down and rested her heavy cast across her

body. Her long fingers played with the edge of her veil and her voice was very soft, dreamy. "The plastic surgeon has told me that it won't be too bad, fixing my face. My lip. He's pretty sure he can do a good restoration. That's what he called it: restoration. Like I was an old painting or something. They can do a lot of things; they've put together worse than...than mine, he said. He said that with time, with healing, with ...time and healing, you wouldn't even be able to...Oh, Lynne, I'm very tired. Sometimes I think it'll be all right. This will all be over with. And then, I look at this...this...thing." She touched the swollen fingertips that curled inward on the edge of the cast. "My God, this was my *hand*. Look at it. You know, someday they'll take the cast off and all the bandages and *I don't want to see it*. It's like a...a horrible growth...something that isn't part of me...something...alien. Oh, God, sometimes I wish I could just turn time back. Very far back, years back. But then, I ask myself, where would I stop it? At what point would I stop time? And I try to find the perfect moment, the perfect time that I would want to start from and I get stuck. There doesn't seem to be a 'perfect moment.' Maybe it's all been one big crock. Goddamn, I'm tired."

I wished I could think of something clever or sustaining or reassuring or wise or important or comforting to say to her. I wished I knew what Lucy would say.

"Can I get you anything, Sanderalee? Anything at all?"

She raised her head. I could see the outline of her face as the veil floated against her. The wiring on her jaws had been loosened considerably; the lower lip torn but healing. Several broken teeth had been removed and she was having dental work as part of the reconstruction process. Her eyes were still beautiful and alive; only her eyes were still Sanderalee. They regarded me with a look of anger and then the look softened, filled with pain and somehow, it seemed, with pity. For me? for herself? Who knows?

"It's all right, Lynne. I get this way sometimes. Tell Lucy..." She stopped speaking and her eyes glazed over. She was having some kind of battle about Lucy. I sensed an anger: that Lucy had let her down. She blinked rapidly and then said, "Tell Lucy that I am *sorry* this happened to her. Really sorry. Tell her that...tell Lucy that I can feel her pain." She spoke very quickly and there was concern now in her voice. "You know, that's what she said to me once and it's very peculiar but I believed her and it helped. She shared my pain and made it easier, if that makes any sense.

"Listen, tell the nurse I want to go to sleep now," she said abruptly. "I don't want to talk about anything else. When it's done and over, when you've gotten the indictment, come and tell me, okay?"

I promised that I would. The nurse came and Sanderalee settled in bed, her right arm extended for the injection that would free her from this moment.

I walked quickly from the room, was called back by the police officer who was established at the desk in the outer room of the suite. I had forgotten to sign out. She was young and pretty and she looked like a recruiting poster in her sharp, well-tailored navy blue uniform. She'd been assigned through Jim Barrow's office since I had no people available for this kind of desk duty. I absently scanned the list of visitors: Sanderalee's network friends; one or two familiar show business names.

"Is it true that all these people party it up here, Ms. Jacobi? I mean, we've heard all kinds of stories."

Her fresh young face was hopeful.

"I hope you've got a good book to read." It was nearly midnight. "What sort of tour have they got you on?"

"I've only been assigned; came on about eleven-thirty. We're all on twelve-hour duty. Emergency overtime." She looked around the pleasantly furnished, hotel-like room. "This beats the streets."

I rode down in an elevator with a couple of cute, sleepy-looking young residents and couldn't help won-

dering what they'd been up to: they reeked of formal-
dehyde. My head began to reel and I was grateful for
the cold blast of air as I exited into the circular drive-
way at the main entrance of New York Hospital. My
driver drove me down Fifth Avenue to my apartment
building. He told me that the city seemed to be settling
down. There were only sporadic bursts of violence, destruction and arson. The perpetrators now were being
pounced on and dragged off.

It had gotten colder and started to rain and the rain
was turning to sleet and the sleet was turning to snow,
which was turning to ice on the streets. The sociologists
and criminologists and all the other experts in mass
behavior could put forth all their theories about the
natural flow and movement of massive disorders and
how to predict the severity and direction of mob behavior. I hold with the cop's prayer: for a good rain
storm or a good blast of cold weather. That generally
winds things up in a hurry.

34

First, it was Jameson Whitney Hale's voice in my ear,
the very tone—low pitched, soft, overly controlled—
advising me of some terrible, if unknown, dereliction.

"My God, Lynne, how could you have allowed this
to happen?"

"Allowed what to happen?" It could have been anything; my mind was blank. There was nothing specific for my guilt to focus on.

"You mean you haven't seen the *New York Post?*"

As he asked the question, the early edition of the *Post* was stuck under my face by one of my Squad people. I blinked, drew back, found my reading glasses.

EXCLUSIVE!
FIRST PHOTOS OF SANDERALEE'S INJURIES
More photos pg. 3 and centerfold

The featured front-page photograph was of Sanderalee Dawson in her hospital bed not long after her initial surgery. It was a very raw, clear and cruel picture: a closeup of her as she lay semiconscious and wounded, her beaten face distorted by swelling; her jaws wired into place; her lower mouth with totally exposed gums, broken teeth and ripped flesh giving her face the appearance of a fright mask.

Inserted into the corner of this page-sized photo was a small, cleanly printed reproduction of Sanderalee at her most *Vogue* beautiful: an Alan Greco photo. Beneath the large photograph were the words "*DO THE POLICE KNOW WHO DID THIS?* Yes, says Dr. Regg Morris, friend and mentor of Sanderalee. They know *exactly* who did this. He charges that the D.A.'s office is sitting on the case for political and/or racial/religious reasons. Pg. 3."

There were indeed more pictures on page three and in the centerfold. Directly from the camera of good friend and mentor Regg Morris.

As soon as the D.A. rang off, Jim Barrow's telephone voice was booming with self-righteousness and accusation. "Lynne, how the hell did *you* let this happen? How the hell did *you* slip up like that?"

Thank you, Chief of Detectives Jim Barrow, but as long as you're on the line: "Jim, who have you got over there with Sanderalee right now? Any chance we can keep her from seeing this paper?"

Which was why he was calling in the first place.

There was trouble at the hospital. There had been a disturbance of rather serious proportions.

No one had instructed the police personnel on duty, specifically the young officer subbing for injured St. Lucy of Assisi, that Regg Morris was to be judiciously and diplomatically discouraged from visiting with Ms. Dawson.

"He arrived at about nine-thirty, I guess to prepare her for the pictures in the newspaper. The girl, I mean the policewoman, police *officer* on duty says Regg just signed in, same as any other visitor is required. She heard them arguing, she thought. She checked it out and Sanderalee herself said everything was okay, they wer just having a 'discussion.' Morris stayed for about an hour all told and then some twenty minutes after he left, a nurse went to check on Sanderalee routinely, and..."

And apparently her good friend, Regg Morris, had prepared Sanderalee for the newspaper photographs. Maybe he even thoughtfully brought along an early edition for her to see. Maybe he even explained to her *why* he had done such an awful thing to the lady he alleged to love so dearly.

The nurse found Sanderalee lying on the floor, in a coma, which was the natural result of her having ingested a collection of Demerols, Valiums, Tuinals, Quaaludes, aspirins and—for good measure—cold tablets. Belted down with a swig of Scotch, which had been stored in a large-sized My Sin bottle.

It was no great mystery as to how Sanderalee had come by all these goodies. Her steady stream of "cleared visitors," good-wishers all, in lieu of candy, which is fattening and we all know that sugar-is-poison, provided the lady with whatever she might like to have on hand in case needed to face a long and scary night. In addition to the lightweight stuff that the hospital people dispensed with such measured caution.

"What's her condition as of right now?"

"Well, thanks to the timing, she was caught almost before any of that junk was effective. There is one serious complication, however. When she fell from the bed, she injured her reattached hand. Might have to go back into surgery. And her state of mind is not exactly what you'd like it to be. That Chinee-shrink was being paged, last I heard. Jeez, Lynne, she should have been placed in protective custody as a material witness long before this."

Jeez, Lynne, *why did you allow this to happen?*

"Just hold it, Jimbo. This was the first fucking night that Lucy Capella wasn't around. Why the hell did *your* people allow that fucking-a bastard Regg Morris in to see her?"

"There's no need to curse, Lynne."

He meant it. Goddamn it, he meant it. Ole Jim Barrow going soppy on me.

"As a matter of fact, Chief Barrow, I am waiting for a signed court order to the effect that Sanderalee is to be held in just such custody. Probably within an hour it will take effect. It is just unfortunate that *your people* weren't *properly* briefed."

"I would have assumed there were standing instructions."

"Blast off, will you, Jim. I have some problems of my own. I really can't get involved with your lax and problematic chain of command. *You* find the *weak spot yourself.*"

I cursed softly *after* I hung up. I wasn't looking for trouble. I had enough as it was.

Lucy Capella had suggested the protective custody some time ago; with Lucy on the job, it hadn't been necessary. The first time she's out: bingo. Fiasco.

"Ms. Jacobi there?" Interesting lilt; Dr. Chan.

"I have just visited with Sanderalee Dawson. She is in a very bad way. She really blew her mind with all that garbage. However, I'm not too sure how much of her behavior at this point is for real, how much is to get what she wants."

"Which is?"

"Lucy Capella. She's insisting that Lucy come and

see her. She refuses to sign the required consent papers for the surgery that seems indicated on her hand."

I tried. No reason why Lucy couldn't convalesce and work at the same time. We could set her up in a bed in the adjoining sitting room and Sanderalee could stagger in and give Lucy her troubles and Lucy could yank on her various pulleys and give a kind and sympathetic ear. Why not? Because Lucy Capella was undergoing surgery on her broken leg and was not in very good condition to listen to anyone else's problems just now.

I had assigned one of our young law-student interns to field telephone calls: several from very angry and irate reporters who thought "we had some sort of understanding with Lynne. Then she lets some jerk of a photographer in right after the beating and now still wants to keep Sanderalee under wraps. What the hell's going on?" The intern, Jeffrey Perfect or something, was a speedwriting expert and not only took down complaints verbatim, he swiftly typed them up and delivered them to me in record time.

Bobby Jones appeared and had two things to tell me. "First, the protective custody order is signed, sealed and delivered. I've sent Carlson and Kennedy to the hospital to set it up quietly and confidentially with the hospital administrator. The plan is to move Sanderalee out of her room late tonight, when we won't attract any attention. There are so many wings and sections in that hospital that a person could totally disappear without a trace. Until then, Kennedy will stand by: no visitors, except authorized medical people, unless cleared by either you or me."

Bobby delivered his information smoothly, professionally, and impersonally: good soldier reporting in. We both avoided direct, prolonged eye contact but in a fleeting glance, I could see the tight control, the contained anger and calculation shining from his blue eyes.

"Very good, Bobby," I told him. Even to myself, I

225

sounded patronizing. He was in no mood for a pat on the head.

"Second thing," he told me sharply, "Regg Morris caught the early morning Concorde flight from Kennedy to Paris. France. For a meeting with some very heavy money men from a mysterious country where the main problem is getting street vendors to cash thousand-dollar bills."

"Run that by me again, Bobby. *What?*"

"Regg is fronting for some oil sheiks. Who have just purchased a five-hundred-acre estate in northern Westchester County under the name of 'The Wisdom of Allah School of Greater Nations.' Incorporated. President and General Director, the Honorable Dr. Regg Morris. A cash deal, Lynne. Allegedly for setting up a country version of his city brownstone private school. The IRS is on this and I've established a liaison with a couple of other federal people. There's going to be all kinds of tax evasion schemes—*i.e.*, that this is a religious enterprise. It's a little fringy for us. But I thought you'd like to know how Allah rewards his favorite loudmouth troublemakers."

"I'll think about all that later. Tomorrow. Or on Saturday when there's nothing on TV but cartoons." It was really too much and too unexpected to fit into anything that was happening at my office at the moment.

A call from Mr. Whitney Hale; fielded, as instructed, by Jeffrey Speedwriter: Ms. Jacobi just left the office, sir. Good boy, Jeffrey.

Dr. Chan: "Lynne, Sanderalee is really messed up. She must have corrective surgery on her hand almost immediately. It's quite urgent. There was some terribly serious damage done when she fell."

"Dr. Chan, I am sorry but surgery is not among my many skills. The only recommendation I can make is *don't* call *Dr. David Cohen.*"

"Lynne, the problem is that Sanderalee absolutely refuses to sign the release for surgery until she talks to someone. I've suggested she talk to you, but no dice.

226

And she won't talk to me, so where do we go? Positively no chance for Lucy?"

No chance. At all. Brief conference with Bobby Jones.

"Dr. Chan, ask her if she'd talk to Alan Greco and get back to me."

Two more phone calls and then Dr. Chan.

"Okay on Alan Greco."

I sent Bobby Jones out to find Alan and bring him to Sanderalee so that she would then consent to the surgery needed to save her hated left hand.

Throughout the past two weeks, other concerns had been crossing my desk. I had Squad members working on various cases and I took a few hours' vacation from Sanderalee Dawson, Regg Morris, David Cohen et al. for briefings and updatings on several pending sex/violence cases. There had been the matter of serious assaults on several homosexuals in a gay bar by on-the-town thugs whose hometown families described them as good boys; good baseball players; one wonderful potential professsional hockey player whose arrest might jeopardize the poor kid's entire future. There were depositions from nearly an entire town as to the healthy, happy family backgrounds, the good citizenship displayed in the home suburban community, the leadership qualities of a couple of the eighteen-year-olds; past membership in Boy Scouts; industrious contributions to community fund-raising events where some of them displayed their skill with basketballs or their strength and dedication by the hard physical labor contributed.

Nowhere, in any of the statements, was the alleged crime referred to: six young men, aged seventeen to twenty, had taken the time, trouble, effort and skill required to carefully stud baseball bats with heavy nails at the hitting ends; had taped the narrow ends for a good grip. They had boarded their local bus to big bad New York City; drifted around while searching for their targets; invaded a pleasant, low-key, social-type gay bar whose regulars were local shop owners, antique dealers, artists, actors: definitely non-violence-prone tax-paying citizens.

I had assigned Karen Slate, young, black, urban: tough, fair and unrelenting in her view of justice.

The defense team had made an approach to my office: would it not be more equitable, more in the interests of justice that this case, involving as it did young white males from the suburbs, carefully nurtured, tended, loved young boys firmly established and connected by lines of family, education, associations with their community: would it not be possibly wiser, fairer, more in keeping with the pure concept of justice that the prosecutor assigned more closely resemble these lads in order to better understand them: as to background? as to misguided motivation? as to childish misbehavior and misconceptions of right and wrong? as to color? as to sex?

The injuries that they had individually and collectively inflicted were horrendous. Not only were heads broken, but lives were broken. Dreams destroyed; careers disrupted. Karen and I went over the case perpetrator by perpetrator and between us we zeroed in on the two most likelies: those who'd go for a deal in return for ratting on their boyhood pals.

A deal: the basis of the criminal justice system.

"If they don't go for it," I instructed Karen, "nail them to the wall and cut their little suburban hearts out."

I spent a little time going over a child molestation case: middle-aged man, six-year-old girl. The defense was seeking a deal: a DOR—dismissed on own recognizance—in return for a promise that the defendant would return to a hospital to continue therapy.

It is my job to consider all sex offenses as serious. I am not as offhand as some of my male counterparts about the passive nature of the acts of exhibitionists or voyeurs. I believe in the possibility of escalation: just give him the time, the place, the opportunity. Same old song; same old story.

"The hell with their promise," I told my assistant,

a bright but slightly reluctant young male Assistant District Attorney who had just recently been assigned to my Squad. "Get the conviction or the guilty plea, then let them persuade the court that this man should be allowed to be hospitalized or analyzed or whatever instead of imprisoned. I don't give a damn about his immediate future. My aim is to have this charge on his record *permanently*. A DOR disappears as though it never happened within a year. And it *did* happen. *And I want it recorded*."

I covered as many pending things as I possibly could; caught up with whatever I had been neglecting and then was ready to turn my attention totally to the presentation of the case against Dr. David Cohen before the Grand Jury.

35

My appearance before the Grand Jury was set for Thursday morning, March 29. I spent Wednesday afternoon and evening with the District Attorney reviewing my plan of presentation.

My list of witnesses was relatively brief for such a heavy case:

> *Tim Doyle would offer his testimony—for what it was worth—to establish in general terms the fact that Sanderalee Dawson did, in fact, return to her apartment with a "tall unidentified white male*

dressed in navy running clothes and wearing distinctive blue running shoes";

Statement by the responding patrolmen as to condition of plaintiff when they came upon the scene;

Affirmation of Sanderalee's injuries by the attending physician on duty at the Emergency Room at Roosevelt Hospital;

Statement by Dr. Adam Waverly, member of the microsurgery team, as to the surgical procedure performed at New York Hospital necessitated by the amputation of Sanderalee's left hand (note to myself: keep this guy within limits; he likes to ramble down the path;

Statement by Dr. Chan re Sanderalee's present emotional condition, physical and mental inability to appear in person before Grand Jury;

Which would lead to the introduction of the taped statement by Sanderalee Dawson, preceded by my statement that I had in fact verified through personal questioning of the plaintiff that the taped statement accurately presented her charges;

Sworn written statement of Lucy Capella, confined to hospital with broken leg, verifying her presence during the original taping of Sanderalee's statement;

There would be a few technicians introduced briefly re: the blue mohair thread found on one of Dr. Cohen's navy blue running jackets, the implication being it matched the blue mohair of Sanderalee's scarf, worn the night of the attack; the sample of type B positive blood found on the remaining tip of the silver unicorn with which Sanderalee had stabbed her assailant (without mention of Sanderalee's similar blood type); verification by a television lab technician that the still photo taken from the initial news conference with the three microsurgeons, and showing a small round Band-Aid on the left cheek of Dr. David Cohen, was in fact what we claim it to be; an indication of a wound prior to his "alleged" accident in his classroom.

230

Whitney Hale and I both agreed we had enough for an indictment on the charges as sought: rape; sodomy; assault with a deadly weapon; attempted murder; dismemberment.

"There is one thing that's turned up and I hope something important comes of it," I told the District Attorney. "Sam Hendrikson spoke with a Mr. Swenson of the Orthopedic Specialty Shoe Company in Pittsburgh. Where Dr. Cohen had his running shoes made up."

"Yes, and?" Jameson raised his eyebrows and waited for something clever. I didn't have much to offer.

"Well, we've confiscated three pairs of Cohen's running shoes. Custom-made; the oldest pair, obviously the pair out in East Hampton, cost one hundred and twenty-five dollars. Four years ago. The two pairs from his New York apartment were ordered...wait a minute..." I dug around in my notebook until I found the information I wanted. "Here we go. Cohen ordered two pairs of custom-made running shoes from this company a year and a half ago: price one-ninety-five each pair."

"Yes, and? Are you trying to show the effects of inflation, Lynne, or what? What's the point?"

"The point: *six years ago*, Dr. Cohen had his *first* pair of running shoes custom-fitted. He went to Pittsburgh and had Mr. Swenson take a mold; went back once for a fitting. The mold is kept on file for future orders. So, the first pair of shoes, costing eighty-five dollars, was delivered some six years ago. Now, Mr. Swenson states that these shoes are practically indestructible. That a pair of these custom running shoes, properly maintained, could last maybe fifteen years. Apparently, Cohen takes good care of them, wearing them on a rotating basis. Two years ago, Dr. Cohen sent his first pair of running shoes back for resoling—'revitalization' is actually the word Mr. Swenson used when he gave this information to Sam Hendrikson. And so..."

"Ah. Yes. And so...we've come up with *three pairs* of custom running shoes. And the question is, where is the *fourth pair?* And I believe, am I not accurate, that the redoubtable Mr. Doyle says that yes, the shoes shown him *resemble* the shoes he observed on the feet of the unidentified male who accompanied Ms. Dawson on her elevator ride but not *exactly*. And the difference being?"

"That the shoes he observed were older. More 'scuffy' was Mr. Doyle's word."

"And the oldest pair of shoes is missing? And Dr. Cohen has not been asked about them? No, of course not. Well, the question at this point is, what do you make of this before the Grand Jury? Hmm, yes." Jameson covered his eyes with his long and elegant hand for a thoughtful moment. "Save it for the trial. Possibly by then..."

"Right."

"The status of Ms. Dawson as of this very moment? I understand she underwent further surgery for damage sustained during an attempted suicide?"

I told him that Sanderalee was resting, under protective custody, in a totally secure and publicly unknown section of the hospital. That her physical condition was good. That her emotional condition was very, very questionable.

"And she had, for a while, refused to submit to further surgery?"

Jameson knew more than he was telling; he always did.

"Right. I guess she was overwhelmed by what goodfriend Regg Morris did to her. He really made good international use of those pictures. My God, they were featured in every yellow rag in the world with headlines ranging from 'Incredible Photos of Top TV Star' to Third World 'Black Heroine Scarred for Life by Zionist Zealot.' Which, I guess, solidly established Morris's credentials with his new financial backers."

I briefed the District Attorney on Regg's whereabouts and future plans.

Jameson Whitney Hale shook his head; quick annoyance. "That's all beside the point of this immediate case, Lynne. Except in one respect: *this immediate in-*
232

dictment will counteract much of the bad publicity. We will generate as much media coverage, as many head-lines as possible to counteract all of this garbage." He narrowed his eyes and focused on me thoughtfully. "We will hold a well-attended news conference immediately the indictment is handed down. You will be front and center, surrounded, of course, by your hard-working staff, but the focus will be on you. *Lynne Jacobi, public avenger.* Your name and face will be fully featured, Lynne. It will be your public introduction. This is the case that will be remembered and we will be sure that your name is linked permanently in the public's mind with the prosecution of David Cohen."

His eyes took in every detail of my somewhat shoddy appearance: my hair needed "doing"; I was wearing a not-great shirt, tails hanging out of not-designer jeans. Working clothes, not media-conference clothes. It is one of District Attorney Hale's finer abilities: he can deliver a specific message without saying one single word.

I shoved a lock of hair from my forehead. "I've been going nearly around the clock on all of this, sir. Of course, I wouldn't dream of turning up before the Grand Jury in less than my best."

"A *nice dress* would be very appropriate, Lynne." He held his hand up quickly. "Of course, whatever you decide." And then, pointedly, "You *do* have a nice dress or two, don't you?"

Not that I've ever seen you so attired, Lynne.

"I will be presentable, Mr. Hale."

"Yes, of course. You always are, Lynne." His eyes slid over me as he rose from his desk to escort me from his office. "Almost always." And then, quietly, he asked, "And what exactly was it that our plaintiff had on her mind that she needed to relay to a 'good friend' prior to consenting to surgery?"

I smiled. He was up on this case without doubt.

"Apparently, it was just that she needed to talk to a friend. I guess she was pretty devastated by what Regg Morris had done to her. I haven't spoken to Alan Greco or seen his statement, but Bobby Jones said it was more or less that she needed reassurance. She needed to have someone affirm that her life was of value. She was pretty destroyed by what this..man...did to her."

"All right, then, Lynne. After your Grand Jury appearance tomorrow morning, let's have lunch, shall we? We've some talking to do. Relative to your future, my dear."

Sounded good to me.

It's a date.

36

I wore a nice Diane Von Furstenberg shirtwaist and my presentation to the Grand Jury went forward smoothly and without a hitch. This is one of those cases where no one coughs, sneezes or blinks too much lest they miss one drop of blood or word of gore. Almost immediately, they gave me exactly what I sought. Dr. David Cohen was indicted and his arrest ordered on Friday, March 30, for the crimes of rape; sodomy; atrocious assault (dismemberment); assault with a deadly weapon (cleaver); assault with intent to kill. They didn't even award him points for having carefully sewn back on the hand he had so carelessly hacked off.

District Attorney Jameson Whitney Hale was as good as his word. There was a wide-open, well-attended media conference held in his office as soon as the indictment was handed down. I was front and center and the District Attorney deferred to me at every question. I modestly awarded a great deal of credit to my hard-working staff, including members of Chief of Detectives Jim Barrow's office. By the end of thirty minutes, my eyes had totally lost the ability to focus. The television lights were not only heat-generating, they were blinding. Particularly in combination with the constant, shocking flash of the newspaper photographers. Glori Nichols was on the job, asking just a few more than her fair share of questions, and her cameraman came practically across Jameson's desk to get a close closeup of me in my quiet and modest moment of triumph.

The only key members of my crew who were missing, but to whom I made reference, were Lucy Capella, who was recuperating from her latest animal venture. And Bobby Jones.

Who was off checking something with the feds relative to Regg Morris and his international cartel. Or something like that, he said.

The arrest was effected quietly, quickly and professionally by members of Jim Barrow's Detective Division. The news media didn't get on to the proceedings until Dr. Cohen and the detectives arrived at the precinct for booking. By the time he was brought downtown for arraignment, of course, it had become a full-fledged media event. Cameras were not allowed in the courtroom, but row after row of benches were filled with bright-eyed eager reporters, male and female, sketching the scene, craning forward, calling out: Who's the lady in the wheelchair? Is that Cohen's father taking care of the lady? Who the hell is the younger guy with them? Must be Cohen's brother, he's an absolute ringer. Hey, isn't their attorney *Arnold Mulholland*? Didn't he practice exclusively in Texas, defending all those rich women who killed their richer husbands? Jeez, doesn't this guy charge ten thou just to appear for an arraignment?

I was a little impressed at the appearance of Arnold Mulholland, legendary glamour-lawyer who had not only been cover-featured by *Newsweek* and *Time*, but who had written one book and co-authored two movies based on his most famous, and invariably successful, cases. He immediately became the center of attention. He exuded star quality, an aura of power, certainty, presence, authority, excitement, tension, yet at the same time easy confidence. He was a large man: or at least he gave the impression of being a large man, of filling the room with his own sense of himself. He turned momentarily toward the family group: a unit clustered around the mother, who was taut and semi-paralyzed, rigid with dignity in her wheelchair. His wide-opened arms embraced and encompassed Dr. Cohen's father, a tall, thin man whose hands seemed frozen on the handles of his wife's wheelchair. Dr. Cohen's brother, a younger version of David, slightly taller, basketball-player legs, more hair, dressed in what seemed to be the family uniform—the good dark suit, the crisp white shirt, the muted expensive tie—this Cohen, Ben, nuclear engineer up at the King's Point reactor, seemed to be focused with great alarm on his father.

Though I was standing in their immediate vicinity, just inside the railing that separates spectators from participants, I couldn't see what was happening. There was a tightening circle around the Cohen family. Arnold Mulholland, back blocking them protectively, practically hid the small family behind the screen of his body.

"David, David, help him. *It's Papa!*"

Dr. David Cohen bolted, pursued by the two surprised arresting officers. He pushed and shoved his way into the tangle of bodies around his mother's wheelchair and then I could see what was happening. We all could.

Samuel Cohen, thin as a weed, originally pale, had turned a light blue color. He was holding on, literally for dear life, to the handles of his wife's wheelchair. As we watched, he pitched forward, falling against his wife and nearly knocking her to the floor, except that Arnold Mulholland caught her in his strong arms. Mr. Cohen was dead before he even settled silently in a small heap against the wheels of his wife's chair.

Dr. Cohen was beside his father, trying to breathe for him, trying for a pulse, but he knew immediately it was a lost cause. Everyone pulled back momentarily and there was a split second of total stunned silence in the large room; suspended motion as we all posed like characters in a still photograph. Into the silence came a small, deadly, nightmare voice.

"*You have destroyed my family. Damn you for all time, you have destroyed my family.*"

The words were directed straight ahead because obviously Mrs. Cohen could not move her head. Her rigid neck muscles gave her the appearance of a kind of chin-up-no-matter-what dignity. She had spoken softly, almost in a chilling whisper, but her words penetrated my brain, the accusation taking on weight as I surveyed the damage.

There were not supposed to be photographers in the courtroom, but cameras began to click; lights flashed and word was relayed to those outside the courtroom who hadn't yet violated its sanctity. There was a scuffle immediately outside the courtroom doors, which burst into the center court corridor as television cameramen pushed and shoved forward to record what was happening, without knowing, exactly, *what* was happening. There were arguments, threats, jostling, shoving among the professional media people and the court personnel and police officers who were trying to evict them. There were cries of favoritism: how come Glori Nichols was allowed in? *Glori Nichols?* Where the hell had she come from? Somehow, it seemed that she had been there all along, right in the center of things. She flashed me a smile, an "okay" signal with thumb and index finger forming a circle. What the hell?

The judge left his bench and came forward after instructing a court attendant to send for an ambulance. This had already been done and it was useless for the judge to try to clear the court; there weren't enough personnel to deal with the situation.

It was a grim family vignette: the two sons knelt beside the fallen father, at the feet of the mother, pale and frozen in her wheelchair. The attorney and his assistants had stopped shielding the Cohen family from the illegal invasion of media people. It was too tragic a scene to be kept hidden.

When the emergency personnel arrived, there was something of a scuffle going on between the Cohen brothers. David was insisting that his brother be taken to the hospital in a separate car, not in the ambulance with his dead father.

He appealed to his attorney, Mulholland. "Please have one of your people take Ben to the emergency room. For God's sake, my brother is an epileptic," he whispered. "He can't take any more of this tension."

The word bounced around the courtroom and all attention swung from the narrow, hardly sagging stretcher that bore the dead father to the gray-faced nuclear engineer brother, who was swept out of reach by two members of Arnold Mulholland's entourage. A third assistant wheeled the mother out of the court.

And then, we all stood and looked at one another in the suddenly quiet courtroom. Dr. David Cohen hadn't even been arraigned.

We all agreed that the process should be accomplished in the privacy of the judge's chambers. Arnold Mulholland used the preceding circumstances as best he could: he asked that Dr. David Cohen be released on his own recognizance. That he be returned to the bosom of his suffering and bereft family immediately. No bail.

I shook off the terrible feeling of guilt, of accusation, of responsibility for everything that had happened in court and found that my voice portrayed a properly professional anger.

"Your Honor, that is unthinkable. This is a *tremendously* serious case. There have been *community implications*. This case is seen by some as a test of the fairness and equitability of the entire criminal justice system. The victim of this man's attack is at this very moment recovering from a second surgical procedure as a direct result of the injuries he inflicted upon her."

I asked for a hundred fifty thousand dollars bail. Mr. Mulholland brought the paneled walls down around me. His theatrical voice reverberated, his entire body seemed to swell and rise with indignation and outrage.

Bail was set at twenty-five thousand dollars and Dr. David Cohen was taken away for the hour it would take Arnold Mulholland to get the bail bond. He walked to the side of the judge's office, his large, strong arm around David Cohen, assuring him that things would be tended to. I could hear David's voice, broken, quavering. I could hear his words. My father. My mother. My brother.

My God.

37

It had been a highly emotional day, a "triumphant-but" kind of day, a totally exhausting kind of day. I decided I was entitled to leave early, to go home, take a hot bath, have a nice quiet dinner and...Where the hell was Bobby Jones?

"No calls, please, at all" had been my instructions to my staff.

"Ms. Jacobi, I know you said no calls, but I really think you should take this one. A photographer..."

"No way. I'm gone. Left. Unavailable. Out of town..."

"Name of Alan Greco?"

"Alan Greco?"

"I may be wrong, Ms. Jacobi," the young man told me as though this remote possibility had just occurred to him, "but I do sense that you'd better take this call from Alan Greco. I don't think it has anything to do with a request for special press privilege."

"What makes you say that, Jeffrey?"

"Mr. Greco said it was a matter of life or death."

"That would make one consider. All right. Close the door on your way out, and no other calls from anyone at all."

I was feeling high-exhausted; playful; exhilarated. Alan Greco's voice was a thin and shaky whisper in my ear and his first words totally destroyed my sense of well-being.

"Lynne, what happened? I don't understand. What went wrong?"

"Alan? What are you talking about? *I* don't understand."

"Lynne, how in God's name could you have proceeded before the Grand Jury? How could you have gone after the indictments the way you did? Why didn't you stop it?"

We arranged to meet in fifteen minutes in a booth way in the back of one of the last remaining old-time luncheonettes in the area.

Alan was seated facing me as I approached and from the look on his face, before he had a chance to say one single word to me, I sensed disaster.

Part Five

Questions of Guilt

38

"Before you read the statement I prepared after my meeting with Sanderalee," Alan Greco said, "there are a few things I want you to know. And to understand." His hand trembled as he wiped his forehead. His voice was heavy with sadness and emotion.

"Sanderalee. Oh God. We see her, you and I, the whole damn world sees her as a beautiful, exotic, stunning woman; a mysterious, elegant, thrillingly special original. Breathlessly beautiful and interesting and exotic. But her history, her life is so terrible. Her formative years were so... Let me tell you that *never, never, not for one single moment in her life* has Sanderalee believed in her own beauty. She's been so scarred by a childhood of being told she was an ugly duckling; a long-legged, skinny, bony freak; a wrong-color child with a witch's green eyes; a sort of monster to be laughed at and avoided, to be jeered at from a distance." He reacted to my expression; he took my hand and pressed it for emphasis. "It's all true, Lynne. During a photo session, she once broke down over something I said. I told her she was beautiful, and she burst into tears—wept hysterically. I held her until she felt able to confide in me. She told me about her childhood. A nightmare! The town freak; school scapegoat. So all of her successes—all the years since she was discovered sitting at a typewriter in that Harlem storefront insurance office and was taken in hand by her French filmmaker, from that day until this, no matter what triumphs she's had—none of these things has ever wiped out the ugly girl just beneath the surface, the girl who one day everyone is going to recognize, and laugh at, and destroy...

"All of this, Lynne, is by way of explanation of why Sanderalee got herself into this mess in the first place. She's never felt that she deserved the success that came to her. She's always felt, beneath the surface, that she's an ugly fraud. And so, she's gone out periodically, masochistically, picking up the kind of brutes who would treat her like the ugly fraud, the faker she feels herself to be. She's actively sought the sadist who will punish her, hurt her, treat her as she feels, deep inside, she deserves to be hurt."

I took a deep breath and exhaled slowly and nodded. I'm a prosecutor. Human failings, even human craziness, doesn't surprise me. "Okay, Alan. I understand. In other words, she's been looking for her murderer for most of her life. And this time, she's almost found him. What have you got for me to read? My God, this looks like an official police report." I flipped through the stapled pages.

He shrugged it off. "Lynne, I've been a photo-journalist and a writer as well as a fashion photographer. If I didn't know the proper way to prepare a report for information, I'd be in a great deal of trouble. The minute I got home, off the top of my head, I typed up, as close to verbatim as possible, what Sanderalee had told me."

I stared at the pages, wished there were more light, hoped they wouldn't be as bad as I expected them to be, and read.

STATEMENT OF SANDERALEE DAWSON TO ALAN GRECO ON MONDAY, MARCH 26, 1979: re events of Tuesday night, March 6, 1979

I jogged up to Columbus Circle that night and started up along Central Park West but changed my mind. It was too cold, too windy. I turned back and headed for the Jog-gon-Inn. I forgot that it was Tuesday and the place was closed.

He was outside, looking in the window. This man. We spoke a little. He said he'd forgotten the place was closed too. He looked familiar, but it was dark and he was bundled up. But he looked like some guy I'd seen at the Jog gon-Inn before. There were so many men. So many. I wasn't sure. And it didn't really matter.

There were no preliminaries at all. None. I wasn't looking for a love affair and neither was he. I asked if he wanted to come back to my apartment and he said yes. It was as simple as that.

I asked him to come up to my apartment for sex. Just that. For straight sex. He came too damn fast. Just bim-bam-boom and out. I asked him what the hell that was supposed to be.

[THERE WAS NO RAPE.]

I felt rotten that night. So uptight, so tense. Mean, so damn mean was how I felt. Mean and rotten and I said things to him. To get him a little stirred up. A little aggressive. I wanted that. A little excitement. You know. I said a few things to him. Jerkoff artist, that kind of thing. He hit me across the mouth and there was the most terrible look in his eyes. I told him to forget it. Get out and forget the whole thing. But I was still excited. Still tense, still ready and went down on him because I wanted to; because I wanted to.

[THERE WAS NO INVOLUNTARY SODOMY.]

And then, afterward, there was still this terrible tension in the room. Instead of relaxing, this man seemed, I don't know how to explain it. He was super-cold; looking at me as though I was something—I can't explain it. As though I was some kind of "thing." He threw my sweater and running pants at me. I was glad to put them on. It made me feel less vulnerable. I was getting really afraid of him. He stood next to me and told me to say all those things to him again. All those put-down things I'd said to him. I had said rotten things to him. He really scared me. He was holding me by the shoulders and his fingers dug in and he kept staring at me and whispering: go on, say it again, say what you said before.

And then he said, "*I've killed women for less than what you've said. Do you know that? I've killed women for less than that.*"

I thought it was some sort of a put-on. I thought he hadn't gotten off completely. That he was playing a game. He insisted I say all those awful things to him again. You know—to taunt him. I was scared to say those things again, but more scared not to.

Then he began to hurt me. Really hurt me. He hit me with the side of his hand, the edge of his hand. It was like being hit with a steel bar. I heard cracking, breaking. My God, he was breaking my face. I could feel the blood in my mouth, I swallowed blood. I tried to pull away from him but he was too strong. I tried to kick, to do something. I reached for anything, I picked up my little silver unicorn statuette and jabbed at him, right in the face. He pulled his hands from me and I tried to slip away, but he had me pinned against the bar with his body. He touched his cheek and he looked at his fingers.

All the blood from me didn't bother him. What he'd done to me was all right. But when he saw his own blood, my God, he seemed to go crazy. I knew he was going to kill me. I knew it. I knew it.

I slipped away from him and ran into the kitchen. I wanted to pick up the house phone because I knew Timothy Doyle would see it flashing. Somehow, I don't remember how, I don't remember how, I had the meat cleaver in my hand. I don't remember this clearly but one minute I had the cleaver and then I didn't and then I had the receiver in my hand and he tried to grab it away from me and I don't remember too much after that.

I remember the pain. I remember lying there and wondering how all that blood got there. And I remember that he was back in the kitchen and standing over me, then he kneeled down and his voice was very quiet and he said what I already told them he said. Something like how "*this has nothing to do with me; I have no control over any of this.*" Whatever that statement was I gave to Lucy was true, was what he said. And then I just wasn't there. I guess he left me for dead.

I woke up once and thought that it was very peculiar; that my hand was still holding the telephone receiver. Over there. In all that blood. Then I blacked out and I was in the hospital.

I woke up once and when I opened my eyes, he was right there, leaning over me, looking down at me. I thought for a second that I was still on the kitchen floor, that he had come back to kill me; but somehow I knew I wasn't in the kitchen. I was in the hospital. Each time I saw him, standing over me, looking down at me, each time I saw him it reinforced my first impression: that this man, obviously a doctor, I knew that by now, this man was the same man who did this to me.

I really thought it was him. Dr. Cohen. The man who did this to me. And so I told Regg Morris. And Regg told me to keep very quiet until he checked this all out.

Then, later, Regg Morris told me who David Cohen was. I began to feel very uncertain. I told Regg that I wasn't so sure anymore. Not really positive. That there had been another man, a couple of times, a year or so ago, that I'd met at the Jog-gon-Inn. That this other man resembled David Cohen. That when we first met outside the Jog-gon-Inn, that's who I thought the guy was. Now, I don't know.

I told Regg I thought maybe David Cohen just looked like the other guy. That maybe it *was* the other guy who actually beat me like this; did these awful things to me.

Regg told me to forget the other guy. He said it would be my fault if we let David Cohen get away with this

247

crime. I was so tired, so confused...so I agreed. It was easier. And maybe Regg was right....

But I'm not sure it was David Cohen who did these things to me.

It might have been the other man. The one who *looks* like David Cohen.

Alan Greco and I looked at each other across the dirty pink Formica tabletop. There were so many obvious questions.

"Why now? Why did she decide to tell all this now?"

"Because Regg released those photographs of her. That he took when she was so wounded. Because of his explanation. Because of what he told her the last time he came to see her, the other day."

"Which was?"

"Regg Morris said he released the photographs because they would tend to keep the pressure on. That the Grand Jury had to be affected by the public climate. And when Sanderalee told him that she didn't feel she could go ahead with things as they were, he said yes, you can. And when she said she was less certain than ever that it was in fact David Cohen, he said just forget that. And when she said, but if it wasn't David Cohen, Regg, then the man who actually did this to me is still out there, walking around, free. Might still be out there ready to hurt other women, just like he said he already had. To kill other women."

"And Regg Morris said to her?"

"And Regg Morris said to Sanderalee, 'Yeah and maybe he isn't a Jew, that other man.' He said, 'We got us our Jew, Sanderalee. Don't mess with this, don't rock it.' And when she said, 'But, Regg, the man who did this to me: *who did this to me.*' And he told her that it didn't matter shit. *That she'd served her purpose and that was all that he was concerned about.*"

There were tears sliding down Alan Greco's drawn cheeks, spilling over from his black, long-lashed, sad eyes. I reached across the table and held his hand.

"And you see," he whispered thickly, "worst of all, do you see what he's done to her? He's made her nightmare come true: he's publicized the 'real Sanderalee.' Those...those pictures, all over the world, showing her, with her face all destroyed. My God, Lynne, he's shown the whole world her secret image of herself. There has got to be a special place in hell for Regg Morris, for what he's done to..."

Alan buried his face in his hands and tried to stifle a sob. I dug out a handful of tissues and he blew his nose and swabbed his face and took a swallow of water, then nodded. Okay. Under control.

It was my turn to face some hard and ugly truths.

"Alan, after you talked to her on Monday afternoon, after you convinced her to have the surgery, God knows how...your love must be so special and strong...then you went directly to your apartment and typed up this first statement?" I touched the first batch of papers and he nodded. My mouth went cotton dry; the words actually had a sour, ugly taste. "And then you went over it, and added to it, and retyped it? And then you took both copies of your conversation with Sanderalee and...?"

Alan Greco nodded reluctantly. Now *he* was holding *my* hand; his grip was crushing but no more crushing than the reality of the situation.

On Monday night, *three days before* I went to the Grand Jury and made my case against Dr. David Cohen for rape, sodomy and the variety of assault charges, Alan Greco had given Bobby Jones the full statement, *the retraction*, made by Sanderalee Dawson prior to the emergency surgery on her hand.

My name, District Attorney Jameson Whitney Hale had assured me, would be forever linked in the public's mind with the prosecution of Dr. David Cohen. *Or did he say persecution?*

Now the tears were sliding down my cheeks and Alan was handing me tissues.

249

39

It did not seem possible that one day could be so long,
could include so many various events. Jhavi was at m
door the moment he heard me come home. He wante
to be sure I had enough copies of the *New York Pos*
and the *Daily News*: frontpage stuff, Lynne. I hav
enough. Thank you and goodnight.

LADY D.A. BAGS SANDERA'S M.D. ATTACKER
That was the late Friday-night-edition headline of th
Post. Beneath the headline, there I was, indeed a lad
D.A., surrounded by all the many males of my Squa
flanked by the Chief of Detectives and by the Distri
Attorney, both of whom were turned toward me a
though I were about to speak words of the most pr
found wisdom. I looked very earnest and profession
as I tried to make sense out of about six questions bein
screamed in my direction at the same time. You cou
catch my response on the eleven o'clock news in ca
you missed the six o'clock edition.

GAL D.A. BUSTS TV GAL'S DOC. Stacks of th
early Saturday-morning edition of the *News* were a
ready on the stands. Some photographer had caug
me in what looked like a sneer. God knows what pa
ticular word I had been saying, but my upper lip wa
pulled sideways and directly underneath my pictur
the copy said I was "sneering at how clever Dr. Cohe
thought he was." I shared the front-page photo spa

with Sanderalee—an old Alan Greco photo. At her very best, at her most beautiful. Inside on page three were Regg Morris's pictures, the ones that would haunt her all her life.

I locked the door, dumped the newspapers on the floor. Headlines. Well, Jameson was right all right. A headline case. Lots of publicity. They'll sure know who Lynne Jacobi is. Jameson said something about an editorial in a later edition of the *News*.

I flipped the switch on my telephone answering machine. The voice of a stranger, cool, professional, midwestern and polite, informed me, "Lynne, it's eight o'clock now. Would you please call me as soon as you get in? It's *very important* that we talk."

Is it indeed very important that we talk, Bobby Jones? What shall we talk about? Shall we discuss Regg Morris's connection with the Arabs? land deals? wheeling and dealing on an international level? Are these the things you want to clear up with me? Or what, Bobby dear?

I took a long hot shower: let the water steam over me, let my hair stick to my face, let the back of my neck be drilled by the concentrated pressure of the needle setting on my shower head. I wrapped myself up in a huge thick terrycloth robe, enveloped myself, hid myself.

I slumped on the couch and tried to coordinate my breathing with Jake Jacobi's breathing: he had sensed I was too totally wiped out to push/shove/command/beg him to get off my stomach. I tried not to inhale when he exhaled through his slightly opened mouth because he had rotten cat breath. He settled down, a huge dead weight. Slowly, he began to happy-foot into my shoulder, gently, just the merest touch of his needle claws getting through the thick toweling into my flesh, as though to distract me from my thoughts. Finally, he dug a little too hard and I gathered my strength and shoved the obese, spoiled, one-eyed cat to the floor. He let out a pitiful cry: the sound of an abandoned infant.

Then he jumped back on top of me and settled down immediately into a deep, snoring sleep.

Absently, I began to rub and pet and scratch and caress his head, his neck. The purring was so loud and the sound on the television was so low, I could scarcely hear what they were saying on the *Tonight* show. I was remembering my own appearance on the TV news.

The first conference, before noon, was when we announced the indictment and impending arrest of Dr. David Cohen. It was orderly, controlled and professional. Jameson Whitney Hale had placed me fully front and center and he deferred to me at every opportunity.

But later, after the arraignment, after the courtroom disaster for the Cohen family, I was interviewed by a jostling, shoving, insistent mob of media people: how did I feel about Dr. Cohen's father's death by heart attack right in the courtroom? about the revelation that Dr. Cohen's brother, the nuclear engineer, was an epileptic and might have blown us all to kingdom come? about his mother's obvious target—me—of her "for all time damnation" curse for the destruction of her family?

I ignored the first questions: for God's sake, how does one feel when an elderly man drops dead of a heart attack at the foot of his semi-paralyzed wife's wheelchair?

I was at a final point of exhaustion, mixed with exhilaration and accomplishment. Had someone been with me, perhaps they would have had the wisdom to clamp a hand over my mouth and escort me from these insistent newsmen.

I made a joke about Mrs. Cohen's curse: her damnation for all time.

"Hey, listen," I told a delighted audience, "when worked in Frauds years ago, my main function was to prosecute gypsies. You want to hear a curse to make your hair stand up straight, you get a gypsy mad at you. Somewhere out there are about fifteen Lynne dolls with pins stuck all over them. Every time I burn my tongue on hot coffee or break a nail, some gypsy curse has been reactivated. So I think I'll survive Mrs. Cohen's."

At the time, my remarks seemed funny. Even as I had watched the interview on the late news, it *sounded* funny. Not clever, not too smart, but yes, funny. Everyone present at the news conference laughed.

However, this particular off-the-cuff interview ended with a closeup of Mrs. Cohen's frozen, stricken, semi-paralyzed, anguished face as she was being quickly wheeled from the courtroom scene of her husband's death and, as she put it, the destruction of her family. The clever television technicians had used my wise-guy reference to gypsy curses as voice-over to a freeze-frame closeup of the shattered Mrs. Cohen, mother of the family Cohen.

Go for the laugh, Lynne. In court, when you sense the need for humor, take a chance. When you know the laugh will turn the jury toward you; infuriate the opposition; devastate a hostile witness. But for God's sake, Lynne, don't go for the laugh at the expense of a semi-paralyzed, newly widowed mother of two sons in desperate trouble.

Now I knew what "final cut" meant.

I rubbed Jake Jacobi's chin and thought of Bobby Jones. Incredible golden boy; my delayed fantasy, fulfilled and now finished. Destroyed. Along with me; along with everything I've worked for for the last fourteen years. How could you have betrayed me like this? destroyed me like this? brought my career, my world down around my head like this?

In a way, of course, I did understand. Another of my marvelous if somewhat bizarre virtues: an ability to understand all sides of a situation. I had told him he was not very good at his job; that Lucy would have been far better. That Lucy was in fact slated for promotion when I was elected District Attorney; that he should look into a new career entirely. He had continued his own investigation. I knew from the very beginning that he doubted David Cohen's guilt. But his reasoning had

been so naive: so stereotyped, ass-backwards discrim
inatory. *Jews don't do that kind of thing.*

He had continued his investigation, suppressing th
new information he had uncovered. He had let me g
for the headline indictment. My name would indeed b
forever linked to the Dr. David Cohen and family trag
edy: the father's falling dead at the paralyzed feet o
the invalid mother; the publicly exposed brother; th
wrongly indicted principal in the case. And my wise
crack response to the oracle-like curse whispered b
the newly bereaved widow would live on as a famou
example of the foot-in-the-mouth.

Bobby had let all of that happen. He had waited. H
could have stopped it, three full days before the in
dictment. That part I could not understand.

The phone rang as the *Tonight* show was ending.
picked it up on the second ring and said "Yes, Bobby
before he even spoke.

"Lynne, can I see you tomorrow? I have some im
portant information to discuss with you."

"Really? I can't imagine what that might be."

"Lynne, what I've got for you is the *real culprit. Th
man who actually did attack Sanderalee Dawson. A
man named Jim McDonald."

"Oh?"

He went on; his voice was steady, calm, Nebraska
slow and flat. "Lynne, may I come over tomorrow eve
ning? At around seven, would that be convenient?"

"That would be fine."

"Lynne, I'll explain everything when I see you to
morrow night. *Everything. We'll work it out.* You'll see
Is seven o'clock good for you?"

"Seven o'clock is wonderful for me, Bobby. Than
you for being so considerate."

I hung up. What can you say to someone who's be
trayed you? When you still love him. Damn it.

I stared at Tom Snyder, who was waving his arm
around and glaring at his guest. Whatever his problem
it had him quite agitated. I stared without seeing;

listened without hearing. Finally, the elusive thought I had been trying to catch all night solidified.

I had been a better teacher than I had realized. Michael Bobby Jones did indeed have the ruthlessness necessary for a good prosecutor.

40

After a sleepless Friday night, I took the E train out to Queens early Saturday morning to visit Lucy, who was in St. John's Hospital.

I followed the usual good-for-nothing advice: I rode in the car with the conductor. I deliberately looked so menacing that prospective muggers and troublemakers of all kinds steered clear of me. Even the conductor glanced at me warily from time to time.

I was dressed like a Nazi and looked mean and vicious in my smart black leather pants and matching jacket. My hands were jammed into my slash zipper pockets as if I could produce a gun or a knife in a moment, given the slightest provocation. Beneath my dark glasses, through which I had a little trouble seeing in the dim subway light, I surveyed a hostile world backing off. Saturday mornings were getting a bad reputation underground and the last thing I needed was to get involved with some joker who wanted to wrestle my shoulder bag from my arm.

I was as relieved as everyone else when the train pulled into my station and I headed for the street. I had

a little trouble getting a taxi until I took off my ha
fluffed up my hair, tied a bright kerchief around m
head, took off my dark glasses, put on a smile an
waved hopefully at some lumpish-looking driver wh
reluctantly agreed, as though doing me a personal fa
vor, to drive me to St. John's.

I am of the generation of women who were raise
not to trust "girls"; not to confide in them too much
not to put too much faith in their intelligence, relia
bility, integrity; to remember at all times that they ar
always and forever potential rivals for a rare place i
the man's world. If I insisted on revealing my intell:
gence, it should be only to a secure and influential ma
in a position to realize that *Lynne's all right; she think*
like a man. This is what I will forever hold against me
in general: that they have carefully selected out an
inculcated intelligent women with a sense of specia
ness: you're not like the other girls. Damn, for a woman
you sure are bright as hell.

Lucy, because of her own particular background an
life, had come to respect, love, trust, admire and expec
a high degree of performance and ability from wome
per se many years before I had learned how to do so
She had become my best friend; in a way, my teacher
my confidante, my strength in moments of stress an
disaster.

I took a long look at Lucy Capella, who appeared t
be enjoying a pleasant dream. Her leg was strung u
inside a stiff white plaster cast; her arm rested heavil
over her body in a similar cast. As soon as I realize
the other bed in the room was empty, that we wer
alone, I burst out crying. Not softly; not in controlle
contained whimpers. I just leaned against the door
had closed behind me, looked at Lucy and cried.

Lucy's eyes snapped open, her head came up, he
expression was startled. "Lynne. Good heavens, Lynn
come on. It's not that bad. All this rigging and ropin
is just for dramatic effect, honestly."

I came to the side of the bed, leaned over, kissed h
forehead, grabbed her good hand and confessed.

"Oh, Lucy, I'm not crying for *you*. I'm crying for *me*. You, for God's sake, you'll be fine. You're tough and strong and you have total absolute faith and confidence...Lucy, my whole life has just gone right down the drain. My whole future has just disappeared right before my very eyes."

"Well, in that case, I think you'd better flop down in the other bed or pull over a chair or take a drink of water and settle down to tell me all about it."

We talked. *I* talked for nearly an hour; about my great lost future as the first woman District Attorney of New York County; of the fact that Jameson Whitney Hale had said *my name would be forever linked in the public's memory with that of Dr. David Cohen*.

Lucy's dark eyes studied the ceiling thoughtfully. She pulled herself up a little and began asking key questions.

"What exactly do you think Bobby Jones has? Actually?"

"I think...that he has the actual culprit who attacked Sanderalee. Beat her up, hacked her hand off. The sex stuff, oh God, Lucy, that damn old male cliché: *She asked for it.*' In this particular case, *she did. Quite literally*." I told Lucy everything that Alan Greco had revealed about Sanderalee's background. "She's been searching for her murderer, and now she's come as close as possible to finding him without being dead."

"Has Bobby told you any specifics yet? About what he's got?"

"No. But Lucy, he's been in and out to see Sanderalee. I checked the hospital sign-in sheet. Whatever he's come up with, she must have verified. She's backed off David Cohen entirely. God, if she'd admitted the pickup and that the sex was voluntary on her part, but was still David Cohen, we'd drop the rape and sodomy charges and still have a good case for assault, attempted murder and dismemberment. But she told Alan Greco she wasn't sure any more about David; doubted it very much, in fact. From the sound of Bobby's voice, from what he's said, I feel that he's shown her pictures of this...McDonald. That the identification is strong enough to go with."

"Why, Lynne? Why did he do this? Why didn't Bobby stop you before you went for the indictment?"

"Because I told him...because we discussed...the future. He learned about Jameson's plan to appoint me as D.A. when he announces for the Senate." Lucy's eyebrows shot up; she didn't know about this yet. I filled her in. "Bobby got this from that Glori-TV documentarian. I told him the truth: that he didn't have what it takes to be a top prosecutor; that you were a better investigator. That his future was somewhat limited within the service of the District Attorney's office. That he should start exploring other areas of the law. I wounded him—his ego; his pride; his macho image— when I said he didn't have the killer instinct. I said he lacked the instinct."

"Like you and I have."

"Like you and I have. I sure was wrong about that wasn't I? My jugular has just about been ripped open."

"Bobby's timing, Lynne. Good grief, his timing. He actually let you go before the Grand Jury and get the indictment and all the ensuing publicity while withholding Sanderalee's statement from you. Was he that wounded by you? Is he that vengeful?"

For the first time, I said aloud what I had been thinking. "Not by himself; I think he's been taking 'getting ahead' lessons. From some very self-interested, self-assured, manipulative little...I don't want to go into this just now, Lucy. I have to think about this for a while. It's...personal."

Lucy nodded. Okay.

"Now, what I want you to tell me: could I throw him to the wolves for this? Bring him up on charges? obstruction of justice by withholding vital information? If it isn't a criminal matter, is it a Bar Association matter?"

Lucy studied me with her dark and serious eyes. Calmly, rationally, slowly and with great care and consideration, she said, "No, Lynne. Not at this point. A tually, Sanderalee Dawson told Alan Greco a new story about the attack. And Alan Greco told Bobby Jones and Bobby Jones didn't tell you. Because...let's play defense attorney for him for the moment: because he needed time to check it out. In the meantime, you went ahead with your presentation to the Grand Jury in perfectly good faith and, based on your presentation, they indicted. So you're covered. And actually, so is Bobby. In a way. He had no reason to either believe or disbelieve Sanderalee's new story; so he undertook an independent investigation. Let's look at the brightest possible side of the situation."

"My Lucy-look-at-the-sunny-side."

"Well, why not? Let's say that Bobby *has* come up with another suspect. A David Cohen lookalike. And now Sanderalee says, absolutely, positively, without an iota of a doubt: yes. Yes. Yes. Yes. That's the man I picked up; took home; had all kinds of slightly kinky sex with. And then he turned vicious and beat me up and hacked off my hand. So, you go back to the Grand Jury and get a dismissal of all charges against Dr. David Cohen. I'm making an educated guess, based on everything we know so far, that this second man is a David Cohen lookalike. You acted in good faith, Lynne: your plaintiff said this was the man. You literally had no choice. Not too much corroborating evidence, but one or two little peculiar things, like the wounded cheek, blood type, missing running shoes. You're in the clear as far as I can see.

"And so is Bobby Jones." Lucy held her hand up to keep me from interrupting. "We're looking at the sunny side, Lynne. Not on the personal motive side, all right? Let me finish. So, okay, David Cohen is cleared. Second man—McDonald, you said—okay, he's charged not with any sex crimes because ugh!—damn and double damn!—'She asked for it.'"

We both made faces and ugly noises but Lucy continued. The longer she spoke, the better I felt. Maybe this whole thing could still be salvaged.

"So, all right, you then ask the Grand Jury for indictments for atrocious assault, attempted murder, dis-memberment, and any et ceteras you can throw in."

"And publicly, Lucy? I have the distinct feeling that the crucifiers will be lined up and waiting. Led by one particularly vivacious and successful young woman who's gotten more than she bargained for—or maybe exactly what she hoped for—by selecting me for her fucking documentary. Sorry, Lucy. Her darn-old doc-umentary."

Lucy ignored my slip; we are all generally careful around her, with that twelve-year-old face and those round dark eyes.

"Okay, Lynne. So what do we have to offer to the public? Well, sir, we show them that the prosecutor's office, the District Attorney's office, is dedicated *to the truth, to justice, to clearing and protecting the innocent, as well as prosecuting the guilty.*"

She ended with a huge, triumphant grin. She had *me* totally convinced. What a *marvelous* organization we represented. What *dedication* to the *tradition of jus-tice.* Oh, Lucy, *you* go in front of the cameras. *You* face the world and tell them what you just told me.

"Lucy, you make it all sound so nice and clean and marvelous and noble. But my God. David Cohen's father dropped dead in court from the stress of seeing his son under arrest and facing arraignment. His brother was apparently a pretty well controlled epilep-tic and now he's publicly disgraced. His mother—oh boy, Lucy, she's put a curse on me forever and ever and you know what? It's beginning to work full force."

She ignored that. "First, Lynne: the father's heart attack was inevitable. From what I've read about him he was on borrowed time. Unfortunate, but there it is. The brother: he lied on his job application. It's too bad the way it all came out, but let's face it, the man had no right at all to a job like that with the kind of re-sponsibility his job entailed."

"So, in effect, you might say that I was instrumental in saving possibly thousands of lives that might have een lost should he have had an attack at a crucial moment and let all that nuclear stuff escape. Right?"

"There you go, Lynne. That's the line to take. Now, he mother's curse." Lucy's face closed up for a moment as though she were searching for something—any-hing—to say.

"You saw it on the news? Was it as awful as I think t was?"

"It was as awful as you think it was."

You ask Lucy a question and you will get a totally honest answer.

"You know it yourself, Lynne. So okay, you learned omething. Be very careful of what you say and who you say it to. Never—ever—trust a media person; keep your guard up. They can do whatever they want to with vhatever you say so be careful what the heck you say, about anything at all times. Lynne, one more thing. Aside from 'showing you,' paying you back for your lack of confidence in his ability, where do you think Bobby Jones is heading with all of this? What does he want?"

I had never even considered. Never thought about t. "Going out in a burst of glory?" I started to laugh; a very gagging sound. "Glory-Glori Nichols. Is he set-ing me up for her documentary? All my shortcomings to be featured in a one-hour news special? And in grat-tude, she'll bring him into the wonderful world of en-ertainment? He's gotten some damn good training in louble-dealing if that's what's behind all this. I'll find ut tonight, at seven o'clock."

Lucy pulled herself up a little, hunched closer to me, it her lower lip. That meant she was making a big ecision: ask this next question or not.

"Lynne. Just between the two of us. No matter what appens later, no matter what turns up, no matter how his whole case is resolved. As of right now, your gut eeling. Forget everything else and give me your best ntuitive gut feeling: *Dr. David Cohen?*"

I answered without a second's hesitation.

"I think the son of a bitch is guilty."

"*I think so too,*" Lucy said.

41

We did not know how to behave toward each other. We had been so intimate and free and honest and loving and knowledgeable with each other. I knew that he had spent a certain amount of time deciding to wear his midnight blue suit. Then he had thoughtfully chosen the sky blue shirt, which intensified the color of his eyes, and then he purposely chose the exactly-right tie that I had bought for him at Saks specifically for that suit and that shirt. He was clean and fresh-smelling down to his skin: the soapy quality of a hot shower somehow lingers on Bobby Jones. He had shaved within the hour: faint hint of recently applied, very light aftershave lotion. I could visualize the motions he had used as he brushed his hair, the way he ran his left palm lightly over each careful stroke.

He had dressed to please me.

I had dressed to please him.

Unfortunately, one look at his blue eyes and smug face was enough to make my choice of clothing a matter of no interest to either of us.

"Bobby. *How the hell could you have done this to me?*" I asked.

There was a careful, tight narrowing of his eyes. He studied me as though calculating, deciding, selecting the proper words. "Actually," he said, after a pause "as of right now, as of this exact *minute*, Lynne, I haven't *done anything to you*."

"All right. Let's start with this. What have you been doing since you spoke to Alan Greco, last Monday night? When he told you about his conversation with Sanderalee. When he gave you copies of the report he prepared immediately after his conversation with Sanderalee."

Bobby focused steadily on me. "Go further back, Lynne. About two weeks back. I've been conducting my own investigation in another direction altogether. Away from Dr. David Cohen. I told you right at the beginning that I doubted he was the perpetrator. But first, I gave you the background report on Cohen that you asked for, I supervised all the Squad members. I coordinated all their findings and kept you up to date. In all areas but one. Because you more or less weren't interested in my *tangential investigation*."

"Tangential investigation? What the hell does that mean? Before you spoke to Alan Greco, before he told you what Sanderalee told him, what investigation were you involved in?"

Bobby held up his hand. "Wait, Lynne. I'll *show* you what I've been doing. *Before* the conversation with Alan." He retrieved his attaché case from the entrance hall. He placed it on my dining table, leaned over, arranging things. "Come on over here, Lynne. I've got a lot of things to show you."

As I stared at the photographs, Bobby stared at me. I looked up, puzzled; pointed to one slightly familiar face.

"Henry. Angel. Henry Angelowitz, our pal from the Jog-gon-Inn. Photogenic devil, isn't he." Bobby moved in closer to me; his hand resting lightly, naturally, on my shoulder, no longer shy of touching. His square fingers searched the small faces on the photograph, then stopped at an indistinct bearded man sitting at a table.

As though he were performing a magic act, Bobby

produced another picture from the folder he had taken from his attaché case. It was an enlargement of the indistinct man with the beard. Vaguely familiar. And then, he showed me an artist's drawing of the face in the photograph; then, the artist's rendition of the same face without a beard: it was David Cohen's face.

"This is what you're showing me? A guy with a beard who looks like David Cohen underneath his beard? Who was photographed at the Jog-gon-Inn?"

Bobby wordlessly handed me his next item: a yellow sheet. The official record of arrests in the name of one Jim McDonald, also known as Donald McGuire a.k.a. Don Finn a.k.a. Donald Tomkins a.k.a. Jim Finn. Not known, at any time, as David Cohen. There was a list of arrests going back to the early sixties: rape; assault; attempted rape; attempted murder; assault; assault; weapons charge (unspecified); rape; assault with a deadly weapon. There were two convictions, bargained-for doubtlessly, for misdemeanors; two convictions for felonies. He had served a total of some six and a half years for his long list of crimes. He was currently on parole, for the last five months, for his latest major felony conviction. Underlined on the yellow sheet was the information that there was an arrest warrant out for him as a parole violator. He apparently hadn't been keeping his required appointments with his parole officer. He could be picked up at any time under the warrant.

Next: mug shots. As Bobby showed them to me one at a time I could see the changes from callow youth to smug tough to streetwise punk. The photographs were dated from 1963 to the last one taken of him in 1977 The last few photographs could have been of David Cohen: alike as twins.

"Now," Bobby cleared the table, glanced up at me as he arranged a series of photographs, one beside the other. "Bear with me, Lynne, for just a minute. Now look. Eight photographs; four with beards, four without beards. I had an artist do the drawings, which were

264

hen photographed uniformly. Pick out who is who. Which are David Cohen, which are Jim McDonald?"

It was impossible. They were too much alike. I turned he photos over again and again, checking the name against the image.

"My God. What's that word, German word... *doppelgänger?* A double—an old folktale about each person having a reverse image or a ghostly twin somewhere on earth. Jesus."

Bobby had other information for me: prison records; employment records; residence records, psychiatrists' reports from prison; statements from all the various officials at all the various institutions through which Jim McDonald eventually passes.

"Right at the very beginning, Lynne, when Sanderalee said she thought she knew the guy—that she thought she recognized him from the Jog-gon-Inn, I slipped a picture of David Cohen to Angel. Henry Angelowitz. He hadn't seen this guy McDonald around for a while. When he showed up with the beard, a little more than a week ago, Angel called me. And..." Bobby gestured to the stack of photographs. "And I've also got a videotape." He set it up on my Betamax. There, indeed, was David Cohen's bearded *doppelgänger*, sitting in the Jog-gon-Inn, drinking beer and eating a hamburger; all in living color.

"Who did the videotape and the artwork and the photos, Bobby? This wasn't done by our people. They were done by an outside agency."

Bobby shrugged. "It was all done on my own time. The rest of this stuff, the yellow sheet, the background, was done as a general information-gathering investigation. We've come up with the information that McDonald is wanted as a parole violator. We haven't approached his parole supervisor yet. McDonald is just sitting around. Under surveillance; very close, total surveillance. We can put hands on him with one phone call. For parole violation. And then for face-to-face identification by Sanderalee."

"You haven't answered my question, Bobby. Who d these photographs? Who made the videotape?"

He didn't answer; he just smiled and shrugged.

"They're *media people*, for God's sake, Bobby. *Med people*. Do you realize what could happen if this m terial is used in the wrong way? Have you any idea..

"It won't be used in the wrong way. That's what th is all about, Lynne. This is what I've come to set u with you."

"To set up with me?"

That dazzling smile: football hero, class practic joker, gleeful "gotcha" grin.

"Bobby, I'm going to tell you that as of this momen I can charge you with obstruction of justice. And you're about to ask me to join with you in some sort scheme involving this case, I'll further charge you wit attempted collusion. At the very worst, you'll face trial and possibly jail. At the very least, you'll be di barred."

"Lynne, come on and sit down and listen to me. Th isn't as terrible as it looks. This can be worked out."

"Worked out? You deliberately withheld informatio from me, you let me go before the Grand Jury and ge indictments against David Cohen when you knew Sa deralee had withdrawn her identification, when yo had all this information about this...this..."

"Okay, Lynne. Here are some facts. *Facts*: not spe ulation. Jameson Whitney Hale is going to announc for the Senate on April sixth. That's next week. He going to appoint you as his replacement and recon mend you as the incumbent candidate and will bac you totally for election."

"Not when this gets out he won't. I'll be lucky if...

Bobby held his hand up. "Lynne, wait. Just let m continue. Now, I've given my own career a great de of careful thought since you last informed me of m lack of ability, et cetera, et cetera. My inability to g for the jugular, something like that, wasn't it? And wasn't as good an investigator as Lucy Capella. Or a good a prosecutor as you." He smiled. "Well, I've g

266

he real culprit tied up and waiting to be delivered. How he gets delivered, *under what circumstances* and conditions and with *what public information*—that's what you and I are going to work out."

"Bobby. Don't say anything more. Not another word. Didn't your pretty little Miss America media-lady tell you what happens to violators of the public trust? Or doesn't she know anything about law?"

"She knows *the law of survival*, Lynne. She's been giving me a few lessons." His feet came off the table, flat on the floor. He leaned forward and stared hard at me. "Our careers are linked together, Lynne. You and I are going to work together, right at the top of the heap."

"I told you before, Bobby, my career has nothing whatever to do with you."

"It has everything to do with me, Lynne. We're tied together because of this case. It can work for you or against you. It's all up to you. It depends on what you decide here, tonight, between just the two of us."

"Where does Glori Nichols fit into all of this, Bobby? First, explain that to me. Before you explain anything else, because I don't know from point one what the hell you have in mind."

"Lynne, Glori Nichols means as much to me as...as Jameson Whitney Hale ever meant to you. You don't have to worry about her any more than I've ever worried about him. We'd still be together, you and I. We'll both get what we want."

That stunned me; it really took me a few seconds to absorb the shock. It had been a long time since anyone had considered me as a bedroom achiever. It was not only grotesque, it was pretty funny, coming from Bobby Jones.

"My God, Nebraska. I'm not sure I can quite see this. You'd be using...both of us. Glori Nichols and me. In exactly the same way you think that Jameson and ...and oh my God, this is too much. Too bizarre. Glori and Jameson; and Glori and you; and me and Jameson.

267

You've come a long way from the rolling waves of grain in Nebraska."

He had the calculated smug grin of a clever child. "You and I would be the team, Lynne. It's not as complicated, really, as it sounds." He shrugged. "I guess you could say I'm a real New Yorker now."

"*An unemployed New Yorker!* I want your resignation on my desk by nine o'clock Monday morning. You can spend Sunday with your TV lady preparing a nice believable story for your resignation." He watched me, expressionless, as I moved around the room; had to keep moving; moving, because what I really wanted to do was something violent. To him.

"As of Monday morning, 9 A.M., we are adversaries, Bobby. I should fire you as of right now, this minute, right now, but I'm giving you the grace period. That's because I really cared about you. I didn't mind your career-building in my bed just as long as your ambition didn't exceed your ability. Tonight, you've crossed the line by a...by a country mile. Either you've overestimated yourself or underestimated me."

"You haven't heard what I have to say, Lynne. You haven't even asked about..."

I took a deep breath, felt it stick in the back of my throat, felt a sense of suffocation. "Don't tell me anything, not a word. Whatever scheme, plan, whatever you've come to suggest to me..."

"You'd better listen to me, Lynne, and go along with me, or you'll be throwing away *your career*. And I don' believe you want to do that. You've worked and planned too long and too hard."

He had perfect control of his face except for one quick little twitch in the left corner of his lip; he knew I'd seen it. He covered his mouth with his hand for a moment; stood up, moved his shoulders around, loosening up; turned to me. Courtroom voice, courtroom presentation: a summing-up whether I wanted to hear it or not.

"It's really very simple, Lynne. You'll stand to lose nothing. We both stand to gain what we want. We si n this information for one more week, until Jameson nnounces. You're appointed as interim D.A. You apoint me as Bureau Chief. *Then*, I make a quick call o Jim McDonald's parole officer. Sanderalee has seen ll these photographs. Yes, she's identified McDonald. nd yes, she's *sure it was him.* She remembers him ow from having been with him before. She hasn't aade a face-to-face ID yet. That will come *after* I'm Bureau Chief; you're D.A. It will move very quickly, ery smoothly. Grand Jury drops the indictments gainst David Cohen. I give the presentation against IcDonald for assault, for attempted murder, for what e did to her. Then, *we*"—he opened his arms to include ie, part of the team—"make a public announcement. et the public know the District Attorney's office is just s interested in the *innocence* of a person as in the *guilt* f a person."

"That's terrific, Bobby. Lucy said something along hose very lines. Only not in quite the same context. o on. You're into it now, go all the way And then hat happens?"

"And then, with all of the publicity you'll get—guarnteed, Lynne, *I* can *guarantee* it she's got a hook ke you wouldn't believe "

"And where do you fit in, Bobby?"

"You'll appoint me as your Chief Assistant District ttorney The good old team, right up there at the top ou didn't think I wanted *your* job, did you, Lynne?"

"Tell me what it is you do want, Bobby? Where will ll this lead to—for you?"

He had a dreamy look now: small-town boy telling is plans for a wonderful future. Only in America.

"I'll have four years to pick my elective spot, Lynne. ou're right about one thing: being a prosecutor is not eally my life's ambition. And entertainment law—foret it. A dead end; an alley. But with four years of eing right up there at the top, being in the public eye uring crucial times, and with the right coverage...in ur years' time, Lynne, I'll make my move. That will ive me plenty of time to figure out my direction. And

no harm done to anyone. If we just wait a week or s
and then proceed on the information I've come up wit
You get what you want; and Jameson Whitney Ha
gets what he wants; and I get what I want."

"And Glori Nichols?"

He grinned. "No one will ever have to worry abo
her. Glori knows how to get what she wants; she's
power collector, Lynne. She'll be behind a president o
day."

"Maybe even you?"

He shrugged modestly. "I'm not quite that amb
tious."

"Let's say that I go to see the D.A. Monday mornir
and tell him that you've suppressed evidence; that y
knowingly let me make an erroneous presentation
the Grand Jury. And that you came here tonight wi
this offer to me. This plan, this deal. What then?"

"Then I would have to respond to your accusation
'Lynne, what are you talking about?' I told you ever
thing Monday night, as soon as I left Alan Greco. I to
you almost verbatim what he told me of his conve
sation with Sanderalee. As soon as he gave me a typ
version of the conversation, I gave you a copy—th
was...sometime Tuesday. But you told me to forget
to sit on it. You told me that you had the man y
wanted; that you were going to get the indictment y
wanted; that you needed David Cohen specifically f
the headline indictment. That it was essential to yo
career to show that you weren't giving special privile
to anyone. You needed David Cohen to cool the bla
leaders down as quickly as possible."

"Why didn't you go to Jameson as soon as I got t
indictment against Cohen? What stopped you, Bobby

"I didn't have the proof. I was in the process of gat
ering my information. Getting the background work
McDonald; the pictures; the face-to-face identificati
from Sanderalee. Which I will get as soon as McDona
is arraigned for parole violation. When that happe
depends on you, Lynne. How about...you got a c
endar handy?...how about a week from next Friday

He looked at a small shiny card calendar he had taken from his wallet. "Hey, that would make it Friday the thirteenth. Good luck for us, tough for Jim McDonald."

I went to the dining room table and tried to steady my hands, so that he wouldn't see the trembling. I collected all of the pictures, the yellow sheet, the background reports that had been done by the men in my squad without my knowledge. I put everything into the folder and held it tightly against my body.

"I'll keep this. I'll bring it into the office Monday morning." My voice was flat and noncommittal. I spoke softly to control the tremor.

"Okay, Lynne. Fine."

"I'm very tired now, Bobby. It's been a long week and I'm very tired. Go home. Or wherever you want to go; just go."

We stood in the hallway of my apartment. His face in the dim light was shadowed and uncertain, waiting for some clue, something definite. His lips were tight against his perfect teeth and there was just a glint of golden stubble along his chin. His hair had fallen over his forehead and my hand reached out, automatic and familiar gesture, and brushed it back into place. At my touch, his face relaxed, a quick grin, almost a reflex action, pulled at his lips. Very gently, I touched his face, traced along his full lower lip and then I reached up and kissed him and tasted again the familiar taste of Bobby Jones. For the very last time. I pulled back when he reached for me and the tension was back in his face, there was a nervous darting movement in his eyes.

"I loved you, Bobby. I'll probably have a hard time learning not to love you. It's because of that I'll still give you the option of resigning by nine Monday morning. Then, I will immediately get a dismissal of the charges against David Cohen. I will prepare the case against McDonald. Your name will not come into this in any way. Otherwise, Bobby, I will nail you to the wall publicly, professionally and personally."

He looked frozen and he struggled to keep his voice

271

under control. It was as terrible as a whispered threat in the dark of night. "It's going to be your head, Lynn. I'll do whatever I have to do. I have more of the kill instinct than you can even begin to imagine."

"That's good, Bobby. You're going to need every ounce of killer force you can get. Because you're going to have a tough time hacking it in prison. Your ass is just too damn cute. They'll fight over you inside the big gray walls, my beautiful Bobby. They won't offer you deals or grace periods. They'll just wreck you right down to your toes. It makes me very sad to think about that. Such a loss; such a waste. *Now get the hell out of my life, Bobby Jones.*"

42

I was in my office at my desk on Monday morning waiting for Bobby Jones. I did not know until later about his arrangement with Glori Nichols, about what they had worked out and decided on and set in motion for that Monday morning. I did not know that he had contacted Jim McDonald's probation officer and arranged for McDonald to be picked up and brought for arraignment into Manhattan Criminal Court at exactly 9:30 A.M. on Monday.

The timing was important. A media event required careful attention to split-second planning. I did not know that Bobby Jones had persuaded Sanderalee Dawson to accompany him to Criminal Court that morning for a face-to-face identification of Jim McDonald as he was being arraigned for parole violation.

Normally, a prisoner is taken from the precinct where he is booked to the back entrance—the prisoner's entrance—to the Criminal Court building. But not this time. Glori Nichols had vetoed that. She wanted the confrontation to be "accidental," in an outdoor setting so that she'd be free to catch Sanderalee's immediate reaction upon seeing the man who had ruined her life and caused damage to so many others.

Two detectives, following their instructions without question, escorted Jim McDonald from their unmarked car up to the front steps of the Criminal Court building.

It was a cold damp gray morning, wet and windy. Sanderalee was bundled deep into her high-collared coat, her scarf wrapped around her face, her dark glasses completing the coverup. She went unnoticed by passersby as Bobby walked along beside her, carefully timing their movements.

I was not there. I learned most of the details later, after the event. I was at my desk, waiting for Bobby Jones. My hand knocked over the container and the remainder of my lukewarm coffee spread in a stain on the desk blotter when I first heard shouting outside my office.

I vaguely remember, as you remember parts of a dream, running down the stairs and shoving and pushing my way through the revolving door, shouldering people aside, coming upon the scene. I remember hearing noises, excited, frightened, shocked voices, cries of pain, fear. Above all else, I remember hearing Glori Nichols' voice, sharp, alert, excited yet totally controlled. She was directing her crew: instructing them to close in on the scene, focus a tight shot, follow the action precisely.

They did a good job, Glori Nichols and her crew. I was able to put it all together, in sequence, later that night on the six o'clock and again on the eleven o'clock news.

It started with a good clear shot of Bobby Jones

emerging from his car, crossing around to the passenger's side. He leaned over and helped a mysterious woman emerge, bundled against the cold, her face hidden. The camera work was terrific: surreptitious, unsuspected, undetected, clear and sharp.

The voice-over—Glori Nichols' voice—told us what we already knew. "Chief Investigator Bobby Jones helps Sanderalee Dawson from the car. This is the first time she's been out in public since the attack on her. They start to walk toward the Criminal Court building. They stop. He says something to her. As he talks, he seems to be adjusting the collar of her coat, reassuring her. He lightly touches her left arm; the sling is hidden by her coat. He is glancing around; she seems reluctant and he seems to be reassuring her and . . .

"*Now!* Watch the three men just off to the right, who've gotten out of that car. They are coming up the steps toward Jones and Sanderalee. Keep your eyes on them. They pass close by; Sanderalee pulls away from Jones and she calls out something. The three men stop and turn. *There. That's him.* That's McDonald, the man in the middle, between the two detectives. Now, watch closely, this happens very quickly, watch Sanderalee's right hand, going into the pocket of her coat and . . ."

Sanderalee Dawson moved so quickly it was hard to follow her action without the helpful voice-over. And it was shown in instant replay and in slowed-down time so that we would miss nothing. Sanderalee's right hand comes from her coat pocket, she moves quickly into the group of three men. You hear the muffled shots: one—two—then see the scuffle. McDonald falls, pulling the detective to whom he's handcuffed down with him. Again, there, focus in close, slow down, two shots, McDonald falls, slowly, slowly, catch the surprised anguish on his face.

Bobby Jones struggles with Sanderalee. They seem almost to be embracing.

The last shot is hardly heard but we see the effect of a body-contact shot; a small-caliber bullet enters Bobby Jones, his hands fly up and press hard against

274

his chest, holding the wound, seemingly trying to stanch the sudden flow of blood that we see spurting between his fingers.

Almost before Bobby Jones falls, the other detective with McDonald has a grip on Sanderalee's wrist, has disarmed her, is holding her. She isn't struggling. She's just standing there, immobile, silent as a statue. The scarf drifts away from her face and the cameraman goes for an extreme closeup.

This part of the narrative was added at the studio: it is carefully enunciated. Glori Nichols' voice is solemn, her words awesome. "There she is, Sanderalee Dawson, there she is as he has made her, this man, this McDonald, who lies, now, dead at her feet. No more hiding. She doesn't even seem to care. She's unaware of the camera or the policeman holding her. She seems lost, gone, unconcerned, unaware of what is happening all around her."

The ambulance arrives and now the camera has caught me: I am kneeling beside Bobby Jones, I am holding his head against my body trying to protect him from the camera, from Glori Nichols' insistent narration, from the ambulance attendants who decide to let me get into the ambulance with him, to let me kneel beside him, to hold him, to hold on to him. Glori Nichols' last shot was of Sanderalee Dawson entering the ambulance; doors slam closed; ambulance pulls away, siren howling.

Bobby lay motionless on the stretcher and I put one hand over his, felt the warm blood from the center of his body, helped him apply pressure, helped him hold himself together. I put my face against his cheek, felt his breath, warm, felt the coolness of the morning on his lips, felt a gentle pressure returning my kiss, traced the slight smile from the corners of his mouth, my mouth tasting his, familiar taste. I touched his golden hair with my fingertips and then I whispered into his ear.

"Bobby, Bobby. Oh God, you dope. You goddamn dummy, why did you set this up? Why did you let this happen to you? This never should have happened. Don't you know we could have worked it out? Oh, damn you, Bobby, I never would have done any of those things I said Saturday, you know I wouldn't have, oh God, Bobby."

He said something softly; it sounded like my name. His eyes were filled with pain; he blinked as though surprised to find himself on this stretcher with me holding him.

Sanderalee began to moan. It was the long drawn-out cry of an injured and frightened animal. I pressed my face close to Bobby to protect him from the sound of her anguish. I felt him shudder in reaction to her terrible cries. I covered his face with mine. I heard him whisper something. I told him it would be all right, that it would all work out. I told him that nothing was important, none of it.

"I love you Bobby, oh God Bobby I love you so much that's all that matters and I won't even be mad at you later on when you can defend yourself. Yes, I will be mad at you I am mad at you I am furious with you. You should not have let this happen to you but it'll all be okay, we'll work it all out together it'll be okay Bobby Just know I love you and we'll be fine both of us we'll be okay"

When we arrived at the hospital there was so much commotion. So many people. Camera crews: how had they gotten there so fast? Voices. Attendants, doctors, people who were taking over. A sharp voice, commanding, in charge.

"Take the girl, damn it, hold her down on the stretcher. Get her to Emergency. No, take her first. *The guy will wait. He's DOA.*"

Somewhere, during the ride to the hospital, I had lost him.

Somewhere, at some point, he had died and I hadn't even realized it.

43

did for him in death what I would not do for him in
life: I lied. I changed the sequence of events. I gave him
full credit for the investigation that led to Jim Mc-
Donald and told Jameson that Bobby had come to me
immediately after he had taken the statement from
Sanderalee Dawson. As the sign-in sheet showed, he
had been in and out visiting with her; talking with her;
getting a strong feeling that she wanted to retract her
accusation against Dr. David Cohen. She kept referring
to the man she had known previously and when Bobby
Jones presented her with the results of his investigation, with all the material he had been collecting, she
gave him the statement he had immediately brought
to me Saturday night, and she agreed to a face-to-face
identification of Jim McDonald.

No one would refute my statement. Alan Greco was
in Europe on assignment; Bobby Jones was dead; Glori
Nichols contacted me and asked for exclusive coverage
of the funeral and followup. I asked her if she understood the words "collusion" and "obstruction." She
changed her mind about any further conversation with
me and wished me good luck. Sanderalee Dawson was
lost in another world that the psychiatrists at Bellevue
had thirty days to penetrate before they shipped her

away as criminally insane, a double murder to her credit.

Jameson arranged for a special session with the Grand Jury and I got the dismissal of all charges against Dr. David Cohen. David Cohen wisely refused any public comment; his attorney spoke for him in terms ominous to the City of New York.

The remaining questions were easily answered. Sanderalee Dawson had gotten the .22-caliber revolver from one of her early visiting PLO friends and had kept it concealed among her nightgowns. It was small and unobtrusive besides being deadly at close range. The Public Relations people were going at the situation around the clock: preparing announcements along the same lines that both Lucy Capella and Bobby Jones had suggested. We would turn it into a public revelation of how the District Attorney's office worked for protection of the innocent as well as for apprehension and conviction of the guilty.

Bobby's father and brother flew in from Lincoln, Nebraska, as soon as his body was released by the coroner and they took him home Wednesday night.

On Thursday night, Jameson Whitney Hale and I along with four others from the Squad, flew into Lincoln, Nebraska, spent the night at their best hotel and the morning at Bobby's funeral. We then returned to spend a respectable amount of time with his family.

There was something of him in all of his family: his mother's clear, bright blue eyes, his father's square jaw, his brother's bright yellow hair, his sister's fair pale skin. And all the family children looked like him: little Bobby-Jones-Americans. You could almost see his life story in stages, just by looking at the various relatives.

There had been a lot of flowers and I heard his mother tell someone, a niece I think, that it would be so nice if she'd collect all the flowers later, and see they were delivered to the children's ward at the hospital, remove the cards first, of course, so we'll know whom to thank. Weren't they kind, weren't they thoughtful, all his friends and colleagues from New York.

278

It was strange to hear him called Michael. His parents and members of his family called him Michael, but all of his old school friends, his pals, called him Bobby and his father told us not to worry about that. He was Bobby and he was Michael. He was buried next to his Bobby grandparents.

There had been no special glance, no special knowledge shared with anyone in his family: I was Michael Bobby's boss. His uncle, a State Attorney General, went out of his way to speak with me about my job, about Michael's job, about the role of women in law enforcement. We were two professionals comparing notes about crime in a changing world. Both Jameson and I told him how well his nephew had performed; what an incredibly fine job his last investigation had been. He was very pleased and told us he'd tell Michael's parents all about it when the right time came.

Flying home, I sat next to Jameson Whitney Hale. He surprised all of us by picking up the entire tab for our flight and the hotel. I didn't know if this was from his personal funds or from petty cash. He and I were in first class, the others flew tourist.

Jameson told me that he thought my plan was a good one: I was going to fly down to Eleuthera for about five or six days. He agreed that I was very lucky to have such good friends. Harley and Jhavi had owned their villa—a neat six-room house by the sea—for a couple of years. I'd been there briefly, twice. I knew some people down there, so I wouldn't be lonely, should I want company. Or intruded upon if I wanted to be alone.

"Take a little time, a little distance before you make any decisions, Lynne. Before we work out what the future should be. There's no rush, no hurry. I'll be working things out, getting a handle on our best approach and when you come back, rested a little and with a nice suntan, we'll talk."

He surprised me. When we parted at the airport, he embraced me, held me against him for a brief moment, pulled back, studied me with sharp, clear, unexpected knowledge of my loss. We had never spoken about it,

279

yet he knew. Somehow, I knew this knowledge was no
from Glori Nichols; it was from his knowledge of me.

His hands tightened on my arms, a friendly reas
suring squeeze.

"You'll be all right, Lynne," he said. And then, typ
ically, pontifically, but appropriately, he told me, "Thi
too shall pass."

As all things do.

I checked into the office for a brief hour to make sur
everything would run smoothly while I was gone. With
out Bobby Jones, with Lucy still laid up, I had a brie
conference with two of my other assistants, set up a
loose chain of command. Everything would hold; noth
ing would fall apart more than it already had.

One of the young interns—I never could tell then
apart—brought over a soft, loosely wrapped package
that had arrived for me. I left it on my desk while
sorted out assignments.

Jameson called to tell me what I had already hear
the moment I arrived at the office. The Corporatio
Counsel's office had informed him that a six-million
dollar lawsuit had been filed on behalf of Dr. Davi
Cohen against the City of New York, the Office of th
District Attorney of New York County, District Attor
ney Jameson Whitney Hale, Assistant District Attor
ney Lynne Jacobi, Assistant District Attorney Luc
Capella, and the estate of the late Chief Investigato
Michael Bobby Jones. That worked out to a millio
dollars per defendant.

Another thought for me to take along to Eleuthera

After the phone call, alone in my office, I opened th
package. Tore open the loose brown wrapping pape
and let the shoe drop on my desk.

It was a well-worn, dark blue, custom-made, right
foot running shoe stained all over with what was prob
ably dried blood. Definitely dried blood. I know drie
blood when I see it.

I held the shoe carefully by the frayed shoelace fo
a moment, then placed it on the center of my des
blotter and stared at it. It was very familiar: an olde

version of a custom-made running shoe we had seen before.

I smoothed the wrinkled brown paper in which it had been wrapped. I didn't have to be careful about handling it: God knows how many fingers had grabbed at it, tossed it one way or another. It would be virtually covered with meaningless fingerprints.

The package had been addressed to me as Miss Lynne Jacobi. My name was written in a large, fragile, clear and spidery handwriting, an old fashioned, schoolteacherish hand. The kind of writing one was used to seeing on the blackboards of one's childhood. The words "First Class Mail" were written in the same spidery, old woman's careful, still elegant hand and were underlined several times for emphasis.

And there was this shoe: this damn familiar running shoe, with the custom-made arch built in to allow for a deformity of a right foot or leg.

I buzzed for my young intern and told him to get an evidence bag large enough to accommodate the shoe, then had him stand by to witness what I was doing.

I carefully folded the wrinkled brown wrapping paper into a packet small enough to fit inside the shoe, stuffed it in without handling the shoe except by the frayed shoelace. Then I put the shoe into the standard evidence bag, sealed it, dated it, signed it and had my assistant countersign as witness. He looked a little surprised when I told him to make out a card and then to mark this evidence bag with a corresponding number and place it in the open file of the matter concerning Sanderalee Dawson, but he did what I told him without comment.

I felt a sudden urgency to get out of the office. I waved as I walked through my staff's office; told them to keep up the good work; that I'd think of them toiling away as I lounged in the golden sunshine.

The cab I had ordered was waiting right outside the building, and I didn't need the driver's help with my suitcase: I travel light. After asking my permission, he

surprised me by singing a soft, melodious repertoire o
the latest hit songs from Broadway shows, and we mad
it out to Kennedy in plenty of time for me to catch m
plane for Eleuthera.

He knelt before her chair and held her hands. He spoke softly, ignoring the uncomfortable, muscle-straining position he had taken in order to be certain she was looking directly at him.

"Mother, I've come with good news. Are you listening? Do you understand?"

He searched her face for some reaction to the news he had brought. It was all over. Finished. Done. He had been cleared. The true culprit was dead.

As he spoke, he was aware of his growing tension, his nervousness, the dryness of his mouth, the dampness of his hands. He felt a slight movement of her left hand in his. It was an attempt to withdraw from him. He looked from her hand to her face. He looked into her eyes. They were no longer blank. They were luminous, mesmerizing. He could not look away. It was impossible.

"Mother? What?"

He looked down and saw her large yellow pad for the first time. It was resting on her knees and her left index finger tapped rhythmically.

"You've written something, Mother? Did you write something for me, is that it? A message?"

He pulled himself to his feet, rubbed his eyes briskly with his fingertips, replaced his glasses and turned toward the window for better light. In the center of the page was her message, written in the large, spidery, shaky letters she had accomplished with her left hand.

YOU HAVE DESTROYED MY FAMILY. GO AWAY. NEVER RETURN.

"Mother!"

He ripped the page from the pad and crumpled it into a tight ball. He leaned toward her, reached out but stopped his hand in midair, then let it fall to his side as her eyes engaged his for one split second of total clarity.

I know. I know.

Then, she closed her eyes and slowly, deliberately, opened them again. She no longer saw him. It was as though he were not there. She did not acknowledge his existence. She had canceled him out forever.

There was a humming sound from his beeper.

He shoved the ball of paper into his jacket pocket. He looked at her once more: the only person in the entire world besides himself who truly knew what he had done.

"Goodbye, Mother," he said softly, but she did not respond. She was already gone.

Dr. David Cohen went down the hall to check with his service.